NOT A WALL IN THE DESERT

NOT A
WALL IN THE
DESERT

NAJUM QURESHI

Matador
9 Priory Business Park,
Wistow Road, Kibworth Beauchamp,
Leicestershire. LE8 0RX
Tel: 0116 279 2299
Email: books@troubador.co.uk
Web: www.troubador.co.uk/matador
Twitter: @matadorbooks

ISBN 978 1800462 618

British Library Cataloguing in Publication Data.
A catalogue record for this book is available from the British Library.

Printed and bound in the UK by TJ Books Ltd, Padstow, Cornwall
Typeset in 11pt Adobe Garamond Pro by Troubador Publishing Ltd, Leicester, UK

Matador is an imprint of Troubador Publishing Ltd

To my father

شوریدگی کے ہاتھ سے ہے، سرِ وبالِ دوش

صحرا میں، اے خدا! کوئی دیوار بھی نہیں

My head seems a weary weight in this frenzied state,
Alas, O Lord, there isn't a wall in this wild desert.

Ghalib

PART 1

JANUARY 2008–SEPTEMBER 2009

ONE

The day was disintegrating in front of me, everything slogging at half pace: an overrunning gynaecology clinic, a disgruntled admissions manager showing me a list of patients breaching government-set targets – and now this phone call. It's never good news when the chief operating officer of the hospital summons you for an urgent meeting.

'Do you have to go now?' the sister-in-charge said.

'I'll be back as soon as I can.'

Shaking her head, and with a worried look on her face, she amended the information board for the patients, which now read: "Mr Mikel Demir clinic running late. Apologies for the inconvenience."

I walked from the bustle of the clinic, considering the pale green lino as if by doing so meant no patient would notice me leave. I shifted weight to my right foot, and it was only mildly achy today. Why would the chief operating officer need to see me urgently? My tongue troubled the inside of my teeth as I thought this over.

'Be careful, Mr Demir,' the cleaner said, holding a mop in a bucket cart, probably noticing my urgent and careless stride. 'The floor's still wet,' she added, pointing towards the floor.

'Thanks,' I said. 'Nice.' The whiff of a clean, mildly antiseptic detergent drifted up to my nose.

Uttering a perfunctory 'Good Morning' a junior doctor whizzed past.

A long management corridor yawned into view as I emerged from the stairwell and saw the gynaecology admissions manager, Jacky Taylor, pacing towards me. As always, she had a large black diary clasped to her chest.

'I've managed to arrange an extra operating list for you,' she said with a triumphant smile glowing her face.

'Could we talk about it later? I'm in a bit of a rush.'

'No problem, I'll e-mail you.'

'Perfect.'

I knocked on James Stevenson's office door, which was ajar. I could hear James talking submissively to someone else in the room.

'Come in, Mr Demir,' said James. 'I thought it would be good if we both see you together.'

He noticed the surprised look on my face upon finding the chief executive officer, Louise Oakley, present in the room.

'Serious stuff,' I said. 'Am I being sacked?'

James sat poised behind a large modern desk with his back to the window. His black leather jacket hung on a peg like a huge bat. He always wore his silver hair long, pomaded behind the ears. He came to the front and sat on the edge of the desk. His burgeoning belly had prised open small eyelets between the buttons of his shirtfront, displaying his hirsute abdomen.

He said, 'Indeed, double-trouble. Take a seat, please. My apologies for dragging you out of your clinic. It's kind of an urgent issue... Would you like tea or coffee?' James did not have a habit of wasting time; his offer of hot drinks suggested something serious was in the offing.

'No, nothing, thanks,' I said catching my breath. 'My clinic is brewing. I need to get back as soon as possible.'

'Louise, is it okay if I explain the background of the meeting to Mikel?'

'Sure,' said Louise before sipping water from a transparent plastic cup, which appeared foggy due to the chilled contents.

James frowned in an effort to attain clarity and said, 'I'm sure you must have heard the news and seen my e-mail, sent this morning, about one of our midwives, Eralia Rose, who didn't turn up to work a couple of weeks ago and was later found dead in her flat by the police.'

'Yes, I did. It's dreadful.'

James wiped his forehead with a wad of tissue paper and said, 'Yes, it's very tragic. We're all very saddened by Eralia's death.'

'What did they find at autopsy?'

'The autopsy report is due this week. We aren't expecting self-harm but some natural cause of death. The police think she died more than two weeks ago.'

Louise balanced the cup on the armrest of the chair and said, 'As you know, the media likes to splash such stories on the front pages. We would like you to lead the inquiry into the sequence of events preceding Eralia's death.'

I said, 'I'm sorry, I don't understand what you want me to investigate? It's a police case. Surely there's nothing I can do?' I was utterly startled by the request.

'We received an anonymous letter of complaint after her death,' James said, looking at Louise. 'Or perhaps we should call it a letter of dissatisfaction from one of her colleagues. We understand the anger and emotions of the grieving colleague who wrote the letter, which raises concerns that the departmental managers missed four alarm bells about Eralia when she didn't turn up for her shifts and study days. It is also alleged that nobody made an effort to find out why she wasn't attending her work and study days or calling in sick.'

James grabbed the letter lying on the table. 'The complainant alleges that if the departmental managers had tried to contact her, either she could have received help in her sickbed, or in the worst-case scenario, her dead body could've been discovered earlier.'

With a visible effort of concentration, James paused to take a breath and then added, 'I'm not too sure about the first point, but I think the second may have some credence. Nevertheless, we'd like you to undertake an internal inquiry in this case.'

Louise said, 'I want this Trust to be open and transparent regarding any complaints, whether they are from patients or colleagues.' Her sentence sounded artificial and worn out as if she'd used it with endless repetition in her speeches. 'James should be able to give you the autopsy report in due course, but in the meantime, I'd like you to go through the sequence of events before her death. I'd be grateful if you could complete your report within two weeks.'

'Don't you think the head of midwifery would be the best person to conduct this investigation?' I said, still battling with the idea of leading the investigation. 'Surely she would know all the policies and procedures about midwives not turning up for their scheduled shifts?'

'Good try, Mikel,' James said. 'Both heads of nursing and midwifery are away on two weeks' holiday. The person deputising in their absence should be able to assist you along with HR but you, as the head of workforce within the Trust… well, we both think… you'd be the best person to undertake this investigation.'

'But, still…'

James said, looking casual, 'This post of head of workforce is a paid job alongside your clinical commitments, isn't it?'

The question itself and its timing were bizarre. I was sure he knew the answer to the question. Did he imply the post was bestowed upon me as a favour and it was now payback time? I looked deeply at him but there was only a benign look on his face. I said, 'Yes, it does have an additional payment.'

'That is beside the point,' said Louise, sharply. 'We'd like you to take the investigation on.'

Finding no room to manoeuvre out of the investigation, I said, 'Did anything unusual happen to Eralia prior to her death? Was she under any sort of investigation for some incident by the Trust?… Or any case with the unsatisfactory outcome with the mother or baby during childbirth?'

Midwifery can be a high-pressure job. The sad case of a midwife who committed suicide after receiving a prank call from a journalist when the Duchess of Cambridge, Kate Middleton, was in labour for her first child sprang to my mind.

'No, none whatsoever,' James said. 'She was under no investigation of any sort by the Trust. We think she died of natural causes. And although we don't know who the real complainant is, we still feel we should complete our internal review within two weeks in case this anonymous person declares their identity and comes forward for a response. We want to be prepared for all eventualities and would greatly appreciate your help.'

'That's right,' said Louise, taking a sip of water and then placing her cup on the table. I noticed her pink lipstick prints on the plastic brim, which looked even more prominent there than on her lips. Louise must have been the result of the recent drive to employ young female CEOs. She had a confident countenance, a natural situational awareness and quick analysis. She passed me a large buff envelope with a red stamp of *Private and Confidential* on it. 'Enclosed are the copies of relevant papers about this case.' She paused, and said again, 'Two weeks for your report.'

I felt a bit annoyed at her insisting on two weeks. They all knew how snowed under I was with clinical work yet still, she was giving me so little time. 'Why two weeks? What's the urgency? Usually, we respond to complaints within six weeks. Is there something I'm missing?'

'No, nothing,' said James. 'We believe that the person who raised the complaint also sent a copy of the letter to the press. We received a phone call from a very insistent journalist this morning wanting to interview us about this sad incident, which we declined for two obvious reasons. A, we don't have the PM report as yet and B, we'd like the results of our in-house inquiry first.'

Perhaps Louise had read my thoughts as she said, 'I'll ask the clinical director of your department to give some of your work to someone else whilst you're compiling your report... I hope that will help.' A smile of success appeared on her face; she knew very well that she hadn't left any option for me to wriggle out of this.

'Okay, I'll see what I can do.'

'Thanks,' they both said.

The meeting had made me uneasy. Why were both heads of nursing and midwifery allowed to go on leave simultaneously? Did they actually go on leave or were they sent on leave? I was the head of the workforce for the medical staff, not for midwifery. Was I being set up here?

As I was going down the stairs, I saw Walter standing at the bottom. Walter was my GP and friend, an extremely congenial and naturally pleasant person. He said with a smile on his face, 'You skiving off work? I came to see you.'

'I wish I was.'

'I heard the headmaster summoned you. Is everything okay?'

'No,' I replied briefly. 'More work for me.' I told him I had been tasked with the internal investigation into Eralia Rose's death.

'Oh no... You should have told them where to go.'

'I know, I should have.'

'But you're the best choice... an excellent clinician, a steady hand at surgery and an eye in any storm. The hospital has every right to make use of your abilities.'

I responded only with a smile.

'Well, you love work,' Walter said, looking really happy. 'How's your foot?'

'Much better,' I said. 'But still needing painkillers.'

Walter said, still relentlessly positive, 'That's good to know, but I still disagree with Mr Shannon. Ten per cent of gout can happen with normal uric acid levels. And what about alcohol?'

'That's not happening frequently, only socially.'

'That's good. Anyway, I came to tell you the news that my back surgeon has given me permission to play squash again. If you're okay to play, I could book a court, and we could have a game this evening.'

'That's brilliant news,' I said. 'I can't wait to start playing again; I need a distraction from hospital work. Please go ahead and book it.'

'Also,' said Walter. 'Are you still okay to come and do some charity work in South America with us? I'm in the process of arranging it with James Shannon. It won't be for several months yet as it takes a lot of organising and paperwork, but can I put your name down?'

'Please do. I'd love to come with you.'

'Great. Will do,' Walter said, taking a twirl and then walking away. 'See you at half seven.'

'You certainly will,' I said, waving goodbye to him.

I repeated Walter's phrase to myself: *You love work.*

Was it true love for work or escapism? To inhabit an empty marriage I had to cultivate some routines. After finishing work for the day, I retreated to my cupboard of an office, where my secretary parked a two-storey, supermarket-like trolley, loaded with patient case notes for my attention. Then I'd hunch over the computer for hours and reply to e-mails, study peer-review articles for publications, fill in workplace-based assessment forms for the trainees and write my research projects.

Today, however, I felt a distorted euphoria at the prospect of finishing my back-to-back clinics and playing a game of squash.

My mobile buzzed before it rang in my pocket. I dreaded looking at the screen in case it was James with some last-minute instructions for the investigation. I was relieved to see that it was not James but my consultant colleague Richard Ponting. He wanted to transfer a Turkish-speaking patient to my clinic, because the hospital hadn't paid their annual subscription to the telephone interpretation company in time and the service had been temporarily disconnected.

I noticed an unexpected ease and lightness in my tread as I walked back to my unfinished clinic.

TWO

'Rohan Singh, get a life,' I said to myself and laughed. 'A final-year medical student like you doesn't have to be that lonely.'

As always, I was alone in my dormitory room. I held the two souvenirs of Ava and looked closely at them, again. For the past three weeks, I'd eyed and caressed them numerous times. I had a strong urge to meet Ava, to refresh her image in my mind, make an attempt to talk to her. I'd never spoken to her, except for a few casual words, and yet her name was like a shot of adrenaline to my foolish heart. I didn't know what to make of my confused adoration. My thought processes remained firmly anchored on Ava and I was unable to think of anything else; towers of textbooks arose from the tabletop, and I had no urge, nor any desire, to read. I wanted to meet her. The closest I could get to Ava was touching her used paper tissues and sunglasses.

It was as if a bonfire that had been built up without my being aware of it were suddenly ignited. The flame leapt up. Without thinking, I pulled my trousers down to my knees and placed the tissues between my thighs. The thought of my privates coming into touch with something that Ava had held drove a surge of pleasure through me. A pulse knocked in my ears; the back of my throat went cold as if I'd sucked on dry ice. The growing tumescence sent a sweet, spreading sensation throughout my body. The image of Ava remained sharply focused in my mind. It was awesome to undress her slowly, very slowly, and I could hear her moan under the touch of my hands. Braided within the fantasy of entanglement, the end came, so full of pleasure that it was agonizing to bear and heralded with pulsatile leaps of secretions, which I caught in the tissues. The thought of my tepid secretions mixing with Ava's propelled me into another elation. A mashed-potato smell crowded the room. The instant gratification relaxed my mind and body. The goal achieved through imagination. There was no feeling of shame in this thing I did.

Anything that had belonged to or been touched by Ava was preciously sacred to me. I didn't wish to discard the relic, and after thinking for a moment, placed the dripping tissue over the warm radiator to dry.

Luscious exhaustion descended after the experience. I remained motionless on the bed and was calmly engulfed by slumber.

I awoke with a lift of excitement, my mind was much clearer, but the compass of my mind was still pointing towards Ava. The fear of a looming examination took me to the study table; I tried *The Textbook of Medicine* but as nothing was going in, I gave up after an hour. I needed to find Ava, or at least to glance at her. A desire to see her had become a resurgent distraction and the only realistic chance of meeting her was in the social club of the medical school.

The club was alive with the chatter of students and throbbing music. A loud gale of laughter pierced the background noise and made me look towards a table, around which my classmates sat. Ava was there, poised confidently, as always.

'Hi,' I said to everyone but looking at Ava.

'Hello, Rohan,' Paul said, raising a hand in greeting. 'You better drink up quick, it'll be your beauty-sleep time soon.'

The comment provoked a candid hilarity.

'We know you, Rohan. You don't belong to the species of *Homo sapiens*,' said Paul with a pleasant smile on his face. 'You belong to the… *Homo pumpkian…* the pumpkin family. When the clocks strike twelve, you turn into a pumpkin.'

It was a laugh-out-loud moment for all, particularly Xhi, who found it so funny that a tiny tear emerged from her palpebral epicanthic fold. I'm sure my Asian face also turned crimson with the embarrassment, but I was relieved when I looked at Ava, who seemed to enjoy the joke.

'Or is this the effect of your birthplace on you, Rohan?' Paul continued congenially. 'Sleepy, fairyland Maldives.'

'Your parents live in the Maldives! How cool,' said Ava with excitement.

Being the topic of conversation, and Ava's focus of interest, infused a delightful confidence in me.

'No, my parents never went to the Maldives before or after my birth,' I said with newly found boldness. 'It was just a freak turn of events.'

'Tell me; tell me what happened,' Xhi said, and drew closer to me.

'I can't remember where my parents were flying to, but Mum went into premature labour mid-air and the plane had to be diverted to the closest land, which was the Maldives. It's a shame the pilot managed to land in time otherwise I would have had a life-long supply of free air travel with the airline.'

'How interesting,' said Xhi.

'Must have been very scary for your mum,' Ava said sympathetically.

'Yes,' I said, feeling a touch intoxicated basking in Ava's attention. 'And for the fellow passengers.'

Helen piped in and changed the conversation. 'I heard the consultant in charge of our teaching recently had a nosejob.'

'At his age? No way.'

'Who?'

'Mr O'Reilly.'

'He could've done with a backjob!' said Xhi, and there was uproarious laughter.

'Is it just gossip?' Ava said.

'No, it's not gossip,' said Helen. 'It's *pukka* news. I overheard a scrub nurse telling Mr Demir in theatre.'

'Who is this Demir guy?' said Paul. 'Everyone talks about him, and I don't think I've met him yet.'

Ava said, dreamily, 'Oh... he's the consultant in gynaecology... the one with grey temples... medium height... wears glasses, speaks with an odd posh accent...'

'He mutters to himself whilst operating,' said Helen, giving Ava a deprecating look. 'A sign of old age.'

Ava completely ignored Helen.

'Okay... now I know which one you mean,' Paul said. 'He's Turkish.'

'Who told you that?' asked Helen.

'He spoke fluent Turkish with one of the patients and I asked him which language he'd just spoken. He told me that he has got Turkish roots. He's quite friendly with students... well, maybe too friendly.'

'Apparently, Mr Demir is quite an influential person,' said Helen as if she was talking to herself.

I said, 'How come? Is he the head of examinations?' It looked obvious to everyone that there wasn't anything more important to me than the examinations.

'No, you roasted nuts, Rohan. He's nothing to do with examinations,' Helen said in an exasperated tone. 'This Demir guy gives training posts after the foundation year training.'

Ava said, 'You mean, he's also the training programme director?'

'Yes, he is,' Helen said with a sparkle of mischief in her eyes.

'Guys,' said Xhi. 'Have any of you met Dr Martin Norton, the gastroenterologist? He is a character! He wears a new baseball cap every day and is actually quite funny.'

'That's right,' said Paul. 'And he has a facial tic which sometimes looks like he's mocking you by making faces.'

'That's so funny, Paul,' Xhi said, gasping a little after the laughter.

'Dr Norton? You mean the little philosopher,' said Helen. 'I've been to one of his lectures. He's very knowledgeable and articulate. I could listen to him all day.'

'Never seen or heard of him,' said Ava quietly.

Oblivious to me watching her, Ava sipped her drink. I'm not a mathematician and can't highlight whether there was any mathematical basis for her beauty. She was slim, and her shoulder-length hair curled upwards. Perfectly placed, blue watery cavernous eyes. The philtrum just a gentle scoop and her lips were so delicate that even Jesus would have liked to kiss them. Her angular jaw appeared to have been carved with a sharp scalpel, giving her a strong and self-assured appearance. She laughed often, displaying neat teeth with incisors slightly broader than the rest. She wore a silver ring on her left index finger. She was perfectly perfect. I liked looking at her but couldn't muster the courage to ask her out.

Ava said, rising, 'I've got to go now.'

'Why?' asked Paul with a frown. 'Let's have another round of drinks.'

'No thanks, I've a presentation to prepare for tomorrow.'

'Why do you have to be such a stick in the mud?' said Paul.

'Sorry,' she said, with a smile, and lifted her arm to thread through her jacket sleeve. In the process her top moved upwards, providing a tantalising view of her slim tummy and a neat belly button. I tingled all over. For the first time, I understood why girls ornament their umbilicus.

There wasn't much point in staying if Ava left. 'Are you leaving too, Rohan?' Ava said and brushed past me as I was getting up. 'Time for your beauty sleep?'

'Yes, definitely,' I said, and my heart raced at her touch. 'I do take my sleep incredibly seriously.'

She laughed, and said, 'Sweet dreams.'

My gaze followed her as long as it plausibly could and she left the club.

The conversation with her provoked delicious, giddy buoyancy and I whistled with a light note as I walked out.

Ava, my love, Ava, one day you'll be mine. You'll be alongside me, I thought as I ambled back to the hostel. *I want you and your company to make my past bearable.*

The memories of my lonely childhood came to mind and brought with them the sound of blood vessels thumping in my ears like waves roaring on pebbles, loud and harsh. I had been the battleground upon which my selfish and stupid parents pursued their narcissistic motives. My mother was a highly neurotic and immature woman. My father was a business magnate, who couldn't get along with her almost from the start of their marriage. They alienated each other, and their only child. Like most Asian parents, they granted themselves deified powers and brought me up comparing, contrasting and judging me against their friends' children. This hardwired me into becoming an unwavering "achiever".

I wanted to achieve Ava. I'd hardly spoken to her, except for a few casual words. I was in a continual state of blue funk. Her beauty frightened me, and sent my tongue into such a spasm that I could not say what I wanted, and I couldn't even imagine hearing 'No' from her.

I remembered sitting directly behind her in the lecture theatre one day, admiring her hair and wanting to touch it.

Paul had elbowed me and whispered into my ear, 'Burnt auburn.'

I had no clue what this nugget of information meant and, certainly, this knowledge had no influence over me to prevent my strong desire to touch her hair. But as soon as I raised my hand, a wave of fear filled my heart as if I was holding a loaded pistol.

Back in my room I took out Ava's sunglasses, and even though they were tight on my face, I sat on a chair wearing them. I got hold of these "treasures" last week whilst we were sitting in the common room waiting to go into the main lecture theatre. Ava had placed her handbag on the floor to grab a can of Coke from the vending machine. Her sunglasses slid out along with a crumpled tissue, which was hardened in the centre due to secretions sticking together the layers, and before anyone noticed, I picked them up and put them in my backpack. To be in possession of what belonged to Ava was a great achievement for me.

THREE

'Thanks for the report.' James passed on his gratitude superficially. 'And thanks for adhering so strictly to the deadline of two weeks,' he added, hissing another hollow compliment.

Why does he have to torment himself by going through all these formalities? I thought. *Of course, he has to*, I reasoned with myself as I sat down, *he's got a tick-box mentality and has to methodically go down the list, and unfortunately, for all us medics, the thought processes of senior management have stumbled from "political astuteness" to "political correctness".*

Today the midwifery manager, Sandra Ashcroft, was also present in the room. Sandra was broad and burly; her body bulging on either side of the capacious armchair. She had sparse shoulder-length hair with a wide central parting accentuating her square face. Her blue-coloured sunglasses were perched on her head like solar panelling. She smelt of cigarette smoke. She hadn't yet changed into her usual knee-length, bright red "matron's uniform", in which she looked like a walking postbox. Someone once made a cruel remark about her – a postbox where no one ever posted a letter.

'There seems to be some disagreement about your report, Mikel,' James said whilst looking at Sandra. The wrinkles on his face appeared more prominent, and there was quietness in his voice, showing concern. 'The whole idea of meeting in person is to clear up any confusion and avoid all the e-mails toing and froing.'

'Okay,' said Sandra, agreeing with the meeting's agenda and appearing contemplative.

'So, Mikel,' James said. 'I think the main issue here is that you feel, and you have written in your report, that Eralia's death may be work-related. And Sandra, you think that her death was due to her ill health. Why, Mikel, do you disagree with Sandra?'

'We missed several red flags showing health concerns,' I said. 'Clearly, Eralia experienced work-related stress. She repeatedly told her supervisor about this, but no one took her seriously. The level of pressure she experienced gave her the health issues. Chest pain or not, she felt compelled to come to work. We missed at least three opportunities to intervene.'

'We were going through a very busy period at that time of the year,' said Sandra.

'Being busy doesn't mean that we ignore the health worries of employees,' I said. 'Eralia's GP told me that he was able to establish a link between her work and the angina episodes, but she was too scared to take time off from the work for her investigations or rest.'

'That's the failing of her GP, not ours.'

'Her GP did write to you with his concerns and you wrote back to him that you'd take the necessary actions.'

'What did you expect us to do?'

'She should have been sent to A & E with her chest pains or to occupational health at least.'

'She wasn't a patient.'

'Perhaps she should have…'

'Honestly!'

'Please, Sandra,' said James. 'Let him finish and then you'll have your say.'

'Whatever.'

I considered Sandra, who was checking her nails as if she was seeing them for the first time.

'There was no mention of any health issues in her last three annual assessments,' I continued. 'And no one showed any concern when she missed two mandatory study days but...'

'I disagree.'

'Sandra, let him finish,' James said as his jaw muscles tensed.

'But...'

'Sandra, you will have the opportunity to give your viewpoint when Mikel has finished.'

'Having interviewed half a dozen of her midwifery colleagues,' I continued, 'it is my distinct impression that one is not treated as a person but just as a number here... Nobody gives a damn about anyone's health or welfare.'

'You're being personal.'

'I'm sorry, Sandra, it's not about *you*... it's about the job as midwifery manager. You may call it harsh,' I added, looking at her – she had very little room to squirm in her chair – 'but I'm afraid you can't extricate yourself from this incident. As midwifery manager, the buck stops with you.'

'I don't necessarily agree with your report,' Sandra said, and a flush of temper stained her face. She wiped the corners of her eyes with a tissue. Her voice was halting and then it cracked like shells. 'There are several flaws in your report. The PM report clearly states heart attack as the cause of Eralia's death. I can't understand why you keep calling it a work-related death.'

I said, 'I'm sorry if my report...'

'In his report Mr Demir has quoted French and Australian healthcare systems,' said Sandra, addressing James, 'and how they investigate workplace-related deaths, but no system like that exists in the UK. I intend to send a copy of Mr Demir's report to my professional union representative... I feel his report has undermined my position in the hospital, and I will be seeking a legal opinion about it.'

'Sandra, you need to calm down!' James snapped.

Sandra was unstoppable. 'There are over 250 midwifery and auxiliary staff working in the hospital. I think, Mr Demir, you need to understand that we can't possibly chase every single staff member that doesn't turn up for work. People have busy lives; sometimes they forget to ring us if they can't come to work. There could be many reasons. It isn't practical or logistically possible to send the police to every person's house when they don't turn up for work. I think you've got it wrong, Mr Demir.'

James said, 'Sandra, can we just talk about the facts, please?'

'But I have a right to say if I disagree,' Sandra said, playing with her fingers.

I said, 'According to the PM, this poor midwife died about two weeks before she was discovered dead. The cold December weather prevented her body from putrefying. The forensic examination of her mobile showed no phone calls or messages from the hospital… till the battery of her phone died too…'

'It's curious,' said James. 'It means her mobile was in working order when she was experiencing chest pains, so why didn't she call the emergency services?'

'Nobody knows why she didn't dial 999,' I said. 'Maybe she was in so much pain or maybe it was a sudden, fatal heart attack giving her no time to ring. The PM report showed a large clot blocking her coronary vessels.'

'Okay. Let's get back to our point,' James said as he clasped his hands over his voluminous paunch and cleared his throat. 'This meeting is to clear any misunderstandings in the report.' He looked worried and, scanning my face, said, 'I think we can amend the report before it goes into the public domain.'

'Amend what exactly?' I said. 'I don't understand what you mean.'

James was clearly making an effort to keep his composure. 'The PM report states that Eralia died of a very bad heart attack. You said in your report that she had some episodes of chest pain during work and was sent home to rest. Could we have done anything differently to prevent this fatal heart attack? I'm just asking; I'm not a doctor.'

I could see rivulets of mascara on Sandra's cheeks; nothing riles me more in meetings than the old-fashioned feminine display of their defences in the form of streams of lacrimal gland secretions.

'Well, we've got to understand the personal circumstances around Eralia's death,' I said. 'She was fifty-nine. I understand she came to the UK some twenty-five years ago and never went back to Jamaica.'

'Was she living alone?' James asked.

'Yes, she had no partner and lived alone in a rented flat,' I said. 'Her colleagues have told me she was a very quiet, very private person. Nobody knew whether she had ever married, but she had a disabled twenty-six-year-old son living in Jamaica, to whom she used to send money every month.'

James was listening intently and said, 'Okay, and what happened on the day?'

'As I've stated in my report, when she complained of chest pains, she should have been sent definitely to A & E... she was warning us of these angina episodes. She was a very conscientious midwife and never took any leave without notice... alarm bells should have been frantically ringing when she failed to turn up for the study days... I'm not saying that we could have saved her... but possibly...'

'Again, I disagree,' said Sandra and her finger punctuated the air between her and me with gathering hostility. 'The shift coordinator of the labour ward didn't send her home. You need to get your facts straight, Mr Demir. When she felt unwell, she decided to go home herself. Secondly, I did refer her to occupational health. The waiting time to be seen in the occupational health department of our hospital is about six weeks. I've got no powers to expedite an appointment with them and her ECG changes due to angina *might* have reverted back to normal. A senior doctor of your stature should know all this.' Her tone was an intricate blend of defence, persuasion and aggression.

'I know,' I said. The annoyance in Sandra's voice did not subdue me. 'In that case, she should have been sent to A & E, and even if no changes were seen on her ECG, she could have been sent for some blood tests, an exercise tolerance test and her angina diagnosed.'

'I disagree with your childish viewpoint, Mr Demir,' Sandra said. 'It's not the job of a supervisor to arrange a supervisee's exercise tests. It's their GP's job. Also, an individual is responsible for looking after their own health.'

'The other issue I felt equally important, as I've written in my report,' I said, looking at Sandra, 'is that the deceased felt bullied and harassed by her manager. She did tell her immediate supervisor both formally and informally about this.'

'You know, Mikel,' said James, fidgeting with a pen, 'you're opening a can of worms here.'

'I don't know what your expectations of me were when you asked me to investigate this,' I said, and I could feel frustration gathering in my voice. 'You expected me to quickly open this can of worms and rapidly drag out only just one worm – a worm of your choice – with a pair of surgical tweezers, and swiftly close the lid shut?'

'And what happened when she reported being bullied and harassed?' James was now sweating profusely; he drew a scrunched tissue paper from his pocket and dabbed his forehead.

'Nothing,' I said. 'Her complaint was brushed under the carpet.'

'That's not true,' Sandra cried. 'She was sent on a training course about how to deal with such situations.'

'That's correct.' I enunciated my words distinctly. 'She was sent on a conflict resolution course and a free-range bully was allowed to carry on bullying.'

'So, Mikel, do you think bullying and harassment is still an issue in our hospital?' James asked with the innocence of a spring lamb.

'The honest answer is *YES*. You need to get off your throne,' I said, waving a finger at his desk, 'to meet people working here to know what's going on. The culture of bullying is rife in our hospital,

Mr Chief Operating Officer. The deceased midwife felt bullied, she made a formal complaint and still nothing was done about it.'

'What did she actually complain about?' retorted James.

'Well,' I said, carefully choosing my words to avoid offending Sandra further. 'She made a formal complaint against Sandra. She felt bullied and harassed by her immediate manager to pick up more shifts, more than she was contracted to work.' I stopped to take a breath. 'Sandra, I'm sorry, but she said that you "used your height and voice" on her to shout at her to "shut up and put up with the work".'

'I have never shouted at anyone!' shouted Sandra.

'Were the bullying and harassment allegations ever investigated?' asked James.

'No, there was no need to carry out any investigations. I had a conversation with her along with her manager and the issue was resolved,' said Sandra.

'Is it not worrying, James, that a formal complaint of bullying was not formally investigated?' I said.

'Yes, it should've been… but Sandra says the issue was resolved,' James said.

'Mr Demir is misreading the truth,' Sandra said to James, tapping her cheeks with a carefully folded tissue paper. 'He's interviewed less than three per cent of the labour ward staff and is making huge allegations which could be harmful to the reputation of our hospital. I don't see any more bullying in our hospital than anywhere else. I feel your report, Mr Demir, should be either amended or discarded as you, Mr Demir, have gone beyond the remit of this investigation.'

'When you say the issue was resolved with the midwife,' said James, 'did she withdraw her complaint?'

'I think she did,' Sandra replied looking at the floor.

All three of us in the room knew what Sandra had just said wasn't the truth. Reality and honesty are closely related like identical twins. Sometimes, it's not easy to bear them together, at the same time, like a blazing fire in a scorching desert. It's easier to take refuge in the dark shade of a lie: we know it's a lie, but we don't have the strength for honesty.

'I have stayed well within the remit of the investigation into Eralia's death,' I said, trying to control my anger. 'It will be all or none. Either you have to fully accept my report as it is or ask someone else to do the investigation again.'

'In that case,' said Sandra, 'we should hold a fresh inquiry.'

'That's fine by me. I'm not precious about my report. I'll feed this report to the shredder.'

'Hold on, hold on,' James said, realising the situation had slipped from his grasp. 'We have two issues here. Firstly, can I clarify, the procedures for staff who don't turn up for work without prior notice were carried out?'

'Yes,' Sandra replied. 'And we do manage such situations quite well on a daily basis.'

James said, 'That's great…'

I said, 'What's the point in having a policy which fails to operate?'

James interrupted me. 'Systems can fail, and this unfortunate incident has unearthed several important issues. I'm extremely worried to hear that bullying and harassment are still happening in our hospital. This was highlighted in the last National Clinical Group report, and it will be very damning to the hospital if we haven't made any progress in rectifying the issue. Mikel, I hope you won't mind if I make some amendments to your report?'

'No, you can't,' I said. 'Management in our hospital has become extremely myopic. Their main interest is to satisfy paperwork, the needs of external inspection teams, to save money. The public image is your main worry, not staff welfare. I'm cursing myself for agreeing to do this investigation in the first place, and I'm sure you're regretting it too.'

'No, *we are not!*' James said belligerently. 'I'll discuss the report with Louise this afternoon. We must consider the public perception of our hospital as our first priority. I quite agree with you that systems for staff absence should not fail, but I feel Sandra has a point too.

Even at annual assessments we can only ask about the health of our employees and the onus is on the employee to provide us with the correct information. If we aren't informed, we simply can't take any action. As far as the bullying issue is concerned, I'll discuss the matter further with Louise.'

'Just "discussing" is not the answer to the problem; it's time to take action. We need to appoint a "Bullying Tsar" in our hospital who could undertake fair and objective investigations and take proper action against these "bullies". But I know you wouldn't like to do this, as some of the "bullies" are the privileged masters, present in the "inner circles" or the "elite classes of the hospital hierarchy".'

'I think we should conclude our meeting,' James said, curtly.

'Ignorance is bliss,' I said, getting off the chair. 'But on a different note, we should not forget Eralia's son in Jamaica. Arrangements should be made for him to attend his mother's funeral and ensure that her funeral costs are paid, and he receives her pension funds.'

'I've already authorised the hospital to pay for her funeral costs,' said James, trying to hide his annoyance. 'And her son will get her pension.'

Sandra remained seated, covering her face with a tissue and sobbing.

James threw a withering glance at me as I left the room.

FOUR

All busy jobs have numerous disadvantages, except one: the days flash by. After my farcical meeting with James and Sandra a month ago, I didn't have the time or energy to follow up whether someone else had been assigned to re-run the inquiry and write a more congenial report for the hospital. I hadn't seen Sandra at work and was told that she had taken sick leave. I felt sorry for her, but not responsible.

Out of the blue, I received an e-mail from James informing me that the three years of my term as the head of the workforce was coming to an end, and the post would be readvertised. The e-mail was devoid of any of the usual niceties thanking me for doing the job, which appeared deliberate, and there was no encouragement for me to re-apply for a second term. It was amusing to a certain extent. I knew I was being punished.

Over the years I've learnt that one cannot negotiate through the mad labyrinth and thermodynamics of the health care service without gangs and allegiances. There were times when one needed a confidant, a stolid friend to whom one could "purge" oneself.

I headed to speak to Alan Taylor, who was a consultant psychiatrist. Alan was thoroughly well read, highly intelligent, articulate and a good friend. I had previously told Alan about my meeting with James and Sandra. He'd predicted, and warned me of, repercussions in the future.

Alan read the e-mail from James, which he aborted in the middle, laughed derisively, and said, 'The problem with management is that they're too bloody predictable.'

We allowed the silence to swell between us, thinking and trying to analyse.

'I'm being punished,' I said.

'Of course you are.'

'I was under the impression that one gets an automatic second term in such posts, without going through the rigmarole of a repeat interview.'

'Yes, normally that should happen. But we know it depends upon who the current post holder is,' Alan said. 'How much are you paid for it?'

'Half a programmed activity per week.'

'If you don't mind telling me, how much does it translate into money?'

'Approximately five... five-and-half grand per year.'

'It's sizeable,' said Alan, frowning.

'True, but I'm not going to die of starvation if this additional income is stopped. I'm not worried.'

'Why don't you reapply? For the fun of it. To make them feel uncomfortable.'

'No, there isn't any point as I won't get reappointed, I'm certain,' I said. 'I couldn't care less.'

Alan said, 'I still don't get why they gave you this paid post in the first instance. People like you and me are doomed to undertake the unpaid work, the donkeywork. The paid work usually goes to the "elite class". Did no one else apply?'

'I think someone did. Perhaps the management was too engrossed in some other business and couldn't pay much attention or none of their favourite choices was available or ready and hence they had no option but to give it to me. It was anomalous in the first place, which they want to rectify now. When they appointed me they were either stupid or crazy.'

'Well, when in power, you could afford to be both,' said Alan and both of us laughed uproariously.

Alan thought for a moment and then said, 'I'm sure they'll find someone from the "inner circles" to reward for their loyalties. Somebody who won't question and will readily and merrily jump when instructed to jump... and may innocently ask "how high?".' The way Alan said this made me laugh again.

'I'm sure they will. They'd prefer a useful idiot.'

Alan grinned and said, 'Someone whose faculties of assent are much more highly developed than that of dissent or protest... compliance over competence.'

I said, 'And there isn't any dearth of such people in our hospital.'

'I know.'

'So sad.'

'Very sad,' said Alan. 'Management is so deluded that they think their "elites" are so pure, so picture-perfect, and I won't be surprised if they think the shit of their comrades doesn't stink.'

We laughed again.

'Let's not be cynical, there must be something special about this privileged class,' I said.

'Yes, I agree there is something very special about them,' said Alan with an indignant expression on his face. 'I think if there's anything special about them, it's that there isn't anything special; nothing at all; zilch, zero, a cypher.'

I said, 'I'm not too bothered about this pay cut of five-and-a-half grand. What bothers me is what else they've got in store for me. They might implicate me in something to punish me.'

Alan smiled affably and said, 'No point in worrying. They're malevolent but at the same time incompetent. Also, even if they wanted, they couldn't give you the sack. You're in a permanent post for your clinical duties. I sincerely hope you'll disappear from their radar after this.'

'I hope so too, but when it comes to teaching someone a lesson, to give someone a bloody nose, they could be ruthless.'

'True, but at the same time, no point in killing yourself with anxiety,' said Alan. 'Just put it behind you.'

'I'm trying my best,' I said as I left his room.

I had a foreboding. The peacock dance of James had just begun and I was sure he had some more colours to show. I needed to be vigilant and grow another pair of eyes to constantly watch my back – a concept I'd always despised but now felt trapped in.

FIVE

The days and months turned, and thankfully we were halfway through another cold winter.

People who care worry about others when they don't show up. It was the first week after the Christmas break. Ava didn't attend the school and I went searching for her at the club. I'd rehearsed several times how to wish her a happy New Year. Fairy lights and lanterns were still twinkling, and people mingled with simultaneous displays of affection and artificiality. Paul and Justin sat drinking around a table. I bought a beer and joined them.

'Hi, everyone,' I said. 'Everyone had a good time off?' My eyes were searching for Ava, but I couldn't see her.

'Yes, Rohan, how are you, man?' Paul said. 'You didn't come to the Christmas party. It was wild... insanely sick.'

'Too wild! It went on till six in the morning,' Justin said with a mindless expression on his face.

'I can't be bothered with such partying.'

'Well, Rohan, your friend certainly had a good time,' said Helen, joining us from another table with a sly smile on her face.

'Was Ava there?' I said in a voice a notch short of a whisper. 'What was *she* doing there?'

Helen swivelled her hips in a carnal, circumscribed fashion and said, 'Dancing.'

I felt caught in the warm jaws of arousal and alarm and could only say, 'Oh.'

'She pulled a fast one. She's definitely scheming for her future training post,' Helen said spitefully.

'What do you mean?' I said, trying to hide my consternation. 'What happened at the party?'

'Well. There was a gynaecology directorate party going on in the same hotel where our party was,' Helen said, relishing the excitement of exploding bombs of information. 'We drank and danced with all the nurses, midwives and doctors. There were also some consultants from the hospital. He was there... I'm sure you must have met him or done a clinic with him... Gosh, I would have never imagined he'd be such a ferocious dancer... epic... Danced like a twenty-year-old with everyone... Probably he fractured his foot... he was limping in the end. What was his name?' She clicked her thumb over the tip of her middle finger.

'Mr Demir,' said Paul. 'Mr Mikel Demir; he was good fun. He danced with Ava all the time... Or should we say, the other way round.'

'Actually!' I said, without sounding despondent.

'Ava proved to be a forward thinker,' Helen said. She was definitely enjoying teasing me. 'We're killing ourselves trying to pass our finals while she's already making inroads for training posts. She covered the distance from the dance floor to the hotel room of this person in a matter of hours. What did you say his name was, Paul?'

'Demir,' said Paul, laughing. 'It's an unusual name but not hard to remember.'

'What do you mean when you say Ava made inroads?' I asked curiously.

'Literally,' Helen said amidst loud, meaningful laughter. 'She got invited to the room of the training programme director... He was sweating like a newly menopausal woman and wanted to change his shirt... and took Ava with him.'

'Did he?' I stuttered. I didn't have the courage to fully verbalise in a sentence what I wanted to know. 'Did she…?'

'Why are you so surprised? Some girls do this to fast-forward their careers. They had a shower together afterwards.' Helen winked and left the table to rejoin her friends.

I almost shouted, 'Did she tell you this?'

Helen turned around and said, 'Of course she did, she tells me everything. Ava will be here soon. Why don't you ask her yourself?'

I was shocked and shaken to the marrow of my bones. I could hear a flustered bee in my ears. Unsure what to do next, I got up from the table and walked across the room. *Has Ava slipped out of my hands before I even can hold her? That can't be right, and I mustn't let it happen.*

I felt my heart reverberating like the black covering of the loudspeaker from which pounding music originated, and I moved away to reach a relatively quiet part of the room. I sipped my beer, and then shook my head several times trying to dismantle the images in my mind of Ava alone in the room with that person, engaged in a consensual act.

I had attended a gynaecology clinic a couple of weeks ago and I tried to recall the name of the consultant. Was it Mr Dimitri or Mr Demir? I wished I was as good at remembering names as I was at remembering numbers. Perhaps it was Demir. Yes, it was him. I recollected not liking this Demir man right from the outset. He belittled me in front of a nurse when he literally asked me to leave the room. 'To eat your apple while the patient is in the room is bad manners. If you're so hungry, go out and finish it.' I didn't like him saying this to me, and had already decided to give him a vile feedback on the student placement form.

Over time, it had become my amusing pastime to make a mental note of the "username" and "password" of a person if someone was silly enough to log into their computer whilst I was in the room. I'd give the impression of a casual glance when someone logged in but would take a cerebral picture and later record it in the *Notes*

App of my mobile phone. To tackle the issue of hoarding so much information, I developed a software, which automatically deleted these passwords three months after I'd originally input them, as hospital IT systems request a new password after this period. I can say with confidence that e-mails provide more information about a person than a private detective. I was also gradually getting better at hacking into computers and thus was able to glean information about politicians, celebrities and big businesses, for the sake of fun. But I found hacking cumbersome and time-consuming and much preferred log-in details. Mr Demir's particulars were already in the safekeeping of my notebook, as I thought they might come in handy someday, and I couldn't have been more right: the time had come sooner than I'd anticipated. I congratulated myself for my foresight genius.

Thoughts of Ava entered my mind again. I shook my head so hard – spilling beer all over the floor – that it began to ache.

Ava, why did you do this to me? I was your true love. I have worshipped you for the last five years of my life. I had hoped that in some alchemy of time you'd be mine and I could fortify the future DNA of my coming generations by mixing mine with your rich and exotic strands. But you fell prey to achieving everything quickly to fast-forward your career. My heart was filling up with a torrent of swelling rage.

Thinking of anything other than Ava and Demir became impossible. Tears bulged from my eyes. Demir had taken away what was a precious part of me. How could I have let it happen? I wiped the tears flowing down my cheeks with the back of my hand. I didn't want to wait to see Ava, or anyone else, and confirm the happenings of the Christmas party. Some truths need to stay unheard, unverified. I just wanted to drown this Demir guy in some swamp so that he could never, ever emerge again on the face of this world.

I couldn't take any more, and I left the club.

The night was dark and thick black clouds padded the sky. There was a mind-clarifying chill in the air and hardly any cars on the roads. By this time people were already tucked up in their beds, whereas I walked aimlessly. I wanted revenge. The easiest way to do this would be to send a romantic e-mail to Ava from Demir's account that would put him in all sorts of trouble, but it might also have detrimental repercussions for Ava. I'd have to do something that harmed Demir but not Ava.

The hospital library remained open 24/7. I could get in now, log in as Demir and go through his e-mails to find something worthwhile, some piece of information to throw mud at him. What a brilliant bright spark of an idea. I patted my back in my imagination. But who went to libraries in this day and age, and especially at this time when there were twenty-four-hour Costas with free Wi-Fi? I found one a few hundred yards down the street which was painfully busy even in the small hours of the night. Drinking a large black coffee, I was distracted by the background noise of chatter, laughter and clinking crockery. I changed my mind and made my way to the library.

The big sixties monstrosity was comfortably warm with the smell of books suffusing the air. No one else was present. I logged in as Mr Demir but the password was wrong. It was most disconcerting, as I had an unblemished record of remembering passwords. I tried again but with the same result. After the third attempt, his account would be locked and only Mr Demir could ring IT to unlock it. A new password would be unknown to me.

Frustrated, I left the library and smoked one cigarette after another. I analysed Demir's password in my mind and realised that a special character was missing. I had recorded his password without a special character. Statistically speaking the majority of people use an exclamation mark as a special character. Should I take a chance? I had to; if it failed then, I would have no option left but the laborious job of hacking into his account.

A combo of fresh air, nicotine top-up and the mental analysis of the password energised me. My fingers trembled, as I was about to type the password for the third time. I paused and looked at the ceiling with palms pressed, made the sign of a cross and then typed in the password with an exclamation mark at the end.

It didn't work.

I was about to blaspheme but then realised that I hadn't pressed return. And it worked! I was overjoyed and repeated the same ritual with the palms and hands.

I went through the search history of the sites Mr Demir had visited recently. It was clear that Demir was the most boring person, who had no life outside medicine. The only non-medical item was a search for a squash racket. Methodically I went through his e-mails, first in his inbox and then the deleted folder. Demir appeared extremely efficient as he'd read and replied to all his e-mails. Again, his inbox was uninteresting. On the left of the screen, he had made folders to sort his e-mails: Education, Publications, Annual Leaves, Actions.

One folder caught my attention: Eralia RIP. I read all the e-mails in the folder including attachments dating back ten months. Three things immediately became quite clear to me: one, Demir was a man of integrity; two, he held a key place in the hospital; and three, his report had led to the resignation of some people in the Trust: Sandra Ashcroft, Midwifery Manager, and Peter Smith, Head of Complaints. I don't know how important these two people were in the Trust but apparently Demir dug his heels in and they had no option but to leave. Was it a principled stance, or did he like to inflict pain? It also became obvious that Demir was a much tougher cookie than I had expected.

I had no desire to go to bed early tonight. The hostel was fifteen minutes' walk from the hospital library but I trudged aimlessly until half three in the morning. My room was small and I rarely invited anyone in, keeping it locked not only when I was out but also when inside. A thinly loaded smell of mashed potatoes hung in the room and I had a habit of sticking notes written on A4-size paper all over the walls.

I lay supine and torpid on the bed with both feet propped high on the wall.

Why can't I forget Ava and move on?

Every rejection and every failure stirred up a towering whirlwind of emotions. Even if I wanted, I could not let Ava go. I could not simply let Ava fade in front of my eyes, and if losing Ava became inevitable, I would do something to lessen the loss.

I pondered whether to serve the dish of revenge cold or fresh to Mr Demir. An image of Ava and Demir formed in my mind behind foggy shower panels. I imagined their nerve-endings firing sparkles at synapses, scurrying signals upwards from touch and pressure receptors lighting up their brain pleasure centres, initiating a downward neural activity leading to stiffening loin muscles, triggering venous engorgement and lubrication. Hypothalamus releasing gushes of dopamine, and pulses of oxytocin from the posterior pituitary, gilding their experience. A pleasing buzz of adrenaline outpouring racing heart rhythms, soaring blood pressure, giving skin pink blooms and emitting a luscious odour.

It was intolerable to imagine any further.

A paroxysm of rage blew off the energy of vengeance from the sparkler of my mind. I had to hurt this Demir guy now; he should face the consequences of what he had done to me.

I leapt up and began reading the instructions from the medical school about the rules, regulations and expectations of medical students regarding their placement in the hospital, which were lying on the table, whilst wearing Ava's sunglasses. I cogitated a scheme and then pounded on the laptop and sent an e-mail to the head of medical students.

I kissed the inside arms of the sunglasses. It was half-past seven. I would only get an hour's sleep before the lectures.

I laid on the bed, felt exhausted, like a woman after a long labour.

SIX

The unrelenting work at the hospital had gathered pace with a vengeance after the lull of activity during Christmas and the New Year.

I was walking out of the hospital car park one morning when my mobile rang.

'Mr Demir, James here.'

The call interrupted my chain of thoughts of the many things which I was planning to do during the day.

'Yes, James. What can I do for you?'

'Can you please come to my office now? Our head of undergraduate medical education, Mr O' Reilly, is here with me.'

'Could I see you later?' I said. I did not welcome the idea of a meeting with either of them. 'I've got to do a ward round and sort some urgent patient matters. I hope it won't take more than an hour.'

'I'd like to see you before you start your ward round,' said James.

I knocked on James's office door, and entering said, 'Hey, how're we doing?'

'Good morning, Mikel,' James said, scratching his newly grown goatee beard. He was tip to toe in a peanut-butter beige suit and a loose tie hung from his neck, like a Premier League footballer's.

Josh O' Reilly was the head of undergraduate education, but I hardly saw him other than at annual undergraduate school meetings.

My colleagues and I considered him a self-congratulatory, smug git. He walked leaning forward; perhaps his habit of continually patting himself on his back gave him this postural disability.

I tried not to look at his nose, but I couldn't help myself. Josh self-consciously ran his fingers over his recent nose job and then offered me two fingers for a handshake.

'Mr Demir,' said James in a formal voice. 'I'm afraid I have bad news.' His facial muscles tensed, and he continued, 'I have to inform you that the head of medical school has received a formal complaint about you from a medical student. The complaint has been forwarded to Josh and the medical director for an investigation. Medical Director Andrew Bailey will join us in a couple of minutes.'

'What? Complaint? From a medical student? What complaint?' I was stunned to my bones to hear this. 'I've been teaching medical students for the past decade and they all seem quite happy with my teaching.'

'We know this,' Josh said. 'The complaint is not about your teaching but about your management of three patients you saw in your clinic with a medical student.'

'I don't believe this,' I said, sounding as exasperated as I felt.

'I know, I know,' said Josh. 'Whenever a medical student raises any concerns, I must investigate and respond within six weeks. Whistle-blowing in the health care service is now a mainstream topic. One may presume that the secretary of state for health blew this issue out of proportion in the last two reports. Whether we agree or disagree with it, the bottom line is that wherever there is any concern about patient safety, it needs to be investigated.'

'Can you come to the point, please?' I said. 'What are the concerns?'

Josh said, 'You're such a seasoned clinician. I'm sure there will be a reasonable explanation for the points raised in the complaint. Hopefully, this won't be a huge problem.'

Andrew entered the room and settled into a chair. 'My apologies for being late. I had to sign an urgent letter.' Andrew was skinny with a giraffe-like neck and quizzical eyebrows. He always ignored me when I passed him in the hospital corridors.

'So, what's the problem?' I said to Josh.

'A medical student has raised concerns about your management of three patients in your clinic,' said Josh, fumbling through his papers. 'The complainant says that you didn't give or discuss management options to the patients, you didn't explain the risks and benefits of the operation to the patient, and finally…' – he hesitated – 'the patient was very uncomfortable during your vaginal examination and the medical student thought you were very "rough". It may be all nonsense, but I'm afraid I have to investigate the complaint.' He looked at Andrew expectantly.

Andrew said in a quiet voice, 'The complainant also felt that some of your vaginal examinations were unnecessary, not clinically indicated, and that you molested the patient during the pelvic examination.'

'What? That's ridiculous,' I said. 'There is always a chaperone present in the room during vaginal examinations and a record is kept about all these examinations. If this student was also witnessing the examination, how could I molest a patient in the presence of two spectators?'

'We understand,' said Andrew blandly. 'We invade our patient's personal space many times a day. It is easy to become blasé and forget the flux of power and vulnerability.'

'What're you trying to say, Andrew?' I asked. 'Could you be more specific?'

'Well, as Josh has already said, we must investigate the complaint, Mikel,' Andrew replied. 'And we are aware that a record is maintained for all intimate examinations.'

'That's right. That's why I feel we should be able to resolve the issue without any problems,' Josh added.

'Have the patients complained?' I asked.

'No, there is no patient complaint,' James said.

'So, what's the fuss about?' I could hear my voice quivering with anger.

'Hang on, Mikel. I know this is all very stressful for you.' There was a sly smile on James's face. 'But we must not lose sight of the fact that there are four parties involved in this issue. One is you, Mikel. The second is this medical student – whom I must say is in a catch-22 situation – about whether to be brave enough to make a complaint or not. The third party is the hospital, and the fourth is the patient. We, the hospital, as employer need to understand that a whistle-blower is… it's anyone raising a concern. We have to follow the correct policies and procedures to be fair and square to everyone.'

I had known several chief operating officers over the years; they were never straight and always pretended to be forthright. Was James representing the views of management to teach me a lesson for being candid in my report about the midwife's death? *I hope you realise; this is a damning report for the management*, his voice echoed in my memory.

'The world has gone crazy,' I said, rattled by the complaint. 'I've been a consultant gynaecologist for over twelve years and taught hundreds of medical students during this time and never had any complaints.'

'We know this,' said James. 'I've dealt with thousands of ugly complaints from the patients, but I've never investigated a complaint from a medical student. It is possible that this medical student is so naïve that in response to the medical school whistle-blower's policy, he felt obliged to make a complaint. I've checked with the complaints department, and no complaints have ever been logged against you from any patient in the past.'

'So, there's been no complaint from the patients?'

'No, none whatsoever, Mikel,' said James.

'If any patients had complained that your pelvic examinations were not required or unnecessary, we would have no choice but to refer you to the regulator,' Andrew said, without making eye contact with me. 'But as there are no patients' complaints, we've decided to undertake an internal investigation first, and then depending upon the results of our investigations a further action will be planned.'

'Let me get this clear in my head,' I said. 'So, there are two issues here. One, from the point of view of a medical student that my management of a patient was not appropriate, but no concerns have been raised by the patient.'

'That's correct,' said Josh.

'So, the second issue of alleged sexual assault or inappropriate internal examinations, who has made this allegation? Patient, or the same medical student?'

'The same medical student,' Andrew said looking at me with his usual cold, dismissive stare.

'What experience has a medical student got to assess and pass the verdict on the management of my patients? This medical student could have had… at the most… maximum exposure to our speciality for five weeks. Even the best student won't have the credibility to pass any such judgements with this experience.'

'I agree,' said Josh briefly.

'This whistle-blowing policy of the medical school is totally bizarre,' I said, finding it difficult to keep up my composure, '… and quite frankly… very dangerous. You're equipping students with a very sharp weapon, which has a potential to cause serious harm in inexperienced hands. I do, on average, twenty to thirty internal examinations each week, which equates to over one thousand each year, and I've never had any complaint from any patients.'

'I'm sure you'll come out of this clean, Mikel,' said Andrew. 'The complaint about patient management is less serious than the allegation of inappropriate vaginal examinations. It is difficult for us to believe. We have discussed this issue with our legal team, and we've consulted the National Clinical Standards Service. We have been advised to suspend you from your clinical duties pending the investigations. It's been a hugely difficult decision for us… I hope you understand…'

'No, I don't. So, I'm suspended until you've completed your investigations. I'm guilty before I'm proven innocent.'

'I'm afraid that is what NCSS has suggested. The default point in any such allegation is suspension and investigations… no matter how absurd the allegations may appear,' said Andrew.

Taking a ragged breath, I asked, 'When does my suspension start?'

'Effective from now. Today. You may go home,' said James.

'But I've got a clinic booked for me. My patients are expecting me.'

'No, *they* are *not* your patients,' said Andrew with a tinge of acerbity. 'The patient belongs to the Trust. *We, the Trust,* asked you to see them and now we're stopping you from seeing any patients.'

The heavy-handed approach by Andrew was palpable to everyone present.

James broke the silence in the room by clearing his throat. 'We as a Trust will give you full support during this time. We fully understand that this will be a difficult time for you. We advise you to contact your defence union. We also have an in-house team to provide support to you, should you wish. I'll give you their contact details. We'll try to complete our investigations as soon as possible.'

'I'm suspended… Can I know the date and day when this particular student was with me so I can go through the case notes myself?' I asked Josh.

'The student has not mentioned the date or time of the clinic but I'm sure I can work it out,' Josh said. 'Don't worry, Mikel.'

'"Don't worry"! I'm suspended on allegations of sexual assault, and you're saying, "Don't worry"! I hope this isn't the student I filled in a yellow card for a few weeks ago.'

'Forgive my ignorance,' said James, 'I know football referees use yellow cards, but I wasn't aware that such cards are used for medical students.'

'We use a yellow-card policy in the medical schools to report medical students for any attitude and behaviour that falls short of the expected standards,' said Josh. 'A yellow-card could be given for many reasons, such as if a student is inappropriately dressed or late or disruptive in class. Thank God drink- and drug-related issues are rare, but they do crop up from time to time. Other inappropriate clinical behaviours or breaches of patient confidentiality would be another area where a yellow card could be awarded. If someone receives three yellow cards in a semester then a meeting with the teaching director needs to be arranged and, sometimes, this could lead to referrals to the regulatory body.'

'As a matter of interest,' James said, 'Mikel, why did you have to fill in a yellow card?'

'A student was constantly texting on his mobile during a clinic. I warned him a couple of times, but he didn't listen… so I had to give him a yellow card,' I replied.

'It's quite possible that this complaint is no more than a clash of personalities,' James said, with a canny smile.

'I think so, too,' said Josh. 'I'll start conducting the inquiry from today. I'll seek an external expert review of the cases and will write a report, Mikel, which I'll show to you before I send it to the medical school.'

'Thanks,' I said. 'Josh, when did you tell James and Andrew of this complaint?'

'This morning,' Josh replied, looking at the floor.

'Is this a stitch-up?… Josh, if you'd just told James about my complaint… how the hell does James know there's been no complaint against me from the patients themselves. It's just quarter past eight now… no one turns up in the complaints office before nine… you're lying… you've told him before… and I suspect you also know the cases the student is referring to. James, you're doing all this on behalf of management to punish me for the midwife's report, aren't you?'

James, who was rolling a pencil between his fingers, gave an incredulous gasp and said, without looking at me, 'You're over-reacting, Mikel.'

'Overreacting… my foot!'

'If you continue to be hysterical, I'll have no option but to end this meeting,' said James.

'Your reaction is understandable,' Andrew said. 'But you're not helping yourself with this attitude. We'll try to complete the investigation as quickly as possible and keep it confidential in order not to tarnish your reputation within the hospital. Please make it easy for us.'

'Okay… answer me one question, just one, James. Did Josh tell you about this student complaint this morning?'

'It's irrelevant. I'm not answering any of your questions now. We will resume this meeting when you're a bit calmer,' James said, pouring tea into his cup from the large flask on his desk, and without looking at me. He had put his management hat on and was proceeding on his own terms.

'Please come with me, Mikel,' Andrew said. 'My secretary's office is next door. I'll give you the official letter about the inquiry and your suspension. The letter will also contain contact details of the support team.'

I felt sick and dizzy as I followed Andrew. Without being asked, the secretary promptly handed Andrew a large brown envelope, which he passed on to me, saying, 'Don't hesitate to contact me, should you wish to.'

The readiness to suspend me was frightening.

'I will,' I said, looking at the secretary, who gave me a sympathetic look in return.

I felt my mind going numb.

My initial thoughts were to go upstairs and tell my secretary of this bombshell, but then I decided against it. I didn't feel like talking to anyone and just wanted to go home. I came out of the management corridor feeling drenched in embarrassment – not just the ordinary variety but a huge, gigantic, soul-mutilating version. I wished I could just evaporate or disappear into some black hole… and become non-existent.

I heard someone calling my name from behind.

'Mr Demir… Mr Demir.'

Reluctantly I turned around and saw a girl striding towards me.

'Mr Demir, I'm Helen, a fifth-year medical student,' she said, struggling for breath. 'Would it be okay if I sit with you in your clinic this morning?'

'Sorry, Helen,' I said, trying to regain my composure. 'I won't be in the clinic today as I have to go to an… er… urgent meeting…' Telling lies was not my forte. I moved the unopened brown envelope behind my back, attempting to hide it. 'Why don't you try some of my other colleagues? I'm sure they'd be delighted to help.'

'It's okay,' she said, looking a bit disappointed. 'I'm interested in gynaecology and may choose it as a career. I just wanted to talk to you about it. Could I meet you next week?'

I looked at her deeply, trying to determine whether she genuinely wanted to see me. Could she be the complainant? Or sent on that person's behalf?

'I'm so sorry,' I said, eventually. 'I'm away next week too. I think it would be best for you to get the exams out of the way first and then I'd be happy to meet and talk to you… I'm sorry… '

'Okay, Mr Demir,' she replied with a look of disenchantment.

I rang Isla but her mobile went straight to voicemail.

SEVEN

Fear was building inside me like dark, whirling clouds as I drove back home.

A cocktail of setbacks began to take effect. I was still bracing myself from the aftershocks of Isla leaving and now I was facing this shocking blow of suspension, not on clinical grounds but on an allegation of sexual assault – a criminal offence. The only consolation was that I didn't have to tell my wife or my mother about either the suspension or the nature of the allegations.

If Isla were here, she would have gone very quiet upon hearing the news and retreated to the study, to process the information in her mind. After a while, she would emerge and quiz me about it from every angle. But, ultimately, she would have been my anchor. My late mother, however, would attempt to console me, hold my face in the palms of her hands, and, in her lovingly misguided way, compare the protuberance of my eyebrow bone and jaw angle with my late father's.

I wiped sweat from my brow with my palm, reflecting ironically that "brow mopping" has always been regarded as a privilege for surgeons, who during long, difficult operations present their brow to a "runner" in theatre to mop sweat from the forehead to prevent it dripping into an open wound. In my entire career I had never required a brow mopping, even in the most difficult operations, but today I needed that cool hand to soothe my troubled brow. My prospects were daunting: complaints have inverted the system and one is guilty unless proved otherwise. Yet the probability of long legal battles looming ahead of me was the least of my worries. It was bad press and bad publicity for the Trust that concerned me most.

My self-respect was on the brink of shattering. Could I end up in jail? The mere thought made me shudder as if my spine was touched with ice. I became a doctor to have a good life, to be respected in society, and to enjoy job satisfaction, but I was now entangled in a nightmare. My speciality was high risk, not only from the nature of the job but also because an inevitable part of a gynaecologist's job is to deal with the organs of patients, which are traditionally described as "private", and despite my professionalism, I could not dodge the risk. The hard declaration – suspended – battered my mind into pulp. I felt depressed, helpless, vulnerable and minuscule.

I recalled a conversation with Alan Taylor, my consultant psychiatrist friend, after we'd completed the Trust's mandatory training about complaints handling.

'I have a definition for a patient complaint,' Alan said. 'It's the gap between a patient's expectations and the clinical reality.'

'You're spot on.'

'The majority of patient complaints in the health care service are due to mistaken memories,' he continued.

'You think so?'

'Definitely. Complaints are based upon the memories which the patient has *chosen* to remember.'

'Interesting concept, Alan.'

'To learn, to reflect, and to look in the mirror is indisputably wise. But it would be more appropriate if hospital management took time to reflect on complaints and analyse why a complaint is made in the first place.'

'I agree. We as doctors can reflect to fulfil the formality of reflection but have no power or influence to overcome the underlying issues. We have time constraints, chronic workforce crises, and only a minimalistic effort is made by management to rectify these problems, but they still wish us to tick-box these mandatory trainings.'

'The complainants I really can't stand,' said Alan, 'are those who have never thought good of anything on this earth and suddenly become all altruistic and philanthropic by ending or beginning their complaint with "… I am making this complaint only because I do not wish anyone else to endure such an experience…".

'What do you think; is getting no complaints a hallmark of a good doctor?'

'Quite the opposite,' Alan said, tensing jaw muscles as if he'd chewed on something caustic. 'To get no complaints, all you have to do is to readily agree to all the reasonable and rubbishy patient requests for their management plans, divorcing clinical judgement which you spent years of training to achieve. This can hardly be right, and no good doctor would ever do that.'

'Is there an acceptable number of complaints before the ever-so-delicate management heads begin to worry about you?'

'Don't know about that but intuitively it could be four to six in a year.'

'But sometimes we do make mistakes; we're humans after all.'

'Our mistakes are part and parcel of our brilliance; they don't stem from some regrettable consequence of a separate and deplorable process.'

I laughed a half-laughter thinking about the complex processes involved in mistakes springing from our excellence.

Yet I was facing no ordinary complaint; it was a complaint by a student… on patient management… and on his perception of sexual assault.

Am I such a dodgy doctor, I thought, *that even a fifth-year medical student considers me a flipping walking, talking disaster to the public? Is this suspension some sort of karma for something hideous I did in my past?*

Have I enveloped myself in so many veils that I can no longer see where I'm going or what I'm doing? Am I consistent with the most prevalent, tri-faceted profile of the doctors who are referred to their professional regulatory body? Male. Yes. Primary medical qualification from overseas. Yes. Middle-aged. Yes.

My head was so full, I had not realised I had driven all the way home. I couldn't remember a thing about the entire journey and my mindless driving was a danger to the public. *Am I going mad?* No, I consoled myself. I was unconsciously competent in driving a car from the hospital to my home, without thinking or causing any danger to anyone else.

But am I unconsciously competent, I reflected, when seeing patients in my clinic? Why is such a question arising in my head? I've been practising for over a decade as a Consultant, so of course, I've become unconsciously competent in patient management. Or maybe I'm not as good as I thought I was? Have I gone bonkers? Am I confessing to my hidden guilt? Have I become double-minded about my position?

My mobile rang as I entered the house, dislodging my tangled thoughts. James Shannon appeared on the screen. I didn't want to speak to anyone, and let the call go to voicemail.

He had left a message: 'Hi, Mikel, James here. Just wanted to say *nil carborundum illegitimis.* I'll talk to you later. I just wanted to tell you that we are *all* with you and fully support you. Take care.'

The suspension had not been kept as confidential as it was supposed to be. I knew James was friends with Josh O' Reilly and to ask Josh to be discreet was asking too much of him. It was bound to happen. The suspension would inevitably make some of my colleagues sympathetic towards me and others bursting with schadenfreude. Andrew's voice echoed again: *'They are not your patients. We, the Trust, asked you to see them. They don't belong to you, they belong to the Trust.'* I switched my mobile off and lobbed it over the study table.

I sat on the sofa and inevitably began to replay recent clinics in my head, like CCTV cameras recording the consultations, hoping to find answers. But I didn't know from which clinic the complaint had emanated. I wanted to analyse it unbiased, as objectively as possible, to look at it through someone else's eyes. I ran the events in my recent clinics over and over again until my head ached, yet I could not detect myself doing anything wrong or objectionable. My only consolation was that whenever a gynaecological examination took place, there was always a chaperone present in the room. Her witness would be vital to my case.

EIGHT

The distress of the suspension orders created a deluge of memories of Isla. It was four years since she'd left me, yet her fragrance still lingered in the house. Isla was my first, and most likely my last, love. The break-up had made me a very quiet person. My friends and acquaintances thought this would be a temporary change and that once I'd got over her leaving I would be normal again, but the greater the blow, the quieter the response. I felt swamped by the need to look into her light-green eyes, confide in her and tell all that had happened.

But all I had left of her was the house. She had a natural knack for interior decoration and had decorated it in her unique style, adding vases and pictures. Her photographs were still on the walls.

Isla had become a freelance war-zone photojournalist following a disagreement with her bosses at the *Guardian*. I was concerned at her choice and, in the beginning, she was intimidated by the enormity of it. We'd been married for three years and I had joked with her saying that she was only doing it because she was an adrenaline junkie.

'Maybe I am,' she'd said. 'I love my job. I simply love it.'

'You're spending your life documenting death. Why not start a life?' I was hoping that starting a family, which we'd often spoken of, would change the course of her priorities.

'When the time is right, I will,' she replied and turned away from me.

Now, I truly believe that ambition is a character trait that is developed and not genetic. Isla's parents had nurtured and nourished the trait of ambition in their children.

I had always liked her looks. Her white skin was delicately drawn across her sharp, regular face features, displaying the distinct benefit of her confident upbringing. There were semi-lunar laugh-lines on either side of her mouth and a faint scar from a corrected cleft upper lip. Her mental organisation was evident through her eyes – which was mostly an advantage but sometimes a drawback, as she was always busy with something. She presented something very special, very modern and highly developed in her features. But Isla became overly job-focused after the sudden death of her elder brother.

'We need to talk,' she said to me one evening six years ago.

'What about?' I asked, sitting on the windowsill, watching her undress.

She went into the en-suite bathroom and, in a minute, I could hear the power shower.

I had become used to Isla going away for a few weeks to war-stricken areas and then spending a couple of months at home.

She came back into the bedroom, tying the bathrobe around her. Drops of water pearled at the edges of her shoulder-length brown hair. Her moist face was glowing, and the rosy gleam of her lips aroused me.

She pressed herself against the length of my body.

'What did you want to tell me?'

'I told you CNN is launching a new headquarters in Qatar.'

I wasn't interested in what CNN was launching, and kissed her.

She separated herself from me and said, 'They rang me today and offered me a CEO post.'

'That's wonderful news,' I said putting my arms around her again.

I could sense her breathing becoming deeper. I freed her of her bathrobe, and we made love.

Dusk was now descending outside, and the room was darker. I closed the curtains and switched on the bedside lamp. We lay face to face, silent, warmth emanating from our bodies.

'You'd allow me to go?' she said in her usual level voice.

'I'll allow you to do whatever you want to do,' I replied, playing with her hair. 'But why would you like to go there? Away from me? Is it the money?'

'Well, they're offering a five-figure salary, plus a home, plus first-class airfare three times a year,' she said, looking at me. 'You did say once that I'd better earn loads of money, and I'm going to do it now.'

'No, I never meant it that way,' I said in a tone tinged with sourness, which I then tried to hide. 'I'm quite happy the way we are. We've got a roof over our head, we drive a relatively new car, our living standards are better than many others'. I never thought you were doing this job for money. I thought it was your hobby.'

She opened her lips to say something but then said nothing. I moved my arm around her and as she moved closer to me, I kissed her hand.

'Are you angry with me?'

'No,' I said. 'I'm not angry, I'm just afraid; terrified. What will I do without you?'

We were lying face to face again. I held her hand, caressing her fingers with my thumb.

Isla sat up on the edge of the bed hugging nakedness. She looked annoyed. I touched the circular vaccination scar on her right arm with the tip of my index finger. She took a breath out sharply, said, 'You'll be just fine. Please try to understand, it's the opportunity of a lifetime.'

'But at a huge cost!' I replied irately.

'There are no costs. I want to do it. I thought you'd be more willing and understanding.' She flung herself off the bed, put on the bathrobe and left the room.

There was silence in the house which had the nature of truce.

We slept in different rooms that night for the first time.

The following morning Isla was up before me, but the aroma of coffee radiating from the kitchen could not negate the baleful air that hung in the room.

'Good morning,' I said brightly.

Isla was reading the newspaper and didn't look up.

'Morning.'

Wanting forgiveness, I said, 'Anything interesting in the papers?'

She answered in the same silent voice and left the kitchen.

Isla accepted the CNN offer. I anticipated the novelty would not last long and hoped that she would quit and get a different job here in the UK. I was known in the hospital for my incurable optimism and I was sure things would work out between us at some stage. I was willing to wait.

However, true, unadulterated hopefulness is one thing; reality could be another, and the former could not influence the latter.

One wretched morning Isla said to me, 'Mike, I feel I've been very unfair to you. I don't want to keep you in limbo any longer.' There was calmness in her voice: the composure that is reached when you've won a raging battle inside you. I felt a shift in the foundations of my optimism. 'I don't think I deserve a good person like you. I feel guilty because I can't give you the happiness you deserve.'

'Don't say it like that,' I said, placing my hands over hers. 'I'm just happy to be part of you. When you're not here, still you're very close to me.'

'That's exactly what I mean, you're so nice, so accommodating… and I'm feeling guilty about putting your life on hold. It's been very hard for me to come to this decision but I think we need to move on.' Her eyes filled with tears.

'What do you mean?' My heart skipped several beats.

'Separation,' she said quietly, wiping her eyes.

'Why? Why separation? I'm worried about your flights and migraines. I don't mind if you're with me every couple of weeks after a few months… It's okay… It's working, and we'll try to make it work better.'

'Relationships shouldn't be made to work; they should work themselves, by default. I don't think this is fair on you,' she said looking at the floor.

'Have you thought through what you've been saying?' I asked, still puzzled by the whole situation.

'Yes, I have,' she said, and a solitary tear escaped her eye and rolled down her cheek. 'I've agonised over this for the past few months. I didn't want to keep you as my hostage.'

She then became angry, and a flush like a port-wine stain appeared on her cheeks. She was unreasonable and uttered a pantomime of absurdities about my inept upbringing with several references to my mother, whom she held responsible for making me an unaccommodating, emotionally unstable person.

'That's enough,' I said, far more sternly than I had intended. Her comments about my mother were hurtful and I would never forget them.

The conversation ended in the dead end of silence.

There was no point in me trying persuasion now that her mind was made up.

Isla's mother felt like a silent spectator, which was highly infuriating.

A crack in our relationship had suddenly progressed to a complete rupture, unexpected and unanticipated.

The curtain had fallen.

I was getting sucked up into the whirlwind of memories from the past and I found it difficult coming to terms with the end of all the promises and pledges we'd made, the books we read together, and the long winter nights we'd spent under a duvet. How could this happen to me? I failed to answer the question again and again.

I remembered the day I met Isla. I still wonder whether we had an accidental connection, or were supernatural forces trying to join us?

I'd been invited to give a talk at a conference in Jordan and after my lecture I had a whole free day on my hands. Instead of sitting and watching TV in my room, I decided to go and see the Petra ruins, which were a three-hour taxi ride away. The plan was simple: I'd leave by taxi for Petra at five a.m. in the morning, spend three to four hours there, and be ready to catch the flight back at seven p.m. The itinerary went like clockwork except on the way back the taxi broke down in the middle of the desert. The road at that time was very quiet. The driver, Abdullah, was extremely apologetic and immediately got out of the taxi to fix the engine.

'Just ten minutes, *Inshallah*, we'll be back on the road,' he said as he opened the bonnet and stooped over the engine.

The desert heat and the temperature from the engine were making Abdullah sweat profusely. Despite this, Abdullah kept smiling. 'Just ten more minutes, sir, we'll be on our way soon.' He spiced up his sentences by using the obligatory word *Inshallah*.

Standing under the thin shade of a palm tree, I adored his optimism. The air was like a blast from a furnace, scorching my lungs. Sweat sprouted and began to flow like an army of ants marching inside my shirt. After an hour, I told the driver I had to reach Amman airport by six at the latest and I could no longer wait for his taxi to be fixed and that I'd be grateful if he could help me find a lift from someone else.

'No problems, *Inshallah*,' he said, walking towards the roadside. He was a silhouette with bright sun in the background of blue sky behind him. His hands were black as coal. 'I'll do this right now.' He wiped his hands over his *jellaba* and began to wave at isolated cars, but none stopped.

I was getting worried that I'd miss my flight but after an hour or so, Abdullah was able to stop a minivan. He had a chat with the driver and pointed a couple of times at me. After these relatively protracted negotiations, he walked towards me, his face beaming with heat and a sense of accomplishment.

'Sir,' he said smiling, 'They will take you to Amman, free of charge.' He took my rucksack out of the taxi and handed it over to me.

'I'm not worried about paying them,' I said. 'I just don't want to miss my flight.'

'No, you will not miss your flight, *Inshallah*,' he said with a hesitation. 'The van driver is travelling with his family, and he doesn't mind giving you a lift as long as you don't mind travelling with them.'

'I should be fine.' I was glad to be on my way. The driver slammed the door shut behind me, and the van made a couple of hiccupping noises before it bolted off.

The family comprised of two hijab-clad women. One had a creased face, and her hospitable smile exhibited a large solitary tooth in her mouth. The other woman appeared much younger and held an infant in her lap. The other passengers in the van were an oblivious-looking goat who sat munching on a seat and a medium-sized donkey sitting on the floor. The older woman pointed to the seat next to the goat. I took it. The donkey raised his nose and upper lip, exposing his front teeth. The young woman noticed hesitation and fear on my face and explained in rudimentary English that the donkey was not going to harm me, and he was just telling us that he felt hot.

'You seem to understand donkeys well,' I said.

'I have been married to him for the past four years,' she said pointing towards the driving seat.

I knew she meant to say that she was married to a donkey-keeper, but the way she said it meant something else and I felt my face redden in the effort to contain my laughter. I was sitting in such a way that my legs were on either side of the donkey, as if I was about to embark on a ride on his back. The donkey was very speed-conscious and whenever the driver picked up speed, he straightened his ears and moved his lower jaw sideways. The driver's wife would then bang her hand on the partition between the driver side and passenger side of the van to slow down. The rest of the journey was relatively uneventful except for when the donkey emitted unintentional burps followed by facial expressions of profuse apology.

I thought I'd made it to the hotel in time to collect my baggage. But when I reached the airport, boarding for my seven o'clock flight was closed, and I was given a boarding pass to travel on another flight three hours later.

I was in desperate need of a caffeine boost and was soon sipping coffee in the first-class lounge, reflecting on the day's events.

'Could I take this seat?' a girl asked me.

I looked around and noticed that every single seat in the hall was taken. 'You may sit at your peril, as I might be smelling of a donkey.'

She laughed out loud, and it was the most beautiful laughter I'd ever heard in my life. 'I'm not joking,' I said, and told her how I had travelled to the airport.

She laughed again, and introduced herself as Isla – my Isla, who had come to Jordan to interview the heir to the throne. But the interview had not taken place as the heir had fallen from a horse and broken a couple of ribs. Isla was supposed to leave the following day but had booked an earlier flight.

Looking back, Nature had put substantial efforts into conjuring events to join us together, and after that hard work, why would Nature make us go separate ways?

NINE

Some events are not amusing when they're happening but become comical as the passage of time tenderises them.

A pile of unopened letters was towering on the coffee table. I opened the one lying on top. Walter had confirmed the arrangements for me to go with his charity to Brazil. I was booked to fly out with him and James in two weeks' time. But how could I leave? I could be summoned to face the investigative committee over my suspension at any time. Yet these committees took weeks to gather some pace, so I made the decision to go to South America and not let the trailing thoughts of this investigation suffocate me.

Isla's departure had left a big void in my life, which I had tried to fill by diving into my work, and that option was no longer available to me. I wondered into her office and gazed at her photographs. I had a routine of going through an assortment of newspapers and magazines and cutting out pictures credited to Isla, pasting them on the walls of her office. My favourite was a picture of a blazing jeep. I had always wondered what story it was telling. To see what Isla had seen through her eyes once brought pleasure to my heart, but now tears of longing bulged and burnt my eyes.

I remembered one Saturday afternoon, not long after she'd left. I was almost done with clearing away the paper trash of cutting and pasting when Martin Norton knocked on the front door. Martin was a consultant colleague from the hospital, a specialist of the digestive system, but with an inherent problem of vomiting blather incessantly. I invited him inside simply for his company.

However, the problem with difficult times is not only that one is going through difficulties but also that everyone appears to have a laser-cut, absolutely-perfect-in-all-dimensions solution to your troubles. All the imperfections and faults in your character become clear to them. They carry a toolbox on their shoulders with every gadget available to dismantle and fix you.

Another problem is that if you have a doctor for a friend they view everything through their clinical glasses.

Martin was well known for his philosophical thinking and speaking his mind: he had a complete disregard for the contemporary culture of political correctness. This approach had landed him in trouble several times with hospital management: he was regarded as a loose cannon. I was certain that the only reason management put up with him was because he was extremely good in his clinical work, held millions of pounds' worth of research grants and churned out publication after publication. Martin wore baseball caps to hide a shining patch on the top of his head. Otherwise, the only thing prominent on his face was his nose, which made his small eyes look deep seated. He always dressed casually and padded around the hospital in trainers.

Martin's visit was akin to a doctor calling on a patient at home. Without any warning shot, Martin began his consultation. He reprimanded me for getting married and pronounced that marriage was a nineteenth-century anachronism, as antiquated as a top hat and chamber pot, and for committing such imprudence of the highest level – I had no one else to blame but myself. This was hardly surprising, as Martin had decided to stay single after a forceful rejection from his cohabiting girlfriend.

I sank into my chair, fearing what might come next. Some of my colleagues were aware of my break-up from Isla, but I never wanted or wished for counselling. Martin had self-nominated and self-selected himself for the job.

'Isla has left you. She's never coming back again,' he said, stating the facts.

'Yes, seems so,' I said quietly.

'Leaving is usually not the first symptom,' he said dismissively. 'Don't you think you ignored some of the prodromal symptoms, some of the tell-tale signs?' He paused, appearing contemplative, and then resumed his talk. 'I'm afraid you're to blame.'

'Go on,' I said with a degree of bravado. 'I'm ready.'

'Is it at all possible that you were far too busy with your own daily grind, your own patients, your anti-social work hours, your gung-ho agreement to being on-call, and that you became preoccupied with the story of your own life and didn't listen or even hear what Isla was trying to tell you? I'm trying to make you think. Was Isla leaving the first symptom?'

Nonchalantly, I said, 'It is possible, quite possible, that leaving was not the first symptom, but it's also equally possible that sometimes the first symptom is the last symptom, like a fatal heart attack, sudden irreversible cardiac arrest.'

I thought my reply would end the conversation, but it didn't. For some people, no matter is too personal or in-house, and every issue is a communal issue, worthy of intervention.

'Did Isla leave you after a big row?' Martin asked, with his eyes still firmly anchored on my face. 'Don't include normal matrimonial skirmishes. I want to hear about world-war type situations to try to understand whether Isla leaving you was a reactive action.'

'Yes, we did have an argument in the end. I suppose everyone has, but that didn't start the separation.'

'Okay. Do you think *love* ever existed between you?' he said with no expression on the face to mellow the pointed question. 'Have you thought about it candidly? Have you searched your heart with the utmost honesty?'

'I think so… I hope so.'

I became uncomfortable with his onslaught. If it were not so well meaning, I would eject him from my house, but the weight of his company was now becoming an unbearable torment.

Oblivious, Martin continued. 'Love is always a retrospective diagnosis. It isn't possible to disentangle love from infatuation at the beginning of a relationship. Time is the acid test.'

'So according to your theory, infatuation can never transform into love?' I said, attempting to divert the conversation from personal to general discussion, and waited for a wacky response.

'It can sometimes,' he said, now looking unsure. 'It's a chicken and egg situation.'

'What length of time proves that it was love, not infatuation?' I asked, feeling better having moved the dialogue in a philosophical direction.

'Twelve to eighteen months.' His response was brief but black and white. 'The passage of time resolves many mysteries of love.'

'Is there any scientific basis for this twelve to eighteen-month figure? Or, is it just your observation?' I said, curious to know. One thing I knew for sure is that life can't be generalised and has many areas of grey in it.

Martin stood up and, placing both hands over his hips, arched his back. The left side of his face twitched. 'Sorry, my back isn't good these days.' After doing a couple of stretching exercises, he sat down again. 'I've discovered a strong link between love and science.' His twitching face beamed with his sense of achievement. 'Lust, infatuation and passionate love are different names for the same disorder. During this period, the neural synapses are flooded with dopamine, the same neurotransmitter that is released when someone does cocaine, which I'm quite sure you know, Mikel. It takes about twelve to eighteen months for the brain to stabilise.'

'Well, we were together for over three years,' I said. 'We did pass your time test.'

'Seemingly so,' he said briefly. 'There are too many confounding factors in love. Many couples perceive themselves to be wearing the crown of love but they don't realise that their crown is fake. It's a crown of illusion, a crown of lust, nothing more.' He paused and a net of wrinkles appeared on his forehead. 'What annoys me most is that love is celebrated like a marriage, which is a definitive event, but these couples are only going out together, and celebrating something which is nothing but a phantom.'

'You're very cynical about love and people falling in love,' I said in a low voice. His perspective on love was from his own personal, bitter experience.

He said, quickly and energetically, 'I'm not cynical at all. Love is a very complex issue. When in love, our sight is studded with blind spots: you only see what you want to see.'

'So, you think that all these very many people living together are not in love?'

My question caused a huge smile to spread across his face, and he stopped twitching. 'Precisely. People think they are in *love* because they're living together but it's nothing more than a symbiotic relationship, like a virus and bacteria living together, a mutually beneficial relationship fulfilling each other's need, but they're not in love.'

'So, you think there was no love between me and Isla,' I said, feeling disgusted and humiliated at being compared with microscopic organisms.

'That's the question only you and your wife can answer,' he said, looking totally unperturbed by insulting me. 'No one can answer this but yourself. You, yourself, have to do the soul-searching.'

I knew very little about his break-up with his girlfriend, but it was obvious that it had formed the basis of his diminutive theory of love.

I said, 'Have you ever seen what happens to a big woolly jumper inadvertently put in a drier?'

'It shrinks.' A wave of anxiety crossed his face, a dread of confrontation. His face trembled. 'What's your point?'

'My point is simple,' I said. 'The heat of your bitter experience has distorted your view of love. The big woolly jumper has shrunk to the size of a child's vest, which is constricting your chest and your views.'

Martin shuffled in the chair and his facial muscles jerked, felt the aptness of analogy.

'My faith in love was strengthened again, recently. A nonagenarian couple attended my clinic. The husband was a year younger. The wife had dementia, stared into space, and there couldn't be any symbiotic needs that could be mutually fulfilled. The concern in the eyes of the husband was nothing but long, deep-seated love. Please don't despise love; it still exists.'

'I agree,' Martin said as he shifted in the chair again. 'Yes, you're right, there may be love, true love. But do remember geriatric love is an entirely different entity, a different species of its own kind. What we think is love, could only be sympathy and compassion. I'm talking here about young couples who remain mistakenly thinking they're in love, when they're simply fulfilling shared needs.'

I'd made him uncomfortable and, teasing him, said, 'So, you don't think that anything like *coup de foudre* or love at first sight exists?'

'Absolutely not! No such absurdity exists. The daydreaming of people creates an image of a person they should like in their minds and whenever they meet a person closer to their mental image, the bargain is struck. People delude themselves by saying that it's their "love at first sight". It's not, but a mere coincidence ornate with lust and infatuation, nothing more,' he said with an expression on his face as if he had just sucked a lemon and looked again at me with his piercing eyes. He continued, 'Love is an exceptional thing. If someone is lucky enough to find it, then its only course is that it increases; it multiplies.'

'So according to your philosophy of love, love cannot diminish, dwindle or cease to exist?' I said, surprised.

'Correct,' he snapped. 'True love is a precious gift from the heavens. It is immortal, it never stagnates, and it's always growing, sometimes slowly, sometimes exponentially but it is *never* static and *never* recedes. If you feel that your love is coming to a standstill or dying, you've got to ask yourself: *Did love ever exist in the first place?*'

He was striding fearlessly through the landmines of his self-manufactured philosophies of love, worrying me in my heart that his wrong footing could not only injure him but also me. His tainted love had distorted him.

After a short pause, he clicked his tongue and said in a mild tone, 'The only thing which nurtures love is a constant booster dose of mutual trust. There is something very childlike and childish in love. It needs reaffirmation and revalidation every so often.' He became silent and stared at the floor, as if he was trying to decipher something written there. Then, with another burst of energy, he continued, 'Nothing has caused more chaos in this world – world wars, atomic bombs, suicide bombers – than one-sided love. Love causes the most havoc, the most distress. Looking at your case, Mikel, I suspect you were in love, but was it mutual and reciprocal?'

He had become intolerable again, but before I could answer, he said, 'I'm sorry, I can't stay any longer, my back is killing me.'

I hadn't even politely objected.

Now, with hindsight, I tried to analyse my relationship with Isla. Where did we go wrong? Did I miss prodromal symptoms of our relationship breaking down?

I had been at the pinnacle of self-righteous despair, convinced that I was the victim. I thought she was a selfish person who had abandoned me to follow her dreams. I was angry with her for ruining my life. Could Martin be right? Should I not point the finger of blame at myself? Was I the person who had been selfish in the relationship? Was it childish of me to expect Isla to love me for the whole of her life?

I returned to the sitting room before beginning the preparations for my visit to Brazil. But first, to unburden my mind, I picked up a poetry book lying on the coffee table beside the pile of letters and opened it randomly. I was startled to read a verse, which aptly described my situation:

Inherent in my own creation lay the seed of my own destruction.
The source of harvest-burning lightening is the fervour of farmer's blood.

TEN

The taxi shuddered and took a deep hiccup before stopping suddenly. This long taxi ride from the airport had set in motion even the most unused joints in my body. The knuckles of my hand ached and were blanched due to a firm grip on the roof handle of the car throughout the journey. The taxi driver ran from behind the wheel to open my door. His manners were not indicative of courtesy and could mean one of two things: either the door of the taxi could only be opened from outside or he wanted to ensure that I vacate his taxi as swiftly as possible.

'That is the charity office,' the driver said, pointing towards a hut on the roadside, and then placed my rucksack and first-aid box on the roadside.

I staggered out of the taxi, my ears buzzing from the vibrations of the engine. The hut had a board nailed on the front with the name of the charity. I had reached the right place.

'You foreigners are very brave to come and work here. It's a dangerous place,' the taxi driver said.

'Why? Is it dangerous?' I asked him, hiding signs of worry in my voice.

He jumped into the taxi, turned the ignition on and, displaying yellow teeth in a vast grin, said, '*Ate logo.*' Then, pressing hard on the accelerator, he took a quick U-turn and sped away. A plume of dark smoke emanating from the taxi's exhaust marked a temporary trail down the rutted track.

The medical charity office had nothing other than the board outside and a broken chair inside. The place appeared to have been ransacked. There were scratch marks on the wooden floor, indicating the furniture had been dragged out, and a pool of black ink on the floor. Doing charity work might not be as easy as I had anticipated. I had been told to wait at the hut until someone came to take me to the makeshift hospital located somewhere in the forest.

Walter, James Shannon and I were all supposed to travel together, but due to an urgent meeting with my defence union representative about my suspension, I had flown separately.

The sun was low on the horizon and there was a smell of earth in the air. I sat on the sun-warmed steps of the hut and, to pass the time, rummaged in the front pocket of the rucksack for a Brazilian Portuguese phrasebook to find out what the taxi driver had said to me. *Ate logo* meant goodbye forever.

A change in the geographical location is not always a successful strategy in leaving behind the past. It was proving futile in my case as well.

Bright meteorites of memories bombarded the gloom of my mind. The pain of separation from Isla weighed heavily on my heart and I wanted to share the descent of the magical evening in this forest accompanied by an orchestra of crickets with her. A giant grasshopper with bulbous eyes was showing off his agility by doing acrobatics on the grass blades. Having remained dull insects throughout the day, flamboyant and fearless fireflies appeared from nowhere, adding greenish-yellow illuminations to the scene.

A heavy hand fell on my shoulder and yanked me out of the magical kingdom where past and present were intermingling. Startled, I looked up. It was just a boy, sixteen years old I guessed, judging by the hair shyly fuzzing his upper lip. A gun was slung over his shoulder.

'Come with me.' There was instruction in his voice. 'Give me your passport.'

I did as he said.

'Hold your hands behind your head and walk in front of me.' He angled his chin into the congealing dusk, indicating the path I should take. 'Any wrong move… and I'll blow your head off.'

'Where're we going? I'm waiting here for my friends to take me to the charity hospital,' I said, applying flimsy bravado over pure terror.

'Just walk,' he said, and I felt a sharp push of the gun muzzle in my back.

'Who are you?'

In response to my question he jabbed another sharp stab into the back of my ribs.

Walter had risk-assessed the charity visit for all possible eventualities, except getting kidnapped.

The boy led me to an area flanked by heavy forestation and then he stopped, looked at the sky and whistled through his teeth: 'Surreettt.'

There was a response to his whistle by another whistle.

He said to me sternly, 'Wait here,' and melted into the night air.

I looked around and tried to assess the situation in my mind: would it be worth taking this chance to run away or was I safer with my kidnapper? Dry ice gripped my throat. Time stretched and stopped.

Before I could decide, the boy rematerialized and led me into an area where armed guards were patrolling. There was a log hut, considerably bigger than the charity office, and a chimney that belched out a wavy tail of grey smoke. A tall, slim man stood by the steps leading into the hut, one foot on the bottom step, the other on the ground. His face was glazed with the sign of deep worries. He shouted something and two men came running out of the hut and took my rucksack from me.

Walter appeared at the top of the steps and descended towards me. I was relieved to see a familiar face. Walter, wearing a smile even in this situation, extended his arms.

'Hi, Mikee. Good to see you. How was your journey?'

'It was okay until I reached here,' I said.

'Unfortunately, we're in a hostage situation here,' said Walter, lowering his voice. 'But it's not as bad as it looks.'

'Where is James?'

'Inside the hut.'

'Who is this man on the steps?'

'This is Solomon. He's in charge of some *pressure* group here,' Walter said, stressing the word *pressure*. 'His wife has been in labour for the past two days. There's a midwife and she's doing whatever she can. Solomon wants us to help his wife. When she gives birth we're free to go, and if we're unable to help, we walk away. Simple as that. I've carried out the negotiations. I've told him you're a specialist women's doctor who may be able to help.'

'Why don't they take her to the hospital? Is there no hospital nearby?'

'The situation is much more complex than that,' said Walter. 'There is a hospital about two hours' drive away but Solomon and his wife are on a wanted list, dead or alive. The hospital is not an option.'

'So, our deliverance is linked to her delivery.' I'd never thought I'd be in such an awkward position in my life.

'Yes, precisely,' Walter said impatiently.

'Can we at least get her transferred to the makeshift hospital, where we were supposed to do the charity work?'

'No. The news of our capture is all over the media. We can't take her there,' Walter said.

'So basically we're stuffed. And what if she doesn't make it? Women do die during childbirth, even in the developed countries,' I said. 'And here we are, literally in the middle of the sticks.'

'Die? Can she die?' Solomon said, visibly shocked. I knew he was listening to us, but I don't know why I assumed he wouldn't understand English.

'Death is a very, very rare possibility,' Walter replied. 'Mikee, go inside and assess the situation and don't be alarmed when you see James. He had a bit of an accident today. A bit of a disagreement... Such things happen in these situations.'

Solomon said something in his usual way of shouting conversation and a timid girl appeared at the hut entrance. 'Please follow me,' she said in an American accent. 'I'm Maria. I'm the midwife.'

The hut was dimly lit with portable halogen lights. I was more than alarmed to see James inside. He was tied to a chair, and an armed guard stood over him. There was helplessness in his eyes. He said, 'Mikel, just be careful, they're vicious.'

Maria walked across the hut and stopped at a closed door. 'Mrs Solomon is fully dilated since this morning. She is pushing well, but the baby's head is not coming down at all. The foetal heart rate is dropping down now and taking longer to recover. The liquor has become heavily stained with meconium in the last hour as well. Her temperature has risen. Ten minutes ago, it was 38.8 C.'

'Why is the head not coming down?' I asked her. 'Is the mother's pelvis too small or some malposition of the foetal head?'

'Her pelvis is fine. I think its brow presentation. I could still feel the foetal head on abdominal examination,' she said, and there was a confidence in her manner. 'The poor woman is absolutely shattered from pushing. I don't care what they say, she needs to go to the hospital.'

'I'd like to reassess Mrs Solomon and confirm your findings. Does she understand English?'

'Yes, she does. She's an Oxford graduate,' she said, and led me into a small room to perform the examination.

The air in the tiny room was suffused with the smell of stale breath and sweat. Mrs Solomon was sitting up in the bed, knees in the air, covered with a crumpled white sheet. Her facial muscles were tense and her eyes were prominent and filled with fear.

'Mrs Solomon,' I said. 'I'm Dr Demir. I specialise in childbirth problems. I have been asked to see why it is taking so long for you to deliver. Is it okay if I examine you and listen to your child's heartbeat? You do look very tired.'

'I'm absolutely shattered,' Mrs Solomon said. 'Please, help me, please save my baby, I don't care about myself.'

I checked Mrs Solomon's temperature, examined her tummy, listened to the foetal heart and performed an internal examination, and then said quietly to Maria, 'She is developing sepsis due to long labour. Her temperature has risen to 39 C. You are absolutely right; the baby is brow presenting and there is severe foetal distress. We need to stop her pushing, give her some antibiotics. She needs delivery now and the only way to deliver her would be by an emergency Caesarean operation in this room.'

Maria's eyes widened in fear. 'Is it safe to do in here?'

'We don't seem to have another option,' I said.

'Mrs Solomon,' I said, sitting beside her on the bed. 'Your baby instead of coming down head first is coming forehead first. Also, you have been in labour for far too long and the baby is getting tired inside you. Unfortunately, the forehead first presents a larger diameter, which the baby could not negotiate out of the pelvis. The only way this baby could be delivered would be by a Caesarean operation. The time it has taken you in labour has made your baby tired, very tired, and you are also showing signs of infection.'

'What are you suggesting, Doctor?' Mrs Solomon said. 'I don't care about myself, but please save my baby.'

'I'm going to do a Caesarean operation, but it could be very painful for you,' I said with my eyes fixed on her face.

'Just cut my tummy open and get this baby out, alive,' she said. 'I'm not worried about myself. I can stand pain. I want to give my people a successor. I beg you, Doctor, please, please.'

'Okay, let me see what I can do.' I left the room to talk to James, who was still tied to the chair. Before the guard could dissuade me, I said to him, 'What have you got in your emergency box?'

'Plasters, orthopaedic screws, bandages, disposable drapes, hundreds of boxes of local anaesthetics, fifty boxes of suture material of all sorts, syringes, two cylinders of Entonox...'

'Antibiotics?'

'Tons. All types, for all situations.'

'Good. You'll be assisting me in the Caesarean section.'

'Let's get cracking.'

I said to the guard, 'You free him now. Right now.' An adrenaline surge had amplified assertion and command in my voice.

Solomon and Walter turned towards me as I walked down the steps.

'Solomon,' I said. 'Your wife has reached a stage in labour where delivery is required straightaway. There are three problems. First, the baby is coming out not the way it should do. Second, the baby is getting tired inside. Third, your wife is showing signs of infection due to a long labour.'

'Will my child die? Is there any danger to the life of my wife?'

'I'll have to do a Caesarean now under local anaesthetic.'

'Mikee, have you been smoking grass?' said Walter, stunned. 'How will you do a Caesarean operation here in the middle of a jungle? Are you out of your mind?'

I said, 'James will assist me in the operation. Walter, you will hold the Entonox facemask over Mrs Solomon's face. Once I deliver the baby, Maria will resuscitate the baby. We have to move quickly. I'm going to set up things for the Caesarean.'

'Are you crazy nuts, Mikee? If anything happens to this woman or child, do you think they will let us walk free... No... They'll kill us all. Have you not seen James? They beat him for non-compliance.'

'We can help his wife and child,' I replied.

'Have you ever done a Caesarean under local anaesthetic before?' Walter was now raging in anger.

'Yes, I've seen it done once before when I did charity work in Africa.'

'Seen? How charming! So, you have never actually done it before? What are you doing here? See one, do one, teach one? We are not in the bloody health care service. Oh, Jesus!' Walter made the sign of the cross and mumbled.

I smiled.

'Mikel,' said Walter. 'Are you absolutely sure what you're going to do is the right thing to do?'

'Absolutely sure.'

My heart raced as I cleaned the operating field with an antiseptic solution and applied disposable paper drapes. With a long spinal needle, I performed a local anaesthetic infiltration. Mrs Solomon was extremely cooperative and didn't wince at all. I had been apprehensive at making the skin incision as she might scream out in pain.

'Are you feeling any pain?' I asked Mrs Solomon.

'No, just mild stinging.'

'That's great,' I said. 'We'll be over and done very soon.'

Dark blood filled the operating field as I swiftly made incisions to deliver the baby. Walter was holding the mask firmly over Mrs Solomon's face. The local anaesthetic, the Entonox facemask, James's assistance and above all Mrs Solomon's compliance made it look all too simple. The baby had some difficulty in breathing at birth, but perked up soon with some gentle spanks on his bottom by Maria.

James said, taking off his gloves, 'Job well done, Mr Demir… Painless, smooth, nimble, non-repetitive. All the traits of a high-class surgeon.'

'And this is a man who hasn't done a Caesarean under local anaesthetic before,' Walter said.

I smiled.

'It's not only shameful but disgraceful,' James said, looking at Walter, 'that those bastards at the hospital are keeping away such an excellent surgeon from his patients.'

'Absolutely disgusting,' Walter said with his expression drawn tightly across his face. 'I shall write a letter to the CEO as soon I return. Your suspension, Mikel, is not protecting patients but harming them.'

I thought if Isla knew about my achievement today, she would also have been proud of me. But not being with Isla or being able to talk to her soon wiped the smile off my face.

Solomon walked around, proud as Lucifer, with the baby boy in his arms, showing him to the guards, who were not permitted air-firing to celebrate the birth. A guard brought out a tray of drinks and thick cigars to the steps outside the hut.

'We celebrate the birth of a son by drinking punch and smoking cigars,' Solomon said.

Walter and James, totally drained from the experience of childbirth, readily accepted a glass and lit their cigars.

'You're God-sent,' Solomon said to me. 'You saved my wife and my child. I wish I could do something in return.'

'Please, don't mention it. I did what I could,' I said, looking at the sky. 'Someone above must be looking after your wife and your child.'

'Walk with me,' said Solomon.

Silvered by the moon, we walked side by side into the forest with rustling footsteps whispering between us. Flitting bats cut ragged holes in the satin air.

Solomon said, 'I looked at your passport. We were born on the same day. Fate had handed you a scalpel and me a gun. We engaged with the world we saw, trying what we knew, used what was within our reach. Fate is very cruel, very strong-headed; it does not give choice, it imposes whatever it wants. We have to do what is right – for me it was for my family, my tribe and my people. Being born on the same day does not change your destiny or mine. I'm glad I've met you, but our paths are different.'

His comments were as sharp as life. Wordless thoughts were oscillating in my mind. The moonlight fell in flakes into forest darkness.

'My people will escort you to a safe area in the morning.' He started walking away but then he turned around and said, '*Ate logo*.'

ELEVEN

After my formal complaint about Mr Demir, the hospital remained as dreary as usual with the only exception that he wasn't around. I suffered no restive pangs but had a nagging curiosity to know the reason for his continued absence, and wasn't entirely sure whether this was the result of my e-mail or that he was simply on leave.

My inquisitiveness led me to the secretaries' office. It was a large room subdivided into small cubicles with the tangled noise of a chicken hatchery: several people talking on the phone at the same time, a hum of energetic fingers pounding over the keyboards and industrial-sized printers churning out pages.

I peeped into a cubicle where a secretary in a bright green uniform and wearing black headphones was typing with religious devotion. The introduction of uniform among some hospital staff was another attempt by the management to "control and curtail" them, echoing in my mind what Dr Norton once said in his lecture.

'Excuse me,' I said, hesitantly. 'Where does Mr Demir's secretary live?'

She continued typing.

'I'm sorry,' I said a bit louder. 'I'm looking for Mr Demir's secretary.'

Without taking her headphones off or looking at me she pointed and said, 'The last cubicle on your right.'

Her multi-tasking skills were impressive.

Mr Demir's secretary, Marlene, was on the phone. I waited for her to finish, but she pressed a button on the phone set, still holding the receiver close to her ear, and said, 'Can I help you?'

'I'm Rohan, Rohan Singh, a fifth-year medical student. I finish my placement here in obs & gynae next week. I need a signature from Mr Demir. Where can I find him?'

Marlene gave me a probing gaze and said, 'He isn't in today.'

'Okay,' I said. 'Not a problem, I'll try again on Monday.'

'He won't be in next week either,' she said. 'It would be better if you try getting a signature from someone else.'

'Okay?' I said, barely containing any hint of happiness in my voice. 'I hope he's all right?'

'Yes, he is.'

'When is he expected back?'

'I don't know,' said Marlene.

I had a strong suspicion that my plot had worked, otherwise who would have an open-ended leave from work?

The realisation that I had been successful in removing Mr Demir from the scene kindled a restless hankering for Ava, and I went in search of her.

Ava, Helen and Paul were sitting in the student room. Helen was munching on a sandwich.

'Hi, guys,' I said. 'Helen, it's not even mid-morning and you're having lunch.'

'It's not lunch. I'm not a breakfast person.'

'Neither am I,' said Ava, typing with both thumbs on her mobile and without looking up.

'I think most women aren't,' said Paul. 'That would be an interesting research topic for you, Rohan. Where have you been, man? I've been looking for you.'

'I just went upstairs to see Mr Demir's secretary. I presented Mr Demir a couple of case histories and needed his signature, but looks like he's off work, maybe indefinitely. Any ideas what's going on?'

'Not a clue,' said Paul, shrugging his shoulders.

Ava put the phone in her pocket. 'I was also looking for Mr Demir. I wanted to show him the results of the audit he asked me to do but he's completely vanished from the hospital. I hope he's okay.'

'I did see him this week,' Helen said, shielding her mouth with the palm of her hand and still eating. 'I think it was Tuesday morning, the one just gone.'

'When? Where?' Ava said with the utmost interest.

'You know the corridor, the one which has the pictures of all the wise heads... where there are a lot of offices,' said Helen.

'It's called the management corridor,' said Paul and looked around to see whether we were impressed with his knowledge and information.

'That's the one,' said Helen. 'He came out of one of the rooms as I was passing by. He looked a bit flustered and pissed off.'

'Did he?' I asked, suppressing glee.

'At least that's what I thought,' Helen said.

'What made you think that?' said Ava, giving Helen a disconcerted look.

'He's generally quite nice and helpful,' Helen said. 'But that morning, he was curt and not himself... I may be wrong. Later though, that morning, there was mayhem in his clinic. I don't know the inside story, but he was supposed to be in the clinic, and he wasn't, and a manager was telling patients that he'd suddenly gone off sick, which was a blatant lie. I'd met him perfectly healthy fifteen minutes ago.'

'Holy shit... What's going on here? Why was the manager telling lies?' I said to enquire further from Helen.

'I don't know.'

'Rohan,' said Paul, 'I've got a book, which I'm sure would interest you.'

'What's it about?' asked Ava.

'It's not up your street. It's about hypnotherapy.' Paul took a book from his bag and handed it to me.

There was a ping on my mobile: a new e-mail landed in my inbox. It was from Mr O'Reilly who wanted to reassure me that the issues raised in my e-mail would be fully investigated. He wanted a detailed statement from me about the complaint.

TWELVE

I was now in the tenth week of my suspension and there was still no further communication from the hospital. The days passed by like shadows. It was two weeks since I'd arrived back from South America and I hadn't ventured out of the house. I did nothing but gaze at the walls in a hypnagogic state, mostly hallucinating. Thumping headaches and surging acid in my stomach made me nauseous. I couldn't remember when I last ate. I sat on the edge of a chair holding my head, feeling that if I didn't do this it might detonate like a bomb. I felt every heartbeat as a shudder and my fingers were as shaky as those of a heroin addict. I had reflected on the whole of my life, down to the smallest details, and I was becoming convinced that knowingly, or unknowingly, I must have sexually assaulted patients in the past. The iceberg of my offences was hidden from the public eye and I deserved the punishment I was now receiving. I must confess my crimes. The only way I could get rid of my problems was to take my own life.

My mother's voice whispered in my ears, *Go out.*

I could feel her breath on my cheek and I looked around, but she was not there. Another illusion.

The thought of her brought memories flooding back. My father had passed away the day I was born. He did exactly what we all are destined to do – to be dead longer than he lived. He was an officer in the forest department near Konya, south of Ankara in Turkey, and they lived in a log hut close to a fiercely flowing river. He had become aware of illegal deforestation and that the river was providing the transportation of the logs. He followed the logs and discovered they were netted out near a village downstream and then sold.

One evening there was a loud thud at the door and two men entered the hut. One of them said, 'You've been watching us.'

'It is my job to report illegal deforestation,' my father replied.

'You'll get your fair share from the log sale and your job is to do what I tell you to do... Understood, son?'

'Don't call me son... and I'll do my job reporting this,' my father said, trembling with anger.

'Just tell me how much money you need to keep your mouth shut and if you come up with a reasonable figure, I'll agree because I'm a reasonable person... otherwise...'

My father said, 'Don't threaten me... Get out of my place. I'm not for sale.'

Both men laughed.

'Not for sale? I've yet to find a person who isn't for sale. I know people like you. This is to increase your percentage... tell us what you have in your mind.'

'Get lost,' my father said. 'I cannot allow this illegal trade to carry on.'

'You want to stop our business? You're a fool. If you don't agree with us, I've other means and you will rot in jail and your child will grow up in this world as an orphan.' He pointed threateningly towards my heavily pregnant mother. 'First, I'll send prostitutes and then the police, who'll find illicit drugs in here. The prostitutes will testify against you,' he added, shoving my father forcefully against the wall.

My father bent over in pain and then vomited and fell to the floor, clutching his fist over his chest. The two men looked at each other and left the hut in a hurry.

Somehow my mother got him to a hospital, but despite the doctors' best efforts, he suffered a fatal heart attack.

Perhaps it was destined this way or perhaps it was the shock of her husband's death that triggered her labour. I was born in the same hospital where my father had died a few hours earlier. It was genuinely clever of him to trick me into this world as he departed, handing me the baton of misery.

Mum used to say that love and death share common dooms: I never understood this until Isla left me, but it was beginning to make sense.

I heard the whisper again. *Go out.*

I put on a pair of chinos that were now so loose around my waist they wouldn't stay up even on the last eyelet of the belt. I punched another hole in it with a pair of Isla's nail scissors I found in the bathroom. The T-shirt hung on me as if it was drying on a washing line. I looked at myself in the mirror and was horrified: unkempt beard, dark circles around sunken eyes, prominent cheekbones. A spray of cologne upon my jugulars brought a little freshness.

I pulled the door shut behind me and walked towards the high street. It was now late afternoon, a warm and humid day after incessant rain waiting to merge into a placid evening.

'Horrible weather,' an elderly lady said to me as she passed. 'This weather is so warm and wet, it's like living in a washing machine.'

Her comments brought a smile to my face. God only knew how long it was since I'd smiled. Maybe, just maybe, I thought, watching and listening to people will get me out of this mental state. It was a good start.

I was walking slowly as if I had just learnt to walk. I looked upwards and saw a flight of swallows darting energetically in the air. I stopped and watched them swirling in the air. A girl whizzed past, jogging with water bottle fixed to the pouch on her waist belt. Before I could raise my hand in an apology for blocking her way, she had run tens of metres ahead of me. The breeze was picking up strength, sending bits of litter kiting up from the pavement. I felt jealous of the entire world, which appeared bursting with energy, and I was barely able to walk in short toddler-like steps, stopping every ten yards or so to catch my breath.

It took me over an hour to walk less than a mile to the café in the high street. Chairs and tables were laid under canopies, inviting customers. The walk had the effect of a long journey, making me exhausted and short of breath. As soon as I saw an empty table, I moved swiftly and fell into a chair. The walk, although tiring, along with fresh air had a miraculous effect on settling my nausea. I felt thirsty and hungry after so many days. I ordered a large coffee and a sandwich.

The food ignited a pleasant warmth inside and lessened my headache. I ordered another coffee, not that I needed it, but to justify being at the restaurant longer.

Beside the footpath temporary safety fencing had been erected, screening work in a man-height deep trench; only the yellow hard-hats and faces of workers were visible. Across the road, an Asian-looking man stood wearing a knee-length cardboard poster over his body, displaying the message: God is love. The attire and movements of this man were not displaying any love towards God's creations; he just made the footpath a tight squeeze for anyone passing.

A teenage girl went past and then halted to give way near the safety barrier. She was minuscule, wearing jeans, deliberately ripped to expose her thighs, with a low-cut plaid shirt and a bow in her hair. She was playing a double act of ambiguity: holding the shield of childhood and at the same time savouring the role of a desirable woman. Someone should tell these millennial teens, I thought, that they are judged first on what they wear and how they look. I wondered if I had the courage to say to this girl, "Little girl, may God appoint an army of angels to safeguard you. My dear, you look too grown-up for your age. Can you not wait for a couple more years? Just give yourself some time. What is the hurry?" However, if I did, I reflected, I would be sitting here wearing my coffee rather than drinking it. Three heads working in the trench bobbed up and one tried a wolf whistle, but failed miserably as he could produce only a faint screech. Laughter emerged from the trench and his head immediately disappeared.

Evening lights were now illuminating the multiplex cinema. There was a film festival and every day, along with the new releases, a classic film was also shown. I walked into the foyer and browsed the film posters, not with the intention to watch a film but to pass the time. An awkward property of time – the more you have on your hands, the slower it passes. The familiar smell of popcorn filtered up to my nostrils. The crowd comprised young couples; watching films together had become an essential part of an unwritten romantic curriculum. There was a long queue in front of a machine, which was gurgling out the pre-paid online tickets. The last time I had watched a film at the cinema was with Isla five years ago. My eyes caught a film poster, which I'd seen with Isla. I decided to see that film again. The advantage of watching a seen movie again is that it immediately becomes inhabitable – no thrills, no frills: you just become a part of it. This film would also act like a time machine, taking me back to a happier period. Sometimes, one has to go back in time to kickstart the halted healing process. No matter how flimsy it seemed, I wanted to make use of every possible opportunity, which might bring me back to normality. The ticket girl behind the window was engrossed in admiring her nail varnish. She looked pleasantly surprised when I asked to buy a ticket, as if she thought I wanted a free car-park voucher.

The film was neither mirror nor flame and didn't do the expected magical turnaround. The act of desperation was making me clutch at straws and deep down inside me, I knew, I was still drowning.

I left the cinema and walked to the furthest end of the road. Church evening service was about to commence. I camped out on a bench and watched people going inside the church. As opposed to the cinemagoers, no one young was entering the church, as if there was an age limit to enter. A spotlight shone on a poster on which a couple of verses from the Bible were written.

'Have you got a light?' A man sat down beside me on the bench. His face was more timeworn than the overcoat he was wearing. An unlit cigarette hung from his lips.

'No, sorry, I don't smoke,' I said.

'I think you *should*,' he said in a commanding tone.

I was surprised at his tone. I couldn't read his expression as he was masking it with smiles, creating permanent lines beside his lips. Certainly, there was no humour in his suggestion.

'I shall consider your advice,' I said, looking away, not wanting to engage in any conversation with him.

'Are you here to attend the service?'

'No, I'm just sitting here… watching people,' I said.

'Good. I'm not either,' he said. He got up and limped towards a man who was smoking.

The man's face was eclipsed by fear and he readily relinquished his cigarette and then walked away briskly. This light-searching person shrugged his shoulders, lit his cigarette and crushed the other man's cigarette with his toe.

To my dismay, he came and sat with me again.

He took a deep drag on his cigarette and said, 'You know, Christianity is a religion for timid-minded people.' He pointed towards the spotlit posters. 'It says you'll inherit the world if you're meek and this second verse from Luke… Oh, I can't read it properly.' He levered himself up and created a shade over his eyes with his hand. 'If you have no friends, blah, blah, blah, then don't worry, you'll get your reward in heaven. Absolute rubbish.'

'What's wrong with that?' I said. 'It's a tough world out there. One needs hope, consolation, support.'

'Only weak people need those. Hardship hardens. If the world gets tough you should toughen up. If you don't have courage, develop it. Confront your difficulties. Deal with them. Overcome them. Don't just walk away saying, "I'll get my reward in Heaven." That's timidity, escapism. It robs life of its full potential.'

'It's easier said than done,' I said, thinking about my situation.

'I've fought in Iraq and Afghanistan. I lost my left leg,' he said, raising his trouser leg to show a prosthetic limb. 'Religion is a potion for idiots. It makes your vices your virtues, your shortcomings into your assets, and above all robs you of creativity. No wonder religious people have lower IQs than atheists.'

He looked at me as if to confirm I was paying attention. Having established that I was, he celebrated by taking another deep puff.

'We're born lazy, both mentally and physically. Religion sanctifies our laziness rather than overcoming it, which requires effort. It's much easier to come to terms with your fate and be comfortable rather than do what's desirable in life. Not making an effort, not getting energised by the pain we experience, drains life of its potential.'

'Did you always think like that or did your placement in war zones change your views about religion?' I enquired.

'I was always like this. Although wars do change your perspective on life.'

'How did you lose your leg?' I asked.

'We'll talk about that some other time,' he said. 'But remember, don't dull the energy which pain gives you by drinking alcohol or going to church.'

'You're an interesting person. If you don't mind, could I meet you sometime again?' I said. This man could be holding a cure-all, a silver bullet to resolve all my problems: I was trying to clutch at another straw.

'Sure,' he said with his eyes fixated on my face. 'I hardly know you but you appear a bit under the weather, but that's fine, we all go through hard times sometime in our lives. Drop in for a cuppa.' He tore off the edge of a newspaper lying on the bench and scribbled his address on it. 'I'm Mark, Mark Davies, and you?'

'Mikel… Mikel Demir. I work at the Cannon Hospital.'

'You're a doctor?'

'Yes,' I replied in a monosyllable.

'Nice to meet you, Doc,' Mark said. 'Food is served in church when the evening service finishes. Would you like to join me?'

He flicked his cigarette away and the fiery ember arched down, landing in a puddle and extinguishing with a hissing sound.

'No thanks, I'm not hungry as yet,' I said.

'Don't give me that strange look. I'm a man of principle in religion and politics but not where there are free meals.'

I watched him walk towards the church door and my thoughts engulfed me again. *What can I do to help my deteriorating mental condition? Should I ask Walter to arrange a psychiatric referral? Would it be helpful, or make matters worse for me by further damaging my already mutilated self-esteem?* But nothing remained confidential in our hospital, and neither would an appointment. I would become a source of schadenfreude for the management.

Mark Davies entered the church and disappeared. Was he a cue from Mother Nature? Was he God-sent? Could he help me? He'd been through a lot. Maybe he held the key? Was I clutching at straws again?

A burgeoning anxiety masticated on me like a medieval goblin.

THIRTEEN

Adescending evening draped the sky with darkness. A full moon had risen and was blinking behind the moving clouds. I was searching for Mark Davies's house. Although he appeared a bit eccentric during our brief meeting a few days ago, I'd developed a great admiration for him: he had faced war and lost his leg, but seemed to have maintained his sanity. His personality mattered little to me if he could help me overcome my deteriorating mental state.

It wasn't too difficult to locate his house, which was old and sombre, and tucked under a large tree in a cul-de-sac. The driveway was padded with the multi-layering of wet fallen leaves. I carefully locked each footstep on the ground and reached the front door. Pale streetlights faintly illuminated the front door, which had a handwritten notice affixed: *No sales or Jehovah's Witness calls.* The message lacked thanks or please, a deliberate omission warning of an impolite reception to anyone who ventured ahead.

I knocked. The door opened almost immediately and a slim lady appeared with every expression of surprise in her eyes to find a stranger at the door.

'Hi, I'm Mikel… Mikel Demir,' I said hesitantly, trying to overcome unfamiliarity. 'I've come to see Mark.'

'Mark!' she shouted, running a scanning gaze tip-to-toe over me. 'Someone at the door for you.'

'Who is it?' I heard Mark in the background.

'I'm Mikel,' I said again, in case I'd confused her with my surname.

'Mikel!' she shouted again, still looking at me.

'Mikel… yeah… that's the doc. Let him in.'

The floorboards protested dismally under my feet as I stepped into the hall and was steered to the room from where Mark's voice had emanated. He was sitting on a sofa. A strong, pungent smell filled the room. The walls were bare: not a single picture, painting, or even a clock. There was flowered threadbare carpet on the floor and the windowsill had an assortment of miniature cactus pots. Mark's prosthetic leg stood aloof in front of him, detached from his body. It looked shockingly bizarre, as if some bionic man was in the process of being built, or it was a war zone without any bloodshed. Oblivious to my distaste, Mark was rubbing some cream over his leg stump.

'Come in, Doc,' he said, cursorily glancing at me. 'By evening my leg gets very sore. The cream eases the pain and numbs it for a few hours.'

'Should I come some other time if you're not too good today?' I said, feeling sick at the sight of his leg stump, which was like a wooden peg.

'No, no, I'm fine. I'm absolutely fine. Do sit down,' he said. I realised the odour in the room was from the cream he had been using. 'Would you like tea or coffee?'

'No thanks, I'm okay.'

'Come on, at least have some juice,' he said. 'Emma, can we have some orange juice, please?'

He pulled the prosthesis over his stump, strapped it, unfolded his trouser leg and left the room.

Emma entered the room with two orange-juice glasses on a tray, as if she had been waiting in the hallway. She placed a glass for me on the coffee table.

'I'm Emma. Mark's wife,' she said and laughed a laugh which was devoid of humour.

'Nice to meet you, Emma,' I said gently, bowing my head.

'I'm sorry… I've not met you before. How long have you known Mark?' She spoke in a low voice and sat on the edge of the sofa, which creaked with a noise akin to the sound produced when walking over freshly fallen snow. Her hands were folded in her lap and her eyes had the uncertainty of a goose separated from its gaggle.

'I only met him a couple of days ago,' I said.

'I thought so. Are you a GP?' she said, staring at her folded hands.

'No, I'm a hospital doctor. I work at the Cannon Hospital.'

'Please ask him to keep his appointment at the hospital this time,' she whispered, looking at the door. 'He was referred there for counselling, but he won't go. He says counselling is for wimps. He needs help.'

The noise of Mark's thumping footsteps, coupled with grunts, reached the room before he did. Emma's eyes flew up at me like a pair of petrified blackbirds out of safe sanctuary. She quickly exited the room; it was obvious she didn't want to talk to me in his presence.

'Are you okay?' I asked Mark.

'Yes. The local anaesthetic in the cream takes a bit of time to kick in. It's getting there now,' he said as he fell onto the sofa.

'Do you have to go to the hospital to get your leg checked?' I asked, to start the conversation.

'No, they can't do anything. It's the nature of my stump. It's sore by the end of the day. I don't like hospitals, anyway.'

'Can they not do anything about it? Why does it give you pain?' I said, to continue the conversation.

'No, not in this country. These buckle-and-strap prostheses cause pain, anyway,' he said. 'One of my comrades, who lost both legs, went to Australia and had metal rods implanted in his thigh bones, which are permanently attached to the prosthetic legs. He's now pain free, even after running all day. It's quite expensive and I don't have the money.'

'How much would it cost?'

'Hundred thousand pounds,' he said and pointed his finger to the room. 'I'd have to sell this house over our heads to do that, and I can't do that to my wife. It's not a huge problem. I can live with this pain. I'm a soldier by profession and by nature.'

'But you shouldn't have to endure pain on a daily basis.'

'I have to put up with it, so why complain?' he replied.

'Don't war veterans get assessment for conditions like post-traumatic stress disorder?' I asked.

'Yes,' he replied. 'I scored high on the Davidson Trauma Scale. Do you know about this trauma scale?'

'No, I don't.'

'Well,' he said, thinking. 'It's American. Seventeen-item questionnaires to measure the severity of symptoms of PTSD and, surprise, surprise, I scored high. Which means I needed not only counselling but also antidepressants. I didn't want either.'

'Why is that?'

'Won't work.'

'No harm in trying.'

'I did go twice. For the fun of it,' he said.

'So how did it go?'

'Total and complete waste of time. The day started with us all gathered in a large schoolroom-like area and some professor of philosophy came to give us a lecture about how philosophy could overcome PTSD... He was a nice enough guy but completely out of touch. For example, he quoted some philosopher... I can't remember the name now... Frederick someone or other.'

'You mean Freud, Sigmund Freud?' I said.

'No, it wasn't Freud. Some German bloke...'

'Friedrich Nietzsche?'

'That's the one,' he said, waving his finger. 'This chap was telling us that Nietzsche says what doesn't destroy you makes you stronger. Excuse my French, but that's bollocks! Such things look nice in thick, leather-bound philosophy books, not in real life. There are traumas in life that weaken you for the future. All the slings and arrows of life don't give you strength.'

'I think I could agree with you on that,' I said, wanting to hear more from him.

'The second half of the day was one-to-one counselling. My doctor really didn't listen to me. The sort of counselling I was getting was more suitable for alcoholics, not war veterans. I felt more disillusioned than ever, but I did try it a couple more times and every time I went there, she wanted me to relive the moment when I got injured. It really racked my memories. The doctor claimed it would help me overcome my traumatic memories, but it was re-opening the wound every time I went there.'

'Did she not suggest to you any exercises to overcome this?'

'She told me to do this when I felt stressed,' he said, and drummed the flat of his hands on his thighs, one at a time. 'This apparently relieves stress, but you can't do it when driving. Useful, though.'

'What about the tablets? Did they help?'

'They made me sleepy.'

'How did you injure your leg?' I asked, feeling as if I was in clinic, eager to progress. 'Did you step on a roadside bomb? What do you call this in military language?'

'Improvised explosive device or IED,' he replied. 'Yes, I did.' His voice had lost its initial vigour. He scratched a nostril with his thumbnail and then ran a hand over his head. Furrows appeared on his forehead, like a ploughed field. 'Do you really want to know this?'

'Yes. If it's okay by you.'

'It was the last day of our duty in Helmand in Afghanistan... We were due to come back home next day after seven months of duty... I was showing the newly arrived guys the area... We spotted an IED and called the specialist unit. They came, excavated and blew the device... It went on forever. Not because of anyone's fault... but that's how things go over there... at snail's pace. We were all tired and hungry after a long day... I radioed the base and was given directions back towards the base.' His voice had become low and brittle. He cleared his throat.

'Do you need water?' I said, sensing he was trying to suppress a sob.

'No, I'm good,' he said, and leaned forward to pick up the glass of orange juice from the table. 'I started walking towards the base. There was a mound with thorn bushes spread over it. This should have been a trigger... and in sixty seconds... maybe less... there was a huge blast... the ground shook and everything changed... There was a huge column of smoke and a massive crater. I fell into this deep hole... noticed some blood on my leg but I clambered out of the ditch. Both my comrades were severely injured... One had lost both legs and an arm, and he died in front of me. I took off my combat jacket and covered him as a mark of respect. A young Afghan boy ran past... He was maybe seventeen or eighteen... I wanted to shoot him but as I tried to move, I realised that my left leg wasn't taking my weight... I can't remember anything after that... I was told that I was airlifted to the hospital.'

There was a long pause. A dense silence suffused the sorrow filling the room.

'It's so sad,' I said, to break the silence. 'These politicians who make decisions to go to war don't understand the consequences.'

'The day I was discharged from hospital,' he said, nodding assent with me. He was clearly still nettled by the past. He took another swig of orange juice. 'I was smoking outside this makeshift hospital, sitting in a wheelchair, waiting for the ambulance to take me to my base, and I saw an Afghan boy being brought to the hospital in a wheelbarrow. He was the same boy who triggered the IED... He was gasping for air like a drowning person... When he was being transferred onto the stretcher... I saw that he was just a torso. I wanted him to die, not because I'd lost my leg because of him, but because his life would be far worse than mine. He'd never be able to walk again and would have to crawl on his belly like an animal until the day he died. If I'd had my gun, I'd have shot him there and then, not for revenge but to free him of all the misery.'

His face had reddened. There was silence again in the room.

'Very traumatic,' I said, looking at him. 'I feel you should persist with your counselling whether you find it useful or not.'

'No, no… Counselling is for wimps. I'm a soldier. I bought a motorbike. I go out on it and forget all that happened. Cutting through traffic, going fast around bends… Better than counselling.'

'You know you could ask your GP to change your counsellor?' I said.

'It won't make any difference. I'll be fine,' he said smiling, pointing towards the windowsill. 'I'm like a cactus; low-maintenance.'

'That's an interesting analogy,' I said, looking at the thorny spikes on the cactus leaves.

'Let me tell you an interesting story from my childhood,' he said, and a warm glow of nostalgia suffused his face. 'We were visiting someone with my parents, I was maybe five or six and these people had a cactus plant with fur-like prickles. I'd never seen a cactus before. My father specifically instructed me not to touch it, but I did.' He laughed. 'Not only did I touch it, I clutched it in my fist.'

'Was it painful?'

'Er… yeah.'

'Sometimes we do what we're stopped from,' I said. 'You may not have even thought of touching the cactus, but the order not to touch made you hold it.'

'It's so funny,' he said, still enjoying the reverie. 'We humans are complex creatures. Anyway, how are you, Mikel?'

'We all have problems in our lives,' I said. 'But after talking with you, I feel my problems are minuscule, Mickey Mouse-like.'

'No, no. Problems are problems; the size is just right for you. Fate never gives you a problem that you don't have the courage to handle. In fact, it's always a bit smaller, otherwise we'd all be decimated. It's a test to push us to our limits.'

FOURTEEN

y conversation with Mark gave me hope and irrespective of the investigation and its outcome, a certain degree of normality was now needed to restore sanity to my life. Having contemplated for a while, I booked a squash court for the evening. I called Walter but his mobile went directly to voicemail. I left a message and immediately felt flustered. Was I doing things in the right order? I should have rung Walter before booking the court. The mere thought that I was losing the ability to think straight made my temples creak.

My phone rang. I picked it up keenly, thinking it might be Walter, but it was Sally Winters, the labour ward lead clinician, who was writing a book whilst on maternity leave. She had asked me to contribute a chapter for her book, fortuitously a day before my suspension order.

'Hi, Mikel,' she said as soon as I answered. 'I'm sorry to harass you but the publishers are hounding me for your chapter. The deadline for submission was last Wednesday. Did you get a chance to cast an eye over the manuscript?'

'I'm very sorry, Sally,' I said. 'It totally slipped out of my mind.' I paused to suss out her response, thinking the news of my suspension must have rippled across to her. 'I've been unwell recently and I'm not at work.'

'Oh, I'm so sorry. Hope you're a bit better.' Her voice did not indicate that she was aware of my suspension. 'What do you think; when would you be able to finish it?'

'Not sure, Sally. I'm sorry to let you down… perhaps you should ask someone else, please?'

'I'll wait for you,' she said. 'You understood my drift. I liked the point you raised about investigating the emotional development of children whose mothers die during childbirth. I don't think anyone would be able to do the job as well as you. I'll deal with the publishers.'

I was in no mood for the honeyed tongue of flattery. 'Your choice, Sally but I can't give you a definitive date to finish it. Bye.' I wanted to keep the chat as brief as possible.

Who could understand better than me the hardship of losing a parent on the day you're born? My birth date was my best-kept secret and precisely the reason why I'd hardly told any of my colleagues or friends. I never celebrated my birthday. Isla understood my feelings but would always find some other reason to celebrate, and I'd end up having a camouflaged birthday celebration.

The sports club had been refurbished and the reception area was gleaming like a five-star hotel. I felt drained and wished I'd had a coffee before I left home. I walked past the water bottles and energy bar dispenser machine. The club had opened an organic food restaurant, attracting not only clients but also the public. Andrea, the receptionist, was the daughter of one of the health care assistants at the hospital who worked for me. She was in her twenties, fully made up, and from a cursory glance I could tell she was wearing artificial eyelashes.

'Good evening, Mr Demir,' she said, politely. 'How's your foot?'

'Much better, thank you. As you can see, I'm back to play.'

'What did you do to your foot?' she asked smiling.

'Too much twiddling my toes,' I said, and noticed a confused expression on her face. Clearly, she didn't understand my joke.

I took the racket off my shoulder and put it on the reception desk. 'My GP thought it was an attack of gout, but the foot and ankle specialist was of the view that the pain was due to degenerative changes in my big toe joint, and gave me a steroid injection. I think the orthopod was right, as I'm totally pain free now.'

'Oh, blimey,' she said, bashing long eyelashes over her eyes. 'I absolutely hate needles. I've got a real phobia of them. Did he give the injection in your arm?'

'No,' I said, becoming amused. 'Into the joint of my foot.'

'Ooh no!' she said, touching her circular earrings, which reached her shoulders. 'I'd rather die than have a needle in my foot.'

'But you mustn't have hated needles that much,' I said, pointing to an elaborate tattoo of a human face on her forearm.

'That's different,' she said, blushing, and changed the topic of conversation. 'It's court number two. Would you like to book a table for dinner?'

'Yes, that would be wonderful, thanks,' I said, and walked towards the changing room.

I wasn't too sure whether Walter would make it. The changing room was empty. I was quite happy not to find anyone there. I had never come to terms with men lounging around naked. The room was clean, and the smell of spicy, fragrant shower gel permeated it from the adjoining shower area.

I began to change, thinking how different this room was from the operating theatre changing room, where the floor was always littered with musty-smelling theatre clogs and scrubs. One of the operating department assistants' lockers had a topless girlie calendar attached, and I was genuinely surprised how in this age of control and command he had managed to escape a complaint about his behaviour and not been disciplined. Some wag in a creative rush had named every single hook on the wall with a black marker pen: "Right hook", "Left hook", "Captain hook", "Fish-hook", "Hooker". The paper-free hospital policy had reached the toilets faster than the clinical areas. There was a urine-bleached area on the floor in front of the commode as a result of constant drips, indicative of a mass prostate problem amongst the staff.

Walter entered the changing room and I was pleasantly surprised:

his timing couldn't have been better. Walter was short and round but very athletic and hadn't changed in years, except he was now as bald as a light bulb.

'I just picked up your message,' Walter said with his usual smile. 'I'm sorry. I won't be able to play. Fortuitously, I was driving by and thought instead of a phone conversation I'd just drop in to tell you.'

'That's very kind of you,' I said. 'It was very short notice anyway.'

'How are you?' he said.

'As well as one could be in this situation.'

'It should never have happened to you.'

'Forget the game,' I said. 'Let's go and eat.'

'I'd love to, but I haven't got permission from my better half,' said Walter, smiling. 'You're a blessed man with no one to hold your reins.'

'I'm sure you're capable of eating twice,' I pleaded.

'That's the last thing I need. But please don't cancel your game. At least do some warm-up knocking about,' Walter said, and opened the door for me to walk towards the courts. 'Does Isla still ring you?'

'No, not any more,' I said, and a current of sadness spread across my heart.

'Yeah, it must be tough,' he murmured, and scolded me: 'You've never told me the meaning of your name and a patient I saw yesterday, with the same surname, told me that Demir means iron in Turkish. You're an iron-man!'

'I feel I'm quickly rusting away.'

Walter laughed. 'I bumped into your friend Martin Norton in a restaurant last week. I think he was with some new lady... some neonate nurse. They both looked very happy.'

'Really,' I said. 'I never thought he'd venture into love ever again.'

Walter laughed again. 'Things change. How's the political situation in Turkey?'

'Settling, I think.'

'Do you still go there often?'

'No. The last time I went there was for my mother's funeral.'

'Mothers generally are a magnetic force. They pull you, and pull you hard. I miss my mother.'

The conversation was making me uncomfortable. I said, 'How's the charity work going?'

'Very well,' Walter said. 'We won't be going to South America after that debacle! We're lucky to be alive. You were Mr Incredible that day. I've written a letter of praise to the hospital and I hope it helps the investigation into your suspension. If you're interested, we're planning a visit to Mali next year.'

'Do you want me to come? I brought bad luck to you all in Brazil.'

'Don't be daft. The unpredictable element is what makes life interesting. Anyway, see you soon.'

As Walter walked away, anger blew up inside me against the hospital management for not concluding my case. I walked to the court and watched a man frantically smashing the ball as if he was working off extreme anger. Perhaps I needed to do the same. I sat on a bench outside the court, wondering if I'd ever emerge from the shadow of this suspension.

The man came out of the squash court. 'Sorry, didn't realise I'd overrun.' Sweat was pouring from the tip of his nose like a tap. 'No partner today.' He collected his face towel and water bottle from the floor.

'I'm not going to play. You may carry on.'

The man gave me a strange look. Wiping his face, he said, 'I'm sorry if I spoiled your mood.'

'No, it's not because of you. I just don't feel like it.'

The man shook his head in disbelief and left without saying anything.

The albatross of suspension around my neck was slowly strangling me.

FIFTEEN

One month later, and what lay on the doormat was a newspaper. No letter from the hospital meant only one thing: I was still suspended from work. Was the pace of the investigation deliberately being kept slow? There could be one – and only one – motive behind such a move: to break me, slowly, piece by piece. The thought generated a pulse of anger, which involuntarily signalled the cells lining my stomach to frantically commence a mass production of acid. I gulped a mouthful of antacid directly from the bottle. Home delivery of daily newspapers was one of the many strategies I was using to distract my mind from the investigation.

I read the headline over and over. There can't be much that is more disturbing than learning from a local newspaper headline that someone known to you has died. Mark, along with his wife and their future son-in-law, had died in a car crash on their way to Scotland. The newspaper reported that the war veteran was caught on camera speeding, moments after passing a digital traffic sign warning motorists to slow down for a dangerous bend ahead. He lost control of his car, crashed through the metal safety barriers, and the car plunged into a ditch. The two passengers died instantly, and Mark died later in hospital.

The paper also reported that Mark and his future son-in-law were amongst the 406 war veterans who had died in road traffic accidents after arriving home from war zones. I wondered if there was a plausible reason for such accidents. Why were soldiers surviving war zones and killing themselves on roads in the developed world? Was it possible that war veterans had developed a distorted perception of dangers and adrenaline insensitivity in their brains as a result of their deployment, and thus exposed themselves to traffic accidents? My heart sank with more sorrow and guilt each time I re-read the report. *Why do I sometimes delay my actions?* Was Mark a victim of "attentional suggestion"? Did he deliberately speed after reading the sign telling him to slow down, just like he had grasped the cactus when instructed not to do so? Did I not take seriously what Emma said to me? Had I let Emma down? Was I negligent? I didn't do anything to stop this happening. *What could I have done?* I asked myself. I could have informed his GP. My suspension from work wouldn't have allowed me, but I could have asked some of my friends at the hospital to speak to the hospital counsellor about his dissatisfaction with his counselling sessions. Sometimes, events happen so quickly that there's no time to build bridges, roads or fences. I consoled myself with the fact that I had only met Mark a month ago but deep down inside me, I felt very uncomfortable.

I left the house and walked aimlessly. A full-blown battle was raging inside me. One part of me was blaming myself for ignoring a plea for help, and that held me responsible for the loss of three lives. Another part was thinking of excuses: my familiarity with Mark and Emma was too short to understand exactly what was going on. I didn't even know they had a future son-in-law and, presumably, a surviving daughter.

I don't know how long I'd walked for or how far I'd travelled, but I found myself in front of Mark's house. It appeared even more sombre than before, as if the bricks and tiles were in mourning too. A small white car was parked in the driveway. I felt compelled to knock on the door. There was no response. I waited and knocked again. I was about to leave when the door opened.

'Yes?'

The young woman who opened the door had a striking resemblance to Mark's wife, Emma. Her eyes were red, as though she had been crying.

'I'm Mikel Demir,' I said. 'I met Mark and Emma about a month ago… I was just passing by. I wasn't expecting anybody home, but when I saw the car parked outside. I thought I should stop and… I'm very sorry to read about the accident in the newspaper today. It's very sad, very tragic. Are you related to Mark or Emma?'

I regarded myself as compassionate, but I've never been good at offering condolences or sympathy. I didn't know whether it was due to shyness of some sort, or inherent inability, or disbelief in the whole process. The whole situation made me unnatural, pretentious and awkward.

'My parents and my fiancé were in the car.' Her eyes welled up with more tears.

'I'm truly very sorry for your loss,' I said, trying to appear genuine. 'I hadn't known them for long, but they seemed an extremely nice couple. Mother Nature didn't allow me a chance to meet your fiancé. May God rest their souls in peace. It must be devastating for you… I'm very saddened and sorry.' I took a card out of my wallet. 'Please, do let me know if I can be of any help to you in these difficult times.'

'Thanks,' she said, taking my card. 'I'm Carys. There's so much to do… and I can't even think straight. I'm trying to arrange their funeral and I'm supposed to be going to the solicitors later. Would you like to come in?'

I sat in the same room, on the same sofa. Carys sat where her dad had sat last month. Only the characters change, the drama of life goes on, seamless and uninterrupted.

Carys was slimly built like her mum and was wearing a black maxi skirt and a white top with a lace collar. Her collarbone winged out from the front of her neck. Her brown hair was moistened with tears around her face and spiralled about her ears. I judged her to be in her late twenties.

'You must be very proud that you were related to two soldiers… Loss of parents is always very painful, and to lose both parents and fiancé must be bigger than a tsunami for you.'

'My world has been turned upside down… I feel as if a violent storm has blown away the roof from my head, exposing me to the outside world. I'm finding it most difficult to come to terms with mum's death. She was my best friend.'

'I understand,' I said. 'Mums and daughters always have special relationships.'

'Mum told me about… she said you were trustworthy.'

'Thanks, it's really nice of her… I feel greatly honoured,' I said, and felt a totally inappropriate smile appear on my face. I made my face blander to counter any offence my smile might have caused. 'Your mum was concerned that your dad wasn't attending his counselling sessions. I work at the Cannon Hospital. In a way, I'm feeling guilty that I couldn't do anything for him, which might have prevented this tragedy. I could have spoken to Mark's GP. I could have requested a change from Mark's counsellor to someone else… I let your mother down. She told me Mark needed help. I should have done something. She told me that, when we met last. I'm not being defensive, but I feel I didn't have enough time to intervene. I don't know whether it would have made any difference to the outcome but at least I could say to myself that I tried. I apologise. Please forgive me.'

'Please don't think like that. I don't think anything would've made any difference,' she said calmly. 'Steve was like Dad, and like Dad he had trouble coming back into civilian life. War had made him very indecisive, very unsure. He seemed to be living in a blur, confused all the time. He had dozens of sticky reminders posted all over the walls to remind him what to do and what not to do.'

'I gather war veterans get completely wrapped up in shocking times,' I said. 'They're constantly drawn back.'

She nodded. 'When he came back from the war zone, he was a different Steve, not the one I fell in love with, but I was hoping one day I'd get my loving and caring Steve back... I was waiting for time to do the healing. Dad and Steve needed help but they both declined it. I don't think you should blame yourself.' She pulled a tissue from the box on the coffee table. 'What really cuts my heart is losing my mum.'

It wasn't the time to console her, but allow her to lighten her heart.

After a little while, she wiped her eyes and said, 'Sometimes I feel like I've woken up in a nightmare and Dad, Mum and Steve will all come back. Dad will come in and sit on this sofa just beside me, take his leg off and tell me about the journey back from Edinburgh. Mum would give me a big hug, and Steve would hold me tight...' She remained silent for a while to regain her composure and then said, 'I'm sorry, I'm breaking apart.'

'No, don't be sorry... crying is a natural part of remembrance,' I said, and felt embarrassed at the shallowness of my words. Her cheeks had turned bright red, like a wild rose, and an iridescent teardrop hung from her chin. 'Do you have any relatives helping you?'

'Steve's brother Jamie is arranging the funeral,' she said, and tears flooded from her eyes again. 'I don't have any relatives from my dad's side, and my mum was adopted.'

'Please, do let me know if you need any help. You've my contact numbers,' I said. 'Also, please let me know about the funeral. I'd like to attend.'

'You can take my card,' she said, and handed me a card from her bag. The card had her name written in bold italics. She was a senior lecturer in English literature at Cambridge University. 'I'll write Jamie's mobile on it. I don't think I'm in a state of mind to remember anything. Jamie's arranging everything from the funeral to selling this house. I'm really sorry, but could you ring him in a couple of weeks – we should have a definite date for the funeral by then. It'll take place here… and then once this is over, I'm never ever going to set foot in this city again… I hate it… absolutely hate it… it's taken all three people I loved,' she said, and her voice was overtaken by her sobs.

'I'm really very sorry. Please don't hesitate to let me know if I can be of any help,' I said.

'Sure,' she said.

A heavy silence descended. Carys was very quiet, playing with her fingers. She appeared to have submerged into her own thoughts, as if she was trying to organise them in her mind. Then she said, 'I feel I'm going mad.'

'Grief has the potential… but you seem okay to me,' I said, hesitantly, as I wasn't sure what the right response was.

'Do you believe in after-death communication?' Her eyes scrutinised my face.

'Communication?' I said, taken aback by her question. 'I'm sorry, I don't know what you mean.'

'My mum was here,' she said, looking at me with piercing eyes. 'She was here with me just before you arrived. She knew how devastated I am, and she told me she could stay with me until I allow her – give her permission – to go to heaven… It doesn't matter how long it takes, she'll stay with me until I allow her… give her permission to go… and… I have decided not to allow her to go… I'll keep her with me… forever.'

I tried to formulate a response in my mind.

'I know what you're thinking. Grief has affected my mind… I've gone mad… I'm hallucinating… but I'm not… I can assure you I'm in my full senses. Mum was sitting here with me just before you arrived,' she said, pointing to a chair. 'I could touch her, hold her hand, look into her eyes. I'm telling you all this because Mum told me that you're dependable. Mum knew you were at the front door before you knocked. I asked Mum's permission to tell you about her presence, and she gave me the go-ahead to tell you. I know you must be thinking I'm out of my mind – I wish I was.'

'No, no, I don't think you've gone mad,' I said, although I was beginning to feel scared in her company. 'Is your mum still here? In this room?'

'No, she went away when you entered the house,' she said calmly.

'How do you call her?' I said. 'Does it involve any rituals or devices?'

'It doesn't involve anything. I don't call her. She comes to me whenever she chooses,' she said, twisting a lock of hair lock around her finger.

'How long has this been happening?'

'Before I received the news of the car crash,' she said.

'So, she visited you in Cambridge, before you had knowledge of the car accident?' I asked her.

'Yes,' she said, and, for the first time a smile appeared on her face. 'Mum had already told me about the death of all three of them before the police came to tell me. That's why I know it's not a grief-induced hallucination. I experienced her presence before I was grieving. I know you don't believe me, but I'm telling you this is happening in reality. My mum was here in this very room. She put her arm around my shoulder, and I could smell her perfume... She's in contact with me.'

'Do you feel her, or could you see her?' I asked.

'I could sense her presence. I could hear her, feel her, touch her,' she said.

'This doesn't happen after every death,' I said, thinking aloud. 'Why do you think your mother is keeping in contact with you?'

'I don't know... maybe Mum knows I'm left alone, no relatives,' she replied. 'Perhaps Mum is trying to save me from grief... I don't know... What I know is that she's been with me. She told me everything would be okay, to get on with my life. I won't let her spirit go to heaven... I'll keep her with me... always.' There was a steely determination in what she said. I was beginning to worry about her; she was diving into a deep unknown world without any safety equipment.

I wasn't sure what was happening and what to say. Was it a grief-induced hallucination based upon wish-fulfilment, a denial or a refuge for her emotional needs? If what she was saying was true, I wanted to tell her that she was being a little selfish. For her own reasons, she was keeping her mother's spirit – her soul – a hostage purely for her own sake, for her own needs. Her mother's spirit was free from the outfit of her body, which was lying in some cold fridge, and her soul should be allowed to fly free and go to a different, better world. I was thinking all this to say to her, but I wasn't sure the timing was right for such a conversation. Both of us remained silent, immersed in our thoughts, until there was a knock at the door.

'I think Jamie is here,' Carys said as she got up to go to the door. 'I feel it was a big mistake telling you all this about Mum. Please just ignore it. I'm really very sorry.'

'No, please don't be sorry. I don't think it was a mistake,' I said, thinking she needs a psychiatric evaluation. *Could she self-harm? I'll do something this time.*

'Jamie,' Carys said. 'Please meet Mr Demir… Mikel Demir. He knew my parents.'

Jamie was a tall, big person. His moustache hung like a limp, slim sausage under his wonky, boxer-like nose. The areas on his face where he had applied aftershave shone like the dome of St Paul's.

'Nice to meet you,' Jamie said amicably.

'I'm very sorry to hear about your brother,' I said, shaking his hand, which was as hard and wide as a shovel.

'I lost my wife last year and now my big brother. It's one thing after another… I think I'm only alive to bury my loved ones… Life is so unfair.' He began to cry loudly without any warning but his mechanical howls were absolutely tearless.

I went over to him, and because of his height, had to fully extend my arm to place over his shoulder, which felt as hard as a concrete wall. In return, unexpectedly, he hugged me and began to sob over my head.

Carys intervened to disentangle him from me. 'I know, Jamie. It's hard, but we'll get through it.'

She offered him a box of tissues and he quickly pulled out several to dab his dry eyes and blow his nose hard and then said, 'Destiny has sent me a skip-load of cow's large bowel movements with no return address. I've no choice but to put up with it... I'm sorry, I just can't control myself.'

The humour appeared borrowed and was majestically incorrectly timed. 'It's quite understandable,' I said, and this time, didn't go closer to console him. 'No need to apologise. It's a huge loss.' I looked closely at him and noticed that his eyes were devoid of any grief.

'Carys,' he said, 'the solicitor's appointment is in ten minutes. Do you want to keep it or cancel it?' It was evident from his voice that he wanted her to keep the appointment.

'Let's just get it over and done with,' Carys said, looking at me.

Jamie appeared relieved to hear that Carys wanted to keep the appointment but looked at me pointedly.

'Definitely,' I said, adding, 'I shall be leaving now.'

'In that case, I'll just nip to the loo,' Jamie said, sniffling. 'Excuse me. I'm sorry.'

I glanced towards the hallway as Jamie thumped up the stairs. There was a hollow-headed decency in his manners, which was hard to disparage, but he didn't appear as innocuous to me as he was pretending. 'Have you told Jamie about your mother's visits to you?' I asked Carys.

'No. Jamie can barely be trusted to drive me to the high street. He has mood swings and he's on loads of medication. I think he's on antidepressants. If I told him, he'd broadcast it to the whole town. You're the only person I've told and I'm already regretting it – I can see you don't seem to believe me.'

Carefully choosing my words I said, 'As a doctor, science and scientific thinking become our first-hand nature. It's not easy to accommodate the spiritual aspects of life. I don't deny the existence of spirituality. And it's not that I don't believe you.' I paused. 'I just feel that there could be a simpler explanation for what you're experiencing... some medical reason...'

'Like what?' Carys interrupted me in an angry tone. 'You think I'm imagining things, making things up, and that I need a psychiatrist assessment.'

'No. I'm not saying that you're making things up,' I said. 'I'm just saying that it's quite possible that there's a simple medical explanation for what you're experiencing. I'm not a psychiatrist, and I can't tell you what it might be.'

'You think I've gone mad? I wish I hadn't told you.'

I said, 'I think this could be your grief reaction. Survivors' guilt is a recognised condition. I'm not calling you mad. Please try to understand me.'

'I'll be willing to see a psychiatrist if it rules out anything sinister happening to me,' she said. A worried expression crossed her face. 'Do you think I need to see someone urgently?'

'I suggest we see how you are in a couple of weeks and, if you feel you'd benefit, I could ask one of my psychiatrist colleagues to fast-track your appointment. There isn't any harm in seeing a psychiatrist, and seeing a psychiatrist doesn't label one as mad. I'm just trying to be helpful, and making sure that this time, I'm able to do what I should do.'

'Don't worry, Doc, I've no intentions of killing myself,' Carys said. 'I don't have a problem with a psychiatric consultation.' A faint smile appeared on her face.

'I think you should let your mum's spirit go,' I said. 'Let her go where she was meant to go. I don't think it's right to keep her with you. Only your memories of her belong to you, not her soul.'

Our conversation ceased at the sound of Jamie thumping down the stairs. We left the sitting room and met him at the staircase.

'I'm sorry about the delay,' he said. 'I'm here now.' He appeared to be habitually apologetic but there was a glint of glee in his eyes, like that of a child going to a candy shop.

'I'm sorry but we have to leave now, Mr Demir. I'll call you in a couple of weeks with the funeral dates.'

I walked out of the house and passed the postman on the footpath. Turning back, I saw Jamie take the letters from him. There was something peculiar under the veneer of Jamie's personality: something not quite right.

I felt frightened and confused. I hadn't been concerned that Carys already knew about me when I first arrived – it was entirely possible that Emma had told her about my visit and given a description of me – but I was bothered about why she had confided such a personal experience at our first meeting.

SIXTEEN

The funeral was well attended by the armed forces and Carys's colleagues from the university. Being the centre of everyone's attention, Jamie seemed to enjoy the occasion. He was shaking hands, pecking cheeks and apologising for no good reason. I wanted to remind him that it was a joint funeral of three deceased, not his birthday party.

There was chattering, clinking of glasses and occasional peals of laughter. Life was moving on undiminished without a hiatus, despite three more additions to the upper crust of this rotating planet. It wasn't long before people began to trickle out and the hall was getting emptier. Jamie was mortified and apologised profusely to a couple for blocking their car, and ran out to move his car. Carys tore away from a clot of the last few remaining ladies and walked straight towards me. She wore all black. The whites of her eyes had red wavy capillaries, indicating tiredness, but she looked composed. No matter how big a loss one suffers, the ability to stomach a calamity descends with time, which is the biggest gift of nature to humans.

'Thank you for coming, Mr Demir,' she said as she handed an empty glass to a passing waiter.

'I truly feel sorry for your loss… the words can't describe,' I said. Her grief-stricken eyes were shadowed, and she looked older. 'How are you?' Will you be here for some time?'

'No. I'll be heading home as soon as I finish here,' she said.

'How are you?'

'I'm fine… just fine… I could do with a strong coffee though. I've got a banging headache.'

'There's a Costa just around the corner,' I said. 'I also need a cup of tea. We could go there.'

She looked around. 'I just need to thank Jamie and tell him I'm going.'

As soon as she finished her sentence, Jamie appeared and said, 'I'm so sorry for leaving you, Carys, but I had to move my car.'

'Thank you for all your help,' she said yet her voice was devoid of warmth and her thanks appeared to be a formality.

'Well done, Jamie,' I said. 'The arrangements were perfect.'

'It's the second time in six months I've done this,' Jamie said and started a tearless cry without any prologue. His laments didn't give him the chance to apologise otherwise he wouldn't have missed the opportunity.

Carys passed a tissue to Jamie, although there wasn't any need, and said, 'You've been very supportive to me during such a difficult time.' The casualness of her sympathy towards him surprised me once more.

Amid sobs, Jamie said, 'I'm sorry…'

I said, reluctantly, 'Jamie, would you like to join us for a coffee?'

'No, no, you carry on,' Jamie said. 'I've got to make the outstanding payments. I would join you if I could,' and as expected and anticipated he added, 'I'm sorry.'

The Costa wasn't busy, and we easily found a table near the window.

'Thank God Jamie didn't come with us,' Carys said. 'I can't take any more of him.'

'What made you say this?'

'He's so different to Steve; miles apart… devious, selfish, opportunistic.'

'Really?'

'How's work?' she asked, totally catching me off guard.

'Work is fine… work is good… busy, busy,' I said, and looked at her, trying to determine whether the question was thrown in to change the conversation or she had somehow found out about the suspension.

'Thanks for arranging the consultation with the psychiatrist,' Carys said, changing the conversation again. 'It went well. The consultant didn't think there was anything wrong with my head. I'm grateful to you… it's given me peace of mind, thanks.' She rummaged through her bag. 'The doctor copied me into the letter he wrote to the GP after the consultation… I had it somewhere in my bag… I wanted to show it to you.' She gave a delightful smile, partially closing her eyes. I liked looking at her.

I said, 'No need to find it. I trust you… I'm glad to hear this.' I wanted to ask whether her mum was still visiting her, but it seemed Carys had read my mind.

'I think you were right… I let Mum go… I set her free. I think that was the right thing to do.'

'I think so too,' I said. 'How are you coping? It's still early days.'

'Life isn't the same and I don't think it'll be the same ever again.' Her eyes filled with tears. 'I miss my mum.'

I laid my hand over hers and said, 'I'm privileged you confided in me in our very first meeting. It must not have been easy for you to talk to someone about your personal experiences of this sort.'

She thought for a few seconds and there was now certitude in her smile. 'I trusted you because Mum told me to do so. I know you still don't really believe me, but Mum was there with me, physically, in person, when you came to our house. I know you thought that I'd gone bonkers, but I'm not.' She laughed and said, pointing to her bag, 'I have a signed letter from a psychiatrist that I'm not mad… I'm certified as sane, officially.'

Her slim hands had a network of pronounced veins with long

fingers. Likewise, her arms were long, pale but powerful, like those of tennis players. She had intricate hazel eyes with a canopy of thick, dark eyelashes. The hatchings around her eyes were deeper than before and the attention in her gaze was that of a marksman.

'You're wrong to think that I didn't believe you,' I said. 'Experiences can change beliefs in today's world. It's easy to believe what one has experienced. Fortunately, or unfortunately, there is no meter, no instrument yet invented to measure and gauge love. I loved my mum dearly, but unlike yours, mine never came back to console me. I was heartbroken and lonely at her death, just like you.'

Carys sandwiched my hand in hers and said, 'I'm sorry… I never meant that my love for my mum was greater or superior than yours.' She paused, scratched the inside of her thumb with the index finger and added, 'I don't know why it happened to me. Certain things are beyond understanding. I'm beginning to believe that outside this known world there are many unknown worlds, circling and whirling, although undiscovered, but they exist. Trust me, she was there… Mum knew and told me that you were at the door.'

'Unknown worlds? Interesting,' I said. 'Is it similar to calling the dead? People sitting around a table and waiting for an upside-down glass to slide. I haven't, but people say that they've seen the glass moving on the table.'

Carys withdrew her hand to make room for the hot drinks and a plate of cookies placed on the table by the waitress.

'Thanks,' we both said to the waitress, who replied in a Polish accent.

'You're welcome.'

Carys locked eyes with me and said seriously, 'No, Mum's presence was different. She was there in person.'

'Did you take a selfie with her?' I asked to lighten the mood.

'It didn't cross my mind.'

'I'm sorry,' I said, realising how insensitive my comment had been. 'When do you leave for Cambridge?'

'In exactly thirty minutes,' she replied, drinking coffee in hasty sips. 'I'll quickly nip to the ladies.'

Jamie entered the coffee shop and glanced around. I waved at him.

'Damn it,' he said as he sat down. 'Has Carys already left? Now I'll have to drive all the way to Cambridge.' His face twisted in disgust; lips pulled backwards, displaying his teeth. Unusually, there were no apologies.

'No, you haven't missed her. She's gone to the loo,' I said.

'Good,' he said, and a sly smile appeared on his face. 'The stupid tyre went flat, just changed it.' He wiped his sullied hands on his trousers and started crunching cookies. He didn't look at me or make any attempt to talk as if he was streamlining thoughts in his mind.

Carys returned. 'Did you settle the balance?'

'I'm sorry, could you excuse us for a minute, Mr Demir,' Jamie said. There was an unknown firmness in his voice.

'No problem, I'll be leaving anyway,' I replied. 'See you sometime again soon, Carys.'

'I'm sure we will,' Carys said, shaking hands with me. Jamie remained busy emptying the plate.

I got up to leave, but tactically delayed my departure by giving way to a waitress and stayed within hearing distance.

Jamie said, 'They're asking for another twenty grand.'

'Another twenty? Why?'

'Stop asking silly questions. I need the money.'

'That's all my savings!'

'Borrow from the bank or friends. I don't care. I need the money. Have no illusions. I will not wait endlessly for your house to sell. I may have to ask you to reduce the price.'

There were no apologies, no niceties but brazen ruthlessness. Jamie's true personality was showing beneath the veneer and an emotionally vulnerable Carys was a perfect catch for him. There was no doubt in my mind that Jamie was trying to make a quick buck out of her.

I stood outside the coffee shop, pretending to wait for a bus. Carys came out, visibly flustered, and hurriedly hailed a taxi. Jamie appeared a moment later, animated on his mobile phone and gesturing wildly with others. Carys jumped into a taxi without looking at him.

I considered ringing her to tell her not to be bullied by Jamie and not to sell the house at a throwaway price. But who was I to her? Why did I need to meddle in her concerns? What evidence had I actually got? Was I jumping to conclusions about Jamie? Had the suspension affected my ability to think straight?

I walked away.

SEVENTEEN

The long-awaited letter arrived from the hospital informing me that my suspension had been extended for a further month. No reason was given for this extension. It was reiterated in the letter that I should not contact any of the hospital employees. I was also informed that Andrew had stepped down as the medical director and his job has been taken over by Adrian Baylis who would be the new head of my investigation. I vaguely remembered Adrian, he was a cardiologist and Andrew's protégé. So, things wouldn't change much in my favour.

Five months had passed since I'd been put on gardening leave and it was now midsummer. The thought precipitated anger and disgust and I felt belittled. I had become a chronic anorexic. I stumbled to the bedroom and fell on the bed like a broken tree trunk.

When I awoke, it was almost evening and I wanted to drink. I headed for the city centre and found a deserted-looking pub close to two others, hoping it would be empty so that I could drink without having to talk to anyone. I just wanted to forget everything.

The pub was dimly lit, which suited me well. I didn't want to see or be seen. I ordered a pint at the bar and sat on a high stool to allow time to adjust my vision. There were three people drinking at a table, two men and a woman. The woman was talking and both men were laughing hysterically and spilling their drinks. Low music was playing in the background. Large black and white photo prints of Marilyn Monroe, Raquel Welch, Sophia Loren paraded over the walls. I took my glass and, without making any eye contact with the other punters, sat in front of the large TV screen showing a T20 cricket match. The sound was switched off.

One of the men walked towards me with his car keys in his hand. His hair was long, curly like a judge's wig.

'Evening,' he said. 'Are you new around here?'

I didn't want conversation, even out of politeness, and purposefully kept my reply as short as possible: 'Yes.'

'I thought so,' he replied.

If you knew that then why the hell would you ask, I thought.

'No fun drinking alone. Why don't you join us?' he said, pointing to the table. 'Olivia is such a good laugh.'

'I'm sure she is,' I said and threw a cursory glance at her. She had magenta hair plummeted over her shoulders. 'I just want to be alone today.' I wondered if he was pimping her. I had no previous knowledge or experience of how to spot a pimp, but he appeared to be a normal person.

'I'm off now,' he said. 'Have to go and pick my daughter up from her tuition class. She's sitting A-levels this year.'

I stood up and shook hands with him before he could volunteer any more useless, irrelevant information about himself or any other family member.

By ten o'clock, I had consumed enough alcohol to feel numb. The bar was now crowded, and a large number of youths had begun to pour in to attend a gig, which was due to start upstairs. The bartender was making the announcement in shrill squeaks of the microphone. I sat with my legs splayed in a high-back squishy chair, sipping from my glass, and watched people traipse towards the stairs.

I had been watching the woman with magenta hair for most of the evening and now she walked over and, without wasting any time on formalities, said, 'Hello, I'm Olivia. Nice to meet you.' She pulled up a chair and sat beside me. She was wearing tight jeans and a denim shirt that had silver embroidery from the collars to the pockets. 'I know everyone who comes to this pub, but I don't think I've met you before.' Her smile, cheerful outlook and ability to be at ease with strangers at the very first encounter were indicative of a salesperson. She spoke with a posh English accent.

'No, you haven't,' I replied.

She extended a slim arm, which was devoid of any hair; to offer me salted peanuts. 'Have some.'

I sensed the strides of a perpetual ancient game, but I had no intention of gaining any further familiarity. I wanted to be left alone. 'No, thanks,' I said.

'Both the hyper and hypos of life magnetise you towards alcohol,' she said with a luminous smile on her face. 'It's none of my business but you chose the right place to drink tonight. There are three pubs at this crossroads. We call it the Bermuda Triangle. Who comes here is lost for at least a few hours.'

I had no intention, but her explanation made me smile.

A thin line of kohl outlined the upper eyelids of her bluish-grey eyes, which had the glint of a faraway stargazer. She had an elegant nose and faint marionette lines which became more pronounced when she laughed. I wasn't too sure, but I didn't think she was looking for a date.

'Here we go again,' she said, angling her chin towards a scantily-clad middle-aged woman who had entered the pub with a yellow python snake dangling around her neck. She was holding a beer glass in her hand that was almost full to the brim with the coins.

'Oh dear,' I said. 'I hate snakes. Why the hell is she allowed to bring such a big and potentially lethal animal into a public place?'

'Don't worry, it's totally innocuous,' Olivia said, smiling. 'She used to be a burlesque dancer and now the snake earns money for her. Although she claims she's collecting money to buy it milk. For a tenner you can have your picture taken with it.'

'No thanks,' I said. 'I don't want any pictures taken with such vicious reptiles. In my opinion, snakes don't fall into the category of animals which should be kept as pets.'

Olivia broke into laughter, revealing her white teeth. 'The snake is not a pet. It's a money earner for her.'

Around the pub people were happily donating milk money for the snake.

'Anyway, it was nice meeting you,' Olivia said. 'I'll see you around. I'm dying for a fag. I assume you don't smoke?'

'No, I don't,' I said to end the conversation. 'It was nice to meet you too.'

'Have a good time,' she said. She walked away, gesturing farewell with her hand.

'Sure, I will,' I said, happy to see her go.

The music upstairs was louder now.

I hadn't smoked in years, but I went to the bar and bought a thick, chubby cigar, which bizarrely reminded me of the Caesarean I had performed on Solomon's wife a few months ago in Brazil. The thought levitated my mood and I hoped the child was doing well with his parents.

People were pouring into the pub in herds now. I was heading outside and had to stop and give way to the incoming traffic. A plump, rustic girl with starch-spiked hair was bouncing in. She had numerous piercings in her ears, nose, lips and the sides of her eyebrows. An effeminate male accompanied her.

'How are you, babe? Long time, no see,' she cooed and hugged another girl in an act of artificial fondness.

I eventually got outside, holding the unlit cigar in my fingers and wondering whether to smoke it or to take it home as a souvenir. Not far from me, Olivia was busy smoking, taking one puff after another. She took a deep drag which temporarily illuminated her fingers and made her windpipe stand out. She looked at me, threw the cigarette on the floor and crushed it with the toe of her high-heeled shoe. This activity made her lose balance and she fell to the ground with a loud thud. I rushed to help her on her feet, but she kept on falling like a cat from a ceiling fan.

'Are you okay?' I asked her. I heard someone snigger and then a wolf-whistle in the background.

'Yes, I'm fine... I just couldn't stand... I think because of my shoes.'

I helped her to stand again. She took her shoes off and slung them over her wrist.

'Do you need a taxi?'

'No, I'm fine... I just live over there... two minutes away.' She pointed down the road. Her cheeks were suffused with red, which was probably due to the embarrassment of falling rather than alcohol consumption.

She was trying to take careful steps like a baby who had just learnt to walk but was tottering and staggering as if she was walking in a strong wind. I kept a distance and followed her in case she fell again.

She sensed me following her, and turned around and said in a loud, harsh tone, 'I told you... I 'll be fine... I'm okay now... leave me alone...'

Before she could finish her sentence, she swayed and was about to fall. I leapt forward and caught her in my arms. The onlookers on the road chuckled. I could feel the warmth of her body, her breasts and pounding heart on my chest. There was spittle on her chin.

She looked into my eyes and said, apologetically, 'I'm sorry... I'm so sorry... I don't know what's wrong with me today... I do look like a drunken dissolute... but I'm not... trust me.'

'It's okay. It's just fine,' I said. 'Has it happened to you like this before?'

'No, never.'

'Are you feeling dizzy?'

'No, I'm not feeling dizzy... I just need to go home and sleep. I had an early morning flight today and it's probably just lack of sleep.'

'I'll help you home,' I said, and she held my arm to walk. 'Who is at home?'

'No one,' she said. 'I live alone. My husband died a couple of years ago.'

'Oh, I'm sorry to hear that,' I said, and wondered whether he'd died naturally, or had she killed him?

'I still miss him.'

I could hear grief in her voice. 'Any children?'

'No, it never happened.'

She was fitting in with the profile of a sexually profligate woman who had acquired every possible strain of chlamydia infection causing a bilateral tubal blockade and rendering her infertile. Was it natural selection that such women were not allowed to procreate or was it a punishment?

The flat doorway was next to a shop. It was dark and small, like a rabbit warren, but neatly decorated, and didn't fit the profile of affluence shown in her personality.

'This was the first place we bought when we got married. My late husband loved it, mostly for its location and convenience for his work. I've kept it to use when I have an early or late flight. Our main house is a bit out of the way… in the countryside.'

I stood in the kitchenette admiring the cleanliness. She slumped onto the sofa, looking tired.

'I don't know whether you're aware or not that British women can't handle wine,' I said. 'It's because they all lack an enzyme which helps to break down alcohol in their stomachs. Alcohol dehydrogenase isoenzyme to be precise.'

'Really?' she said, and her eyes widened in surprise. 'Help yourself to coffee.' She remained on the sofa with her head held firmly in her hands.

'Would you like one?' I asked, filling the kettle with water. There was an unopened envelope beside the kettle, which confirmed the name she had given me.

'I don't drink coffee after eleven,' she said, still holding her head.

'You've got an interesting surname, even telling your nationality…
English.' I held up the envelope. 'What do you do for a living?'

'I sell yachts… luxury, top-of-the-range stuff,' she said slowly.

'What is your role in the company?'

'I sell yachts,' she replied curtly.

'So, if you don't have coffee after eleven, what do you have
instead?' I said, realising that she didn't want to talk about work.

'Depends on where I'd like to land. It's a different powder for a
different mood. Would you like some?' she said casually.

'Are you talking about the powder which women apply on the
face for make-up?' I asked in a way to appear naïve. I leaned against
the kitchen counter and folded my arms across my chest.

'Drugs, man… What's wrong with you?' she said irately.

'I beg your pardon… drugs… I've never done drugs… I didn't
know what you meant by "powder".'

'You seemed to have lived a sheltered, petty life. What did you
say your name was?' She was no longer holding her head. Faint
wrinkles had deepened around her eyes and mouth, adding grace to
signs of age. Although circulating oestrogens in adolescence give girls
the magical capability to transform any facial and bodily features to
a gold-plated beauty, I thought she was probably a lot more striking
now than in her youth.

'I didn't,' I replied. 'Mikel. Do you inject or snort?'

'Snort. I have needle phobia,' she said. 'I have an assortment of
powders which vary in their strength. Tonight, I'm going to do *moon-
raker* as I have to go to work tomorrow… can't go very far tonight…
but at the weekends, I often do *atom bomb* which takes me to the
furthest parts of the universe… to the remotest planet, Pluto.'

I was quite impressed with her understanding of the distance of
planets from the Earth. 'Sadly,' I said, 'Pluto is no longer a planet.'

'Why? What happened to it?'

'It's been downgraded.'

'Oh, holy fuck. These bloody scientists have nothing better to do.'

There was a degree of transparency and translucency about her and I reflected that she would be very popular with her friends.

She leaned forward, fumbled both hands behind her back and, like a magician, pulled a bra out of her shirt sleeve and slung it over to the back of a chair on the other side of the room. She dug into her handbag and brought out two neatly folded pieces of paper. She unwrapped one, looked around with searching eyes and not finding what she was looking for, she took her purse out of the handbag, made a tube of a crisp five-pound note and snorted the contents in a single breath. A glistening white patch hung from her nostril like a pearl.

'I'm done for the day,' she announced, and then tossed the other wrapped piece towards me and said, 'Be my guest tonight.' She stood up, pulled a bed out of the sofa, fell on it, and was snoring in no time.

I held the drug bag in my hand. I could be another Neil Armstrong if I used it tonight, I thought, and smiled at my stupidity. A wailing police car went past the flat, filling me with fear: if this house was raided and I was caught red-handed with drugs, I'd be arrested and ruin any remaining chances with the regulator of the medical profession. I looked at Olivia who was oblivious to anything happening in this world. Her white belly peeped provocatively through her shirt.

I left the drug packet on the kitchen top and tiptoed out of the flat, quietly shutting the door behind me.

EIGHTEEN

The glowing summer arrived with good news: we all passed. I was well pleased to become a fully qualified doctor, but there was a constant undercurrent of anxiety playing over in my mind, damping the happiness: the Demir investigation still lingered and apparently he was still suspended. Could this have any damaging effect on my nascent career? Would I join my very first training post with a black mark against my name?

Xhi had thrown a sumptuous celebratory party at her home, inviting thirty or forty of us. Her parents were holidaying in Hong Kong, and their absence meant one thing: alcohol flowed freely. Bob, one of the porters from the hospital, who also did some part-time work as a gardener at Xhi's home, was operating the bar. The bar was as well stocked as a high street pub. He pulled pints and filled glasses with a permanent smile residing on his face. He was in his forties with long, greyish hair like a thick rope, tied at the nape of his neck with a red rubber band. His left eye was blue, like a ripe fig.

'How did it happen?' I asked.

Bob said, 'Fist-fighting. I'm not a street fighter, bro. I'm a pro. I earn more money from fist-fighting than from that lousy hospital job.'

'Nice one,' I said, although I didn't believe a word he said.

There was a variety of food available for everyone's fondness or preference – vegetarian, vegan, kosher, halal, gluten-free.

Xhi had told me that she had invited Dr Norton and Mr Demir to the party. I doubted very much that Mr Demir would attend.

Ava was wearing a black dress with high heels and looked stunningly beautiful. I positioned myself beside Paul and observed her from a distance. She was indulging in alcoholic drinks more than food. Her slowly opening lips and her smiles tugged at my heartstrings.

Paul nudged me and said, 'This might be your lucky night!'

I just smiled. Ava had achieved several distinctions in the final exam, and I expected that Mr Demir would become a distant, forgotten past for her.

Dr Norton arrived, a baseball cap planted over his head, and announced that he would be leaving soon because he had to go to the hospital for some semi-urgent case. He looked at the food table and said, 'Xhi, have you invited the whole class?'

'Just this lot… everyone has arrived,' Xhi said, laughing.

'This amount of food could feed the whole of your year group. All 300 of them!'

Everyone laughed and continued to fill their stomachs with rich food.

'Ah, hello there, Rohan,' said Dr Norton whilst heaping his plate. 'Which hospital are you starting your new job at?'

'Ava and I got a placement at the county hospital,' I said.

'Good. You must be extremely careful in the first few months,' he said, adjusting his cap and looking at me with his small, penetrating eyes.

'Why me? Why did you say this?' My heart thumped.

He seemed surprised at my question and said, 'Everyone must be careful in this day and age. We all are vulnerable.'

I was almost certain he was aware of my troubles with Demir. 'Mr Demir is also invited,' I said, and scrutinised Dr Norton's face. 'He should be here soon.'

Dr Norton stared at me blankly and said, 'I don't think so. He's not well these days.'

I wasn't prepared to let the topic slip away from me and said, 'There's a Chinese whisper going around that he's suspended.'

'Is he?' Dr Norton said. The left side of his face twitched and made his surprised look appear artificial. 'I have no knowledge of this.' His facial muscles convulsed again.

Telling lies with conviction, I thought, is bloody difficult.

'Paul,' said Dr Norton, turning towards him. 'I was just telling Rohan that we don't live in a developed society, we live in a consumptive society. We consume more food than we need, and food which is meant to give us life is giving us death.'

'I saw a whale of a woman,' said Paul, overtly relishing the privilege of Dr Norton's personal attention, 'in my last gynae placement. She had cancer of the lining of the womb which I hadn't realised is linked to obesity. You're absolutely right, excessive eating is killing us.'

'We're not only consumed by food but also consumed by rules and regulations,' Dr Norton said, and gave me a meaningful glance. 'Yet we empower management and governments to make these absurd rules. My friends, this is all consumption and consumption is a pernicious disease. Consumption gives us the illusion of vitality and progress but what it delivers is death and dependence.'

One of our class-fellows, whom I have never liked, approached Dr Norton laughing hysterically. He opened his fist and said, 'Fancy trying some whippets?'

He held a couple of bullet-shaped silver canisters.

'What're these?' I asked.

'No thanks,' Dr Norton said and turned towards me. 'These're nitrous oxide, laughing gas canisters. Once inhaled, they give you thirty seconds' head rush.'

'That's what they are,' I said. 'I had recently seen such cylinders lying in the detritus channel beside the road kerb and didn't know what they were.'

'My friend,' said Dr Norton placing a hand on my shoulder. 'We humans like to go in circles. The laughing gas parties were in great vogue among the high elites in the eighteenth century and they're back in fashion again. You can try them if you fancy, pretty innocuous stuff, but don't fall off.'

He looked at his wristwatch and like the white rabbit added, 'Must go. Where is Xhi? Please all, do keep in touch.'

Paul said, 'It's always great to talk to you, Dr Norton.'

I called Xhi. 'Dr Norton wishes to leave now.'

I headed towards the bar where Ava was waiting for her drink. I wondered how long I could hold my feelings for Ava in my chest. I'd like to tell her today.

'Get me one!' Paul shouted.

Helen reached Ava before I did. She was drunk and threw her arms around her and said, 'Baby, I love you.'

Ava looked perplexed as though she wasn't sure what to say, and in the end said, 'I love you too, baby.'

'Ahh… that's so nice,' said Helen and gave Ava another prolonged hug. They looked like Siamese twins.

'Can I speak with Ava?' I said, trying to separate them. Helen stumbled aside, air-kissed Ava and tottered away.

I stood in front of Ava, holding her hands. The warmth of her breath, the smell of her perfume was slaying me. I looked into her eyes; her pupils were dilated under the influence of alcohol. I could feel the firmness of her gaze on my face.

'Ava,' I said. 'I meant to tell you this all those years, but I couldn't… I just wanted to tell you that I like you…' My heart pounded. 'I've been secretly admiring you all these years. I love you…'

'That's so sweet, Rohan,' Ava said and placed her lips on my cheek. 'I love you too, baby.'

I contained myself, although I wished to pump both my fists in the air. 'Would you like to risk going out for a meal with me?'

'Why not? We'll be working in the same hospital,' Ava said, still holding my hands.

'Your drink,' said Bob, passing a glass to Ava. She released herself from my grip, picked up the glass with a trembling hand and spilt the fizzy drink all over the counter.

'I'm so sorry…'

'Never mind,' said Bob, smiling as he cleaned it up. 'That's why I'm here.'

Ava wandered back to her bunch of friends.

'Where's my drink?' Paul asked when I returned without it.

'Forget about the drink,' I said, feeling vertiginous and heady with excitement. 'I told Ava!'

'What?'

'What I've been holding in my heart for years.'

'Did you?'

'Yes.'

'And?'

'She kissed me.'

'You lucky bastard!'

'That's what I am.'

Xhi was passing and I said, 'Does this room have a CCTV camera?'

'Er… Yes.'

I looked at my wristwatch. 'Could I have a copy of the recording from half-eleven to quarter to twelve, please? Not for the whole of the room, just in front of the bar.'

NINETEEN

My mobile phone pinged, and a message appeared from Olivia asking me to come over. I'd met up with her several times over the summer. Apart from her indulgence in drinks and drugs, she was a genuine sort of person: thoughtful, caring, and at times philosophical. I liked her company and, subliminally, had drawn a line in our friendship, not to be crossed – the mummified emotions need to remain mummified. Anyway, she was seeing a humourless, pencil-shaped Italian called Albert Rossi.

I had received a letter from the hospital reminding me that I was still suspended. The threat of adverse outcomes if I contacted a colleague remained. The letter brought an acid surge in the stomach, which made me nauseous. I reached her flat, limping.

'What's wrong with your foot?'

'Painful big toe. Perhaps a nasty combination of gout and arthritis.'

'What can you do about it?'

'Stop drinking.'

She laughed and said, 'Not an easy solution then!'

'Unfortunately.'

'What did you do all day today?'

'The same I do every day. Drink gin and miss Isla.'

'Have you tried ringing her?'

'Yes, but couldn't speak, her mobile was switched off.'

'Why not ring her TV channel? Why don't you go and see her?'

'I will, once I come out of this suspension fiasco, if at all I'm able to,' I said, and felt engulfed by another rising tide of sadness.

'Is there a possibility of them sacking you?'

'Everything is possible.'

'Bastards.'

'Exactly.'

'Well,' said Olivia, cheerfully. 'I'm going to do powder. The choice is yours: would you like a drink or powder?'

'Powder.'

She unfolded a baggie and I recalled my first intrepid snort through a short, stubby straw. It felt like inhaling hot air from a hairdryer. In a moment, I was a swaying kite in the sky whose string had been severed. Now I realised that everyone has a finger on his or her self-destruct button. There is a moment in your life when you either lift your finger off the button or press it.

Late that afternoon I told Olivia of the letter which had arrived that morning. She sat on the sofa, lit a cigarette and listened intently. Silence resided in the room under the ticking sound of the wall clock.

'Your hospital has hung you out to dry,' she said. 'Aren't they legally bound to start the investigation and conclude it within a specific time frame?'

'They are… but they first want to break me, break me into small pieces. So that I become weak, so weak that I bring myself to their submission,' I said and lit a cigarette. I took the first hacking inhale, and then the long-forgotten but familiar rush.

'I'm afraid this can happen,' said Olivia. 'It's a standard practice. You need to acknowledge it and put it behind you; just don't fall into their trap. This time will pass… all time passes… good or bad… You just have to persist.' Olivia paused and took a deep pull on her cigarette.

A silence pregnant with the sorrow of victimisation swelled in the room again.

I could feel Olivia's gaze on my face. I turned to look at her. A woman's face make-up, her hair colour, can hide her age but her neck, the loose skin of the neck tells the story of age truthfully.

'It's easier said than done,' I said. 'I'm trying my best, but bit by bit I feel I'm losing this battle. I'm grounding like a sandcastle.'

'Why won't the bastards allow you to contact your colleagues?' she said fiercely. Recently, she had started referring to the hospital management as "the bastards", which always amused me.

'Perhaps they feel that I could influence them to put pressure on the management.'

'The bastards.'

I laughed.

'You're missing Isla too? Aren't you?'

'Yes, I am,' I said, sounding like an obedient pupil confessing in front of a forceful teacher. 'I couldn't exorcise memories of her which haunt me. I think I've developed a habit of missing her and this seems to get worse when I'm under stress.'

Olivia laughed and said, 'You men pretend to be strong, but the fact is you're weak and dependent. You need emotional help from women all your life – mothers, sisters, secretaries, girlfriends. The bodies and brains of men can't function unless they off-load physically and emotionally. Poor little creatures!' She was delving into deep waters without any breathing apparatus. Without thinking, I nodded in agreement with her.

'Why did your wife leave you?' Olivia asked suddenly whilst fishing in her bag for something. 'Was there another man?'

Her questions took me by surprise, and I said quietly, 'I don't think there was another man. She was just too ambitious.'

'You know how to insult a woman but sound like you're paying her a compliment,' Olivia said angrily. 'You talk in code. If a woman seems a little dim to you, you say, "You're so nice!". If she's not particularly attractive, you say, "She has beautiful hair". And if she's pushy, or annoying in any way that you can't put your finger on, you say, "You're so ambitious" which is code for so many things and nearly all of them bad. So, what was Isla? Be honest with me.' She rolled a five-pound note into a tube and spread the powder on another note and then snorted it, making a noise resembling someone trying to prevent watery nasal secretions running down their nose during flu.

My first impressions of Olivia were collapsing fast. She seemed to understand life far better than me. 'No code words, it's a plain truth. She had a laser-focused ambition to succeed in her career,' I said.

'Naked ambition in women is problematic for men,' Olivia said, coughing and now appearing a bit more sympathetic towards me. 'Ambition in women is tricky and misleading for them.'

I felt aggrieved as memories of time spent with Isla gushed over me. 'I wanted her to settle down, stay at home and raise my kids.' My voice seemed caught up in my throat as I struggled to form the words. 'But she had this atomistic view of ambition and success. I couldn't stop her. She got the job of a CEO in a major TV network in the Middle East.'

'Sometimes we don't know what we want. We make good money and we think we're happy,' Olivia said. 'But, in fact, what we're doing is just making money and deep down we aren't happy. And we keep running like a horse with blinkers. The problem is that we're unwilling to break this cycle. We're afraid of quitting and what other people might think. We mess with our lives and our definitions of success because of what other people think. As soon as we realise it's my life and I'll do what I want to do, the fear of what others think evaporates and we're liberated. Was Isla afraid of quitting?'

'I don't think so, or should I say I'm not too sure,' I said.

'Never mind,' Olivia said and passed me a baggie of the drug and the folded note. 'Don't waste any powder this time!'

Insanity hovered over me like a giant moth circling around the light. I spread the powder thinly over the crisp five-pound note and looked at it with my heart hammering in my chest. I snorted every single particle in one deep breath.

Am I also afraid of getting sacked from my job? was the last thought which went through my mind as I slumped on the sofa. I could hear Olivia's laughter in the background, but I was free from this world – at least for the time being.

TWENTY

A continuous telephone bell interrupted the resounding silence in the room. I disliked it. I was sitting a yard away from the phone but didn't feel like talking to anyone and let it go to the answering machine. No one left a message. The phone remained silent for a couple of minutes and then became noisy again. Reluctantly I lifted the receiver.

'Well, hello, Mikel,' said someone in a cheerful voice. 'This is Amjad Chaudry from the hospital. Well, how are you?'

It was quite strange to have a phone call from Amjad. He was a consultant ophthalmologist at the hospital, and I'd delivered his twins some years back. Amjad was also the chair of the local consulting committee for the Doctors' Industrial Union. The purpose of the committee was to protect the rights of employees, but unlike the previous chair, Amjad did nothing of the sort and had proved toothless as a pangolin, which was precisely the reason why he was given the job in the first place. I had known him for over a decade and he had the annoying habit of starting every sentence with the word "well".

'Yes. I'm okay. What can I do for you?'

'Well, I'm very sorry to hear about your suspension.'

'How did you come to know?' I said, realising it was inevitable. The news could not lie dormant forever. 'Am I becoming the talk of the town?'

'Well, not really,' said Amjad, laughing. 'Well, I was at the regional clinical group meeting last night and overheard Adrian talking about you.'

'Adrian?'

'Well, yes, Adrian Baylis. The medical director.'

'What was he saying?'

'Well, that he had hung you out to dry to teach you and your colleagues a lesson.'

'How did you know he was talking about me?'

'Well, initially, I didn't know who he was talking about but then he said your name.'

'Are you sure?'

'Well, there aren't many doctors with your surname.'

'Did you not stop him? He was breaching the confidentiality clause.'

'Well, I didn't have to. The meeting started and he had to stop.'

'It's very sad to know that he was talking about me in places where he isn't meant to. It's not only a privacy breach but also spoiling my reputation.'

'Well, he's also deliberately prolonging the investigations to torment you,' Amjad added.

'Unbelievable stuff. Did he actually say this?'

'Well, he indicated that he was taking his time.'

'Okay,' I said. 'Thanks, Amjad. Based on what you've just told me I need to speak to my legal team. Could I ask you something? Will you be willing to be a witness if I decide to take any action?'

An unanticipated urgency appeared in his voice as he said, 'Well, yes, sure. I thought I'd just let you know. Okay, then, bye…'

'Amjad, before you go, is it okay if I contact you about this again?'

'Of course.'

The phone line went dead and my stomach acidity flared.

I rang Nafeesa Reis, my industrial union representative, and sought her opinion. Nafeesa concurred with me that it was inappropriate for a responsible person within the Trust to talk about me in an external meeting. She suggested that we should file a complaint about Adrian Baylis to the chief executive based on Amjad Chaudry's phone call, adding, 'Will Dr Chaudry be willing to act as a witness to the conversation?'

'I think so. I hope so,' I said. 'I have asked him.'

'Okay. I'll prepare a complaint and ask the legal team to cast an eye over it. I'll email a copy to you before the end of the day,' said Nafeesa. 'Get Dr Chaudry to sign it, post the signed copy back to me and then I'll send it to the chief executive.'

Amjad Chaudry and his wife, Sarah Vaughan, a physiotherapist at the hospital, lived out of town. It wasn't difficult to locate his barn-converted cottage; I'd been there before with Isla.

Sarah Vaughn opened the door and seemed genuinely upset to see me. 'Oh my god, Mikel! You've lost so much weight. Are you okay? Come in, come in.'

'Yes, I'm fine. Just under the weather.'

'Have you had yourself checked?'

'Yeah, don't worry, there isn't any underlying malignancy, just work-related stress,' I said, laughing.

Amjad entered the hall and shook my hand warmly. 'Well, it's good to see you, buddy.'

Sarah, still unable to overcome the shock of my weight loss, said, 'The hospital has done this to you. Amjad has told me all about it. They are bastards!' She led me into the kitchen.

Their twin sons burst in through the back door wearing cycle helmets and with an anxious ruddy glow on their cheeks. 'Daddy, Fluffy isn't in his hutch,' they said in unison.

'Well, boys,' said Amjad with affection. 'Say hello to Uncle Mikel.'

Both very obediently came over to me and I shook their hands. 'It always gives me so much pleasure to meet children growing up which you have delivered as tiny babies. How old are they now?'

'Seven in October. Next month,' said Sarah. 'Time flies.'

'Yes, it does.'

'Well, excuse me, Mikel,' said Amjad apologetically. 'I need to find the fugitive rabbit.'

I followed Amjad and Sarah into the garden. It was a large garden with a quietly flowing stream along the far boundary. Amjad looked around, raised his index finger to his lips and then pointed towards a white ball of fur underneath a bush. He lay down on his belly, crawled clandestinely underneath the bush like a commando and grabbed hold of the rabbit. He screamed as he came out of the bush.

'Did he bite you?' Sarah rushed towards Amjad with a worried look over her face.

'Well, it's the thorn in the bush,' he said, running a hand over his cheek. 'I'm bleeding.'

Amjad handed over the bunny to one of the twins and said, 'You see what I do for you… tears, sweat and blood.'

'Thank you, Daddy,' both said gratefully and took the rabbit to its hutch.

'Put some aftershave on it,' said Sarah, inspecting Amjad's cheek closely. 'It'll sting a bit but it's antiseptic.'

Amjad went upstairs to do what he was instructed and Sarah made tea. I sat on the sofa and took the envelope out containing the witness statement for Amjad to sign.

Amjad returned and noticed the envelope lying on the table. 'Well, I didn't know about the suspension until… How long ago did it happen?'

'Eight months and eighteen days.'

'Well, are you still on full pay?'

'Yes, but minus the on-call supplement.'

'Well, full pay and no work! How did you manage that? I'm very envious.'

I just smiled.

'Well, I'm sorry for what you've been through, Mikel, and… er…still going through. I hope it all settles down soon for you,' said Amjad.

Sarah joined us with three mugs and a plate of mini croissants.

'It hasn't been an easy time for me and perhaps they didn't wish to make it easier either,' I said, sipping the tea, which was too weak for my liking.

'We can see that,' replied Sarah. 'It must be awful.'

'Well, you remember Sandra Ashcroft? The midwifery head?'

'Who can forget Sandra?' I said. 'What about her?'

'Well, she went off sick for six months and then took early retirement on the grounds of ill health.'

'I'm sorry to hear that,' I said.

'I'm not,' said Sarah. 'The bitch knew the system too well and used the pension clause Tier 2 to get an enhanced pension, double her entitlement.'

'Really?' I said. 'I need to try that.'

'One of our banker friends told me she's setting up a business of some sorts,' said Sarah.

'Amjad,' I said, opening the letter. 'Thanks for informing me about the meeting. I've discussed it with my legal team. We've decided to log a complaint against Adrian Baylis to the chief executive on the grounds of breaching trust and deliberately delaying the process of investigation to victimise me. As you were present there in person, we'd like you to act as a witness to this. Could you read it to ensure it's factual and then sign it?'

'We're not signing anything,' Sarah said assertively. 'Look what they've done to you. I don't want my husband in the same position. Amjad is not signing it.'

Amjad looked embarrassed at his wife's sudden intervention and said, 'Well, Mikel, how will this complaint help your case?'

'We need to inform the chief executive that what is being done is wrong. It was a confidence breach and victimisation. Sackable offences.'

'Nothing would touch them,' said Sarah. 'Nothing would change. I've been with the Trust for nearly twenty years. It hasn't changed, and it won't. Anyway, you can't raise a complaint just on the basis of gossip. They'd simply refute it. Bin it.'

'It's not gossip,' I said. 'Amjad has heard them saying my name.'

'Don't rely too much on Amjad,' Sarah said, smiling. 'He hears so many things. Probably too many.'

'It's serious, Sarah,' I said. 'It would help my case.'

'It may or may not, but signing that could potentially put Amjad in all sorts of trouble. I'm sorry, but he has to look after his family.'

Amjad stared at his shoes and made no effort to take part in the conversation.

Sarah continued, 'It was silly of Amjad to tell you this. He admitted to me that it was a mistake... an innocent mistake, nonetheless. We've discussed this and we'd love to help you... You've been an excellent colleague and a good friend, but I'm afraid the consequences of it backfiring are far too high. I'm sorry, but we're not going to be part of this mess. Anyway, Amjad isn't well these days.'

There wasn't much point in further persuasion. Their minds were made up. I folded the deposition and put it back into the envelope. 'I'm sorry to have disturbed you. It's okay.' I looked at both Amjad and Sarah and added, 'I'll take my leave now.'

Sarah said, 'Please understand our point of view and don't take it personally.'

'Of course, I don't. It's entirely your prerogative.'

'Well, thanks for your understanding,' Amjad said. 'Please don't take any offence. I just don't want to get on the wrong side of senior management. They can be vicious... as you know.'

'Don't worry, Amjad,' I said, and looked at his face. There were no signs of ill health. 'What's the matter with you, anyway?'

'Nothing serious,' Amjad said, again looking embarrassed. 'Maybe a touch of irritable bowel syndrome.'

'So, we can assume that the matter is closed and that Amjad will not be involved in it in any shape or form?' said Sarah. 'We'll continue to be good friends and colleagues and no hard feelings, I hope.'

'I give you my word,' I said. 'Amjad's name will not appear in this matter.'

As I left the house I decided to lodge the complaint based on the information provided by Amjad, but not mentioning his name.

TWENTY-ONE

I t was not unusual to receive a phone call from Olivia at two in the morning. 'I think I'm dying,' she said as soon as I answered. 'I don't want to die alone. Please come over.'

'Have you called an ambulance?'

'Yes, but something's going on in town. They'll be ages.'

It was hardly the time to argue. 'I'm on my way.'

Olivia was indeed in excruciating pain and was struggling to breathe. She clutched the bottom of her chest with both hands and said, 'It... feels,' she was stopping at every word 'as... if... someone... has... pushed... a dagger... into... my chest.'

'Don't worry. I know you're not well but hopefully you'll be okay soon,' I said, taking her hand, which was pale and cold.

Could it be a pulmonary embolism? A life-threatening emergency. I dialled 999 again and was told that due to a major incident in the town there would be a delay of at least thirty minutes before the ambulance could reach us.

Every passing minute was critical.

'Olivia, it looks like I've got to take you to A & E. The way you're presenting, there is a possibility that a clot might have travelled up from your legs to lodge in your lung. This is called a pulmonary embolism. I'm not too sure about this at the moment, but if it is the case, then this could be serious and needs urgent treatment. We can't wait for an ambulance. We have got to go now, in my car.'

Olivia tried to put on a brave smile and said, 'No... no... I'll wait for the ambulance... I don't want... You... will see... your colleagues... Don't ruin your case because of me...'

'We'll worry about this later, let's not waste any time,' I said, hoping and praying that I wouldn't see any familiar faces.

The emergency room was heaving with drunks and ambulances were bringing in casualties like buses from a shooting incident in the town centre.

Olivia was given painkillers at arrival. Her ECG and her blood gases were not indicative of a clot in her lung. The CT scan request form was fast-tracked to exclude a bleeding duodenal ulcer. Olivia became calmer under the oxygen mask and her breathing was settling.

She removed her mask for a few seconds and said, 'I'm sure I'm in good hands, but is it true that the mortality rate in hospitals doubles over the weekends?'

I laughed. 'First, don't worry; you're not going to die. Second, it's all media hype, misinterpretation of the results. Olivia,' I added to tease her, 'I never knew that you would be so much afraid of death.'

'I'm not afraid of dying,' she said. 'I just didn't want to die alone, and I don't have enough words to thank you. You've put me above your suspension and the investigations and I'm grateful. I'm in your debt. You're not only a good doctor but also a good human and a good friend.'

I just smiled as I listened to her compliments.

The CT scan was normal, and she was admitted to the observation ward. I left the hospital but told Olivia I would speak to the on-call doctor about her in the morning.

Olivia had been assessed and a gastroscopy had been performed. A severe inflammation of the stomach lining at endoscopy was found, most likely linked to her drinking habits. This inflammation could be treated with tablets, but she had to curtail her drinking.

Later that morning, my mobile pinged and there was a message with a smiley face from Martin Norton asking me if I was in. Before I could answer the text, there was a forceful knock at the door.

'I knew you'd be in,' said Martin smiling, unashamed of his audacious beating at my front door. 'I've just dropped Connie, my girlfriend, at the hairdressers and thought I could come in for a chat. To see how you are.'

'Thanks for dropping by,' I said, devoid of any warmth, and mustered a faint smile. 'Thank God it's you. I thought I'd been raided by the police... Please do come in.'

'Thanks,' Martin said without a hint of embarrassment.

'I'm very pleased for you and your girlfriend,' I said, showing him into the sitting room. 'The last time we met you seemed quite averse to the idea of taking any more chances with the incursions of love into your life.'

'True, but Connie is the best thing that has ever happened to me.'

I smiled and reflected that if someone else had made such a statement about a new girlfriend, Martin would've shredded him to the cellular level.

He continued, 'She is so beautiful, so perfect. Her voice is like a harp to my soul. Her radiant smile illuminates the dark deep alleys of my heart. I feel truly blessed... Yes, Mikel, I'm in love. Do you know Connie? She's a staff nurse in neonates. You must've seen her.'

I smiled at what he had said. 'I can't remember having met your Connie, but I'm pleased and envious of your luck.'

'Thanks,' he said, and hitched his trousers above his ankles before sitting on the chair. 'How's life treating you, my friend? Any contact from Isla?'

'No. I feel the relationship has snapped,' I said, and I'm sure I reeked of gloom.

'The trouble with the smart women is that they get bored easily. They need to manufacture new challenges. How's the investigation going?'

'It's a free-range sense of learned helplessness,' I said. 'They're purposely prolonging the investigations to punish me, both mentally and physically.'

'I'm not sure about that. Investigations take time.'

His platonic words blew my fuse. 'Have you come here to defend them?'

'I'm just saying what I understand to be true. I know it's been a difficult time for you,' said Martin and left the side of his cheek contracted.

I didn't want to get into an altercation with him and said, 'I don't know what's the cause for the delay. There's muteness and there isn't any transparency.'

'There's a triad of factors in such cases,' Martin said as he counted on his fingers. 'The persons, the situation and the system. Most systems have shields and therefore aren't transparent.'

An alert critical silence resided in the room and I wondered whether he had actually come to kill time whilst Connie was at the hairdressers or that he had a hidden agenda.

'How long is it since you were suspended, Mikel?' asked Martin to kick-start the stumbled conversation.

I weathered my disappointment and said, 'It's more than nine months. A full-term gestation length. I suspect the stress is giving me duodenal ulcers.'

Martin said, 'I could arrange an endoscopy for you.'

'I met Amjad about a month ago,' I said, changing the topic. 'You know Amjad? Married to Sarah, the physio?'

'I know Sarah very well,' Martin said meaningfully. 'We were an item for a couple of months a long time ago. Amjad was the perfect catch for Sarah. She was a recent divorcee desperately looking for a new relationship and Amjad was on the verge of deportation needing a technical legality to stay in the country. So, they got married. A perfect match for a symbiotic relationship.'

I laughed and said, 'That's typical of you! Cynical... mistrusting love. The Asians are generally well-behaving husbands. They prove more enduring than their white counterparts. Cultural inhibitory influences have programmed them not to become "hoppers". So, you've discovered your true deep love?'

'Seemingly so,' Martin said. 'So, your issue of suspension… The golden rule is: if you're in a hole, stop digging.'

'What do you mean by that?'

'Making a complaint against Adrian Baylis wasn't your smartest move.'

'You're quite well informed, my friend,' I said, feeling alarmed. The mainspring of his visit was becoming clear. 'What made you say this?'

'Even if the investigations conclude in your favour, senior management could still make your life difficult,' said Martin.

'By doing what?'

'Questioning your clinical practice, for example.' His face twitched. 'I can guarantee you if we looked into the clinical notes of the most astute clinician, we would come up with something objectionable. Senior management would then be in a position to recommend supervised training. I don't know! I'm only postulating, thinking laterally.'

'To tell you the truth,' I said, and I'm sure my face was glowing like a tanning lamp, 'I couldn't care less about them any more.'

'I'm afraid you do, my friend,' said Martin. 'We both know the nature of our colleagues. The moment they're wearing a managerial hat, they transform from clay kings into monsters. There's no point in prolonging your ordeal. If the investigation concludes in your favour, just close the chapter, retract the complaint against Adrian and move on.'

'So, Adrian Baylis likes to investigate others but doesn't like himself investigated?'

'I'm just making a suggestion,' he said, and his face jerked again.

'Come on, Martin, be honest with me. What favour do you want of Adrian if I do decide to withdraw my complaint?'

'You're being cynical. I want no favours from Adrian. You should know me by now… I'm trying to help you. When you're back, you'll have to work with your colleagues in the Trust. Try to make it as painless as possible,' said Martin. He leapt to his feet and looked at his wristwatch. 'Time to pick Connie up. Think about what I've said, Mikel, and let me know if you'd like the endoscopy. I could always squeeze you in as an urgent patient. I keep an empty slot at the end of my clinic for urgent cases.'

'I'll let you know. Thanks for your kindness.'

'Don't be daft. Look after yourself.'

'I will.'

'Oh, I nearly forgot,' Martin said. 'Hospital gossip. The midwifery manager Sandra Ashcroft wrote that anonymous letter of complaint that kicked all this to put the management under pressure. She was on the verge of being fired and was about to go on intermittent sick leave with stress for a couple of years but Eralia Rose died. Sandra planned to write a series of letters to rattle the management but then you came along with your report into Eralia's death and threw a spanner in the works by exposing the issue of bullying and harassment.'

'I hope you're planning to report her to the counter fraud office.'

'No chance! I'm not a fool like you!' he said, laughing.

After Martin had gone, I sat in the cocoon of my own silence, trying to decipher the real purpose of his visit. Did he come of his own accord, or was he sent? I didn't believe he would oblige Adrian Baylis on some trivial matter relating to my suspension and the investigation, but had he done something significant for which he needed exoneration?

I had never suspected that Sandra Ashcroft had been playing a double game and I felt naïve and gullible, wondering why Martin had shared the gossip about her with me.

A maddening nausea was building up in my chest.

TWENTY-TWO

I carelessly signed the recorded delivery receipt for the postman under a faint 'Thank you'.

I slammed the letter down hard on the top of my study table and threw myself into the swivel chair. A gush of acid was burning my chest. I could feel the prickles of cold sweat over my forehead and, with a trembling hand, I wiped it. *I really will develop duodenal ulcers if I don't take care of myself,* I thought, and went to the kitchen in search of the liquid antacid in the fridge. I took a big swig of the cold, chalk-like fluid from the bottle to calm the acid and it gave me instantaneous relief. I braced myself against the fridge, wishing I had such magical solutions to all my problems.

A relentlessly ringing landline phone in the study jolted me back.

'Hello,' I said tersely, thinking this might be some marketing call.

'Hello, Mikel, it's Alan Taylor here. Are you okay to talk?'

'Sorry, Alan,' I said, feeling a bit embarrassed. 'I wasn't expecting your call. Yes, I can talk. How are you?'

'I'm fine,' said Alan. 'How are *you?*'

'Not sure. Perhaps *surviving* is the best word to describe it.'

'I fully understand. I've been trying to ring you for a couple of days, but your mobile kept going to voicemail. So, I got your landline number from HR.'

'So, what's the news?' I said, fearing the worst.

'Well, you should by now have received a letter from the hospital for a meeting regarding your suspension,' said Alan. 'I hope common sense will prevail, and that we can sort it all out for you.'

'I'm not too hopeful,' I said. 'I think they're out to get me.'

'I'm very sorry that they've taken so long over this. It's been blown completely out of proportion.'

'I did receive a letter this morning,' I said, 'but I've not opened it yet, fearing this might be a repetition of the same letter I've received routinely over the past nine/ten months.'

'No, no. Don't be afraid. Read the letter. It's an invite for the meeting,' said Alan. 'I'll see you at the meeting. Take care. Bye for now.'

'Bye, Alan.'

I opened the letter. The meeting was scheduled for the next Tuesday in the HR block. The list of people invited to attend the meeting consisted of:

Myself
James Stevenson, Chief Operating Officer
Adrian Baylis, Medical Director
Josh O' Reilly, Head of Undergraduate Teaching Academy
Ebony Precious, Head of Medical Staffing
Alan Taylor, Consultant Psychiatrist and Head of Research and Development
Professor Saunders, Professor of Medical Education
Anusha Willets, lay observer
Nafeesa Reis, industrial union representative

I wanted to go through all the paperwork including my statement with Nafeesa before the meeting. We agreed to meet an hour beforehand in one of the quieter hospital cafés. I had spoken with Nafeesa several times over the phone during the past nine months. She had a posh Scottish accent and a habit of speaking with an economy of words, always to the point.

As I entered the café, a rudimentarily slim woman wearing a flowery hijab waved at me.

'Nafeesa Reis?' I said to the woman.

'Yes. Mr Demir. I'm Nafeesa Reis,' she said, smilingly.

'Oh, nice to meet you. It's always good to put a face to a name,' I said hastily to hide my embarrassment. 'How did you know it was me?'

'From the hospital website. It has your picture.'

'Indeed, it has.'

Nafeesa had been provided with all the statements and she was cautiously optimistic about the outcome of the case.

The blamestorming was scheduled to take place in the HR block. The wall outside the designated room was covered with photographs of the current management board, smiling at the opposite wall. The room itself had the intimidating horseshoe arrangement of tables with a chair placed at the empty end, which I suspected was where I'd be made to sit.

In an attempt to appear unruffled by the proceedings, I'd put on an ash-grey suit, which had become a bit loose over my shoulders due to weight loss, a crisp white shirt, and a maroon Royal College tie. There were a series of continuous whirs and clunks from the coffee-dispensing machine placed at one end of the room as everyone made themselves a hot drink and chatted together. I had poured myself a glass of cold water from a water dispenser that gurgled loudly as the glass filled and I stood by the window, which provided a bleak view of the jam-packed car park.

Copies of all documentation for the meeting were placed upon the table. The proceedings of the meeting started, and everyone introduced themselves even though their names were on plastic signs in front of them. Ebony Precious, Head of Medical Staffing was to take the minutes. Nafeesa's request to voice-record the meeting was disallowed immediately by James Stevenson, Chief Operating Officer, because she hadn't made a written request in advance. She said she would also make her own notes.

James, as the head of the firing squad, read the indictments made by the medical student. 'There are three points: One, Mr Demir did not give treatment options to the patients in question; two, Mr Demir did not explain the risks and benefits of the procedure during his consultation with the patients; and three, Mr Demir performed inappropriate and unnecessary pelvic examinations thus sexually assaulting the patients. However, the patients themselves have not logged a complaint against Mr Demir.'

James then directed the attendees to a copy of the witness statement made by the chaperone nurse from the clinic in the bundle of documents in front of them, which vehemently dispelled the concerns raised by the medical student.

Alan Taylor, Consultant Psychiatrist and Head of Research and Development, cleared his throat and said, 'It is a matter of clinical judgement what a clinician decides to tell his patients. This judgement is learned by experience gained day in, day out in the clinic and questions such as what constitutes sufficient information for a particular patient to make a meaningful choice and give consent is where discretion is embedded. No matter how many medical students might wish it were otherwise, clinical practice cannot be definitely captured by a list of learning objectives, however enormous and far-reaching.'

'I agree with Alan,' Adrian Baylis, Medical Director, said. 'One size does not fit all.'

'Absolutely,' said Alan. 'Well-motivated and well-qualified clinicians can reach different judgements for different patients and need to exercise their discretion. I believe Mikel would have informed the patient with what he thought was important for that patient at that time and that is what matters most to the patients.'

'Sometimes there may be an error of judgement and that would be a concern,' Anusha Willets, the lay observer, said. 'In recent weeks, politicians' careers have been derailed by a lack of forethought in something they have said or done.'

'Oh, let's not digress to politicians and their judgemental lapses,' said Alan, waving his hands in the air so that everyone laughed.

'I'd like to make a point about judgement here,' Professor Saunders, the pofessor of medical education, said, looking thoughtful as always. 'Judgement is about discretion and it is required when a situation is contested or uncertain. Does a lack of judgement mean anything other than a person has acted in a way that we all may have done at some time? Are they not mere disagreements?'

James passed copies of an external expert's report and said, 'The experts, three senior consultant gynaecologists, strongly felt that all pelvic examinations were clinically indicated.'

'That's a relief,' said Alan, looking at me.

James said, 'We have also reviewed our Patients Advice and Liaison Service records and there are no complaints registered against Mikel for poor communication.'

'That's correct,' Nafeesa said. 'Mr Demir's 360-degree assessments by his patients and his colleagues have always been extremely gratifying.'

'Yes, we looked at his colleagues' assessment as well,' said James. 'The Trust has no concerns about Mikel's practice whatsoever. We also made enquiries from the gynaecology nursing and auxiliary staff who provide chaperone attendance for Mikel during intimate examinations and none had recollections that his examinations had hurt or upset any patients or were sexually motivated. Similarly, we have found no evidence of this sort of complaint against him in the past.'

Professor Saunders said, 'In my opinion, all three points raised by the medical student against Mikel are indicative of a lack of experience and perhaps contain a degree of malicious intent. Realistically, it is not possible to molest a patient in the presence of a chaperone and a medical student. This simply does not make any sense.'

Anusha raised her hand for permission to speak. 'For the record,' she said, 'what exactly does a pelvic examination constitute in the field of gynaecology?'

Everyone looked at me for a response. I said, 'A routine pelvic examination consists of three parts: one, to look at the outside area and lips; two, an instrument called a speculum is inserted inside to inspect the lower genital tract including the cervix – it's a bit cold and stretchy examination...'

Anusha interposed, 'Is this what we women have when we're having a smear test?'

'Exactly,' I said. 'And the third part is the insertion of one or two fingers into the vagina to feel for the uterus and the ovaries and a flat of a hand on the abdomen. This is called bi-manual examination.'

'Okay,' said Anusha, contemplating my explanation. 'Is it possible that the medical student got the wrong end of the stick – so to speak – and thought the bi-manual assessment was a sexual assault?'

'I don't know,' I said, and looked at James who shrugged his shoulders.

'Would I as a patient know the difference between a normal vaginal examination and being molested?' said Anusha.

'Definitely, Anusha,' said Alan. 'You'd certainly notice the difference between the two.'

Anusha blushed, and to hide her embarrassment took a couple of quick swigs from her bottle.

James said, 'Just to reiterate: no patient has raised any concerns about Mikel.'

Professor Saunders said, 'As so well articulated by Alan, the student who has raised these concerns against Mikel has not fully comprehended the use of judgement and discretion by a clinician. I think, Josh, you as head of undergraduate teaching need to take this to the medical school as an agenda item for a future meeting, indicating that the idea of whistle-blowing, or raising concerns by a student, is theoretically sound *but* they need to be given *explicit* training in such matters.'

Josh spoke for the first time, displaying his teeth, which appeared unnaturally white. 'I've reviewed the statement provided by the medical student.' He paused for a moment and then continued, 'I also feel that his concerns are based on a lack of knowledge and experience, but what worries me more about this particular student is that almost every year he has been given a yellow card. Without going into the details, I have a medical school meeting this afternoon and I believe that this student will be referred to the regulator on probity issues. He may – will – say we're being vindictive, but we will consult our legal team and, if we decide that this is the right course of action, we will refer him to the regulator on probity issues.'

'What will that achieve?' Professor Saunders said, removing his half-moon glasses and sucking on their temple-tips.

Josh said, 'It will put him on the regulator's radar and, depending upon the case examiners, he could be issued with a warning which remains in force for five years.'

Professor Saunders said, 'So the case could have a detrimental effect on his future career?'

'Possibly,' said Josh briefly.

Alan said, 'Do we have another "doctor in difficulty" in the making?'

'Possibly,' Josh repeated. 'But we'll worry about that later.'

James turned to me and said, 'We've fully reviewed all the paperwork and we've also looked into your personal circumstances... that you're separated from your wife and...'

'Excuse me, James,' Nafeesa interjected sharply. 'Why are you raising Mikel's personal issues? Mikel's personal circumstances bear no relation to the complaint made by this student whatsoever.'

James looked embarrassed, but before he could respond, Alan said, 'It is quite outrageous to bring up such a matter in this meeting.'

'I agree,' said Adrian. 'Ebony, please don't include this in the minutes.'

'Hold on,' said James, overcoming his discomfiture. 'Could I finish what I was saying before you come at me all guns blazing?'

James looked around and continued, 'My apologies for referring to Mikel's personal life. I just wanted to acknowledge that sometimes we can behave differently under stress, but I'm willing to retract my words.' James had not expected such a strong reaction, I thought. He continued. 'We, as a Trust, have a duty not only to protect our patients but *also* our doctors. We have been sympathetic towards you, Mikel, although you did violate the suspension rules by performing a Caesarean operation in Brazil when you were explicitly told to stop all clinical activities. We could have reported you to the regulator, but we decided to look away.'

Nafeesa looked at James in disbelief. 'Excuse me! That is an unjustified accusation.'

'We have the evidence. A letter of praise written by Mikel's friend Walter to the CEO. We could easily have used it to show that he wasn't being compliant.'

'Unbelievable,' Alan said. 'James, you are attempting to use a letter of praise not to support Mikel but to harm him?'

'Let me answer this please, Alan,' Nafeesa said. 'Mr Demir has informed me of his charity visit to Brazil with his friend Walter, and what occurred there. Firstly, you cannot prevent a suspended medic from helping someone in an emergency. Isn't that your Hippocratic Oath? Secondly, it was outside the UK and beyond the bounds of Mikel's suspension, and thirdly, you cannot prevent anyone from doing charity work in this country or any other.'

'Anyway,' James said with an air of benevolence. 'We have decided not to take any action against him.'

'The law is very clear. It does not allow you to take any action against Mr Demir,' said Nafeesa.

James's cheek muscles tightened and then twitched. He was purple with rage. He squeezed his lips into a circle and said, 'Mikel, considering your clean slate and the number of senior medical and non-medical staff who have sent messages of support for you to the senior management team, and as the allegations from the medical student against you have not been substantiated, the case is concluded without any further action. Adrian, is there anything you wish to add?'

'No,' Adrian replied. 'Mikel, the case is concluded, and you can return to work. But as you've been out of the practice for more than six months, the hospital insurers will require you to work under direct supervision for a period of two months. Then, once we receive a satisfactory report from the supervisors, you'll be allowed to continue independent practice.'

'Why is direct supervision necessary?' Professor Saunders asked. 'Just remind me, Mikel, aren't you the most senior consultant in your department?'

'Yes, I am,' I said. 'All my consultant colleagues have been my registrars at some point.'

Alan didn't give Adrian chance to reply. 'This is not only bonkers but insulting. Effectively what you're saying is Mikel has to re-train.'

'No, it's not re-training,' said Adrian, looking flustered.

'You want his juniors to supervise him and write reports about him?' said Professor Saunders. 'I agree with Alan, this is an affront. Did you insist that from your colleague *and* friend, who went abroad for a six-month sabbatical to work under supervision when he returned back?'

'Well, a sabbatical is different,' said Adrian. 'And, he didn't work in a surgical speciality.'

'No,' Alan said. 'This is ridiculous. Time off from the hospital is time off, whether it's sabbatical or suspension. The same rules should apply.'

'Okay,' said Adrian, raising both hands. 'I understand. Mikel… to satisfy the insurers, could you do one Caesarean and one hysterectomy assisted by your consultant colleagues… and no written reports will be required?'

'If I was you, Mikel,' said Alan, 'I would not agree to this stupidity.'

'It doesn't bother me,' I said. 'Instead of operating with a junior doctor, I'll at least have an experienced assistant. No, I don't mind operating with a consultant colleague.'

'Thanks, Mikel,' said Adrian. 'The Trust would like you to self-reflect on this complaint in your annual appraisal. I think it would also be useful if you attended a course about issues surrounding consent.'

'This is what I don't understand,' Alan said with a disgruntled look. 'If the case is closed and nothing could be proven, why the heck does Mikel have to self-reflect and go on a course? It's outrageously insane.'

Adrian did not appear happy at Alan's words, but said, quietly suppressing his anger, 'There is always something to learn from reflection and attending courses.'

'Bollocks! Excuse my French,' Alan said furiously. 'Reflection is yet another rope we're tied to now. Lawyers may use an honest reflection as a weapon against us. I'm afraid it could be dangerous.'

'You're quite entitled to your views, Alan,' said Adrian, who turned his face towards me and added in a way that was more of an instruction than of an option, 'Could you return to work tomorrow?'

'Good grief, Adrian! Give Mikel a break,' Alan said laughing. 'I'm sure spiralling locum costs aren't going to break the Trust. Give him time to recover. What do you think, Mikel?'

I felt both James and Adrian expected a rush of gratitude from me for their generosity and understanding in exonerating me, but I merely nodded and said, 'The whole process has been extremely stressful and difficult for me, to say the least. I think I'd need some time to recover.'

Nafeesa said, 'I don't think Mr Demir should return to full-time work until he's been assessed by occupational health.' She looked at me and I nodded again. She said, 'I can't see him returning to work full-time immediately. He could start with a few sessions – which could be gradually increased to meet his contractual obligations –

and may take three or four weeks. In addition, we would like to see the case closure letter before his return to work.'

'The letter will be done today,' Adrian said. 'I'll instruct occupational health to give you an appointment – tomorrow.'

Adrian's keenness for me to return to work was not his love for me but to curtail the locum bill.

Anusha said to James, 'What I fail to understand is why has such a simple and straightforward complaint case took almost ten months to resolve?'

James's discomfort with the question was visible on his face.

Adrian replied instead. 'Well, we have to follow all the procedures, policies and practices laid down by the Trust and, as such cases are of a very sensitive nature, and the Trust necessarily holds zero tolerance towards such allegations, we have to be extremely careful throughout, and I'm afraid this all takes time.'

Nafeesa said, 'I agree with Anusha. The Trust's handling of the case and excessive delays are open to question.'

'I'd already said the reasons for the delay, which were not intentional,' Adrian said, looking bored.

'I assume the Trust will pay for the course fees which Mr Demir has been advised to attend,' said Nafeesa.

Adrian replied immediately, 'No, the money will come out of his study-leave budget.'

'That is not appropriate,' said Nafeesa. 'Mr Demir's study-leave budget is for his own personal development, not for this course about issues surrounding consent. If you want him to go on this course, the Trust will have to fund it separately.'

James looked at Adrian and said, 'Perhaps the Trust could fund the course expenditure as an exception.'

'Thanks,' said Nafeesa. 'Ebony, please include that in the minutes.'

James thanked everyone for attending with artificial politeness.

Finally, I was off the hook and left the room, still feeling deflated.

Alan walked over to me and put his hand affectionately on my shoulder. 'What a farce! Unbelievable! It took them ten months to resolve this. The case was not only meant for you but also to send a clear signal to all the consultant body that the traditional power structure is being dismantled. They want us to be subservient, marching like the geese, slaves to the elites.'

'Thanks for standing up for me, Alan,' I said.

Alan said nothing, smiled and walked away.

Nafeesa came out of the boardroom and said, 'I've asked Ebony to send me the minutes and a copy of the letter from Adrian. I'll check them for factual inaccuracies against my own notes.'

'Thanks, Nafeesa, you've been very helpful,' I said.

'You're very welcome. I hope you're satisfied with the outcome and I hope all goes well for you from now on. I'll be in touch.'

Instinctively, I dialled Isla's number, but her mobile was switched off.

TWENTY-THREE

I rejoined the hospital with a mutilated ego and crushed confidence. But the gossip of my return to work was completely eclipsed by Martin shooting dead Connie and then killing himself. The news was splashed all over the TV and the newspapers.

My last meeting with Martin flashed back over and over again in my mind. I felt sad not only at having lost him but that I had failed to pick up any clues about this impending disaster. If it was not premeditated, then what could have changed so drastically for him that within a month he'd shoot both himself and Connie? Or could it have been a spur-of-the-moment decision?

A meeting had been held between the medical director, the nursing matron and the chief executive of the hospital and it was decided that as it was a police matter, the hospital wouldn't issue a press release or any staff communication. I thought this was a vile decision: an ostrich policy. The hospital should communicate something to the people who had worked with Martin and Connie and at least set up a colleague support group. But nothing like that was announced and no one knew the cause of this horrible incident; everyone had assumed they were happily living together.

'There isn't much admin work for you to do,' said Marlene, my secretary, who looked pleased to see me back. 'I'm sure there will be thousands of e-mails. I'll make you a coffee while you go through them.'

'That would be good,' I said. 'A phased return to work is planned for me by the clinical director. Initially, I will be working sixty per cent of my clinical sessions with no on-call commitments, and the work hours will gradually increase to full-time in four weeks.'

'That's good,' said Marlene. 'I'll check the clinics and make sure they're reduced for the registrars.'

'Thanks,' I said. 'How is your dog-breeding business?' Marlene bred designer puppies, producing three or four litters every year and selling them at £1200 each. She had a year-long waiting list for prospective buyers.

'It's good. I love it,' she said. 'Much better than listening to whingeing patients over the phone all day. When I've got enough money to buy a farm, I'll quite happily quit this job.' Her last sentence was indicative of hospital staff morale.

'Is dog-breeding that lucrative?' I asked her. 'That you can buy a farm?'

Marlene laughed and said, 'I wish it was. When I say a farm, it's not a big farm but a suitable size to breed dogs.'

I smiled back.

The whole experience of the investigation had completely dis-incentivised me. It appeared the aim of the saga was to humiliate and bring me down in the Trust. I had lost my vigour for work.

After careful thought I sent two e-mails. One to the clinical director asking for an urgent job-planning meeting with the aim of reducing my working hours so that I could become "maximum part time", and the second to Pensions enquiring about the earliest date I will be eligible for retirement.

There was a faint knock at the door followed by Amjad Chaudry entering. He said cheerfully, 'Good morning… Welcome… It's so nice to see you back.'

He warmly shook hands with me.

'Thanks, Amjad. I'm glad it's all over.'

'I'm very happy for you. I've been feeling guilty for being unable to help you. I'm extremely sorry. I feel bad.' He changed the subject quickly.

'Have you heard about Martin Norton?'

'Yes.'

'Well, it's strictly prohibited in our religion to gossip about the dead,' continued Amjad, 'but a rumour is floating about that he was being investigated for having sex with Connie whilst he was on call – in the on-call room.'

'Who was investigating him?'

'Adrian Baylis. Who else could it be?'

Was this the reason Martin came to see me? Had he wanted me to retract my complaint against Adrian? Was he trying to trade off this favour with Adrian to gain concessions for his own investigations?

I thought for a moment and decided to stay discreet. 'Martin had far too serious allegations made against him in the past and he always came out clean. He was too clever for them. I'm sure he wouldn't take his or someone else's life to avoid such allegations, which are always difficult to prove.'

Marlene entered the room and placed a mug of coffee on my table and said, 'Dr Chaudry, would you like one?'

'No, I'll be going now,' said Amjad and looked at me with pleading eyes, and said, 'Please, Mikel… Please forgive me for not helping you.'

Amjad hurriedly left the room and I heard him say 'Good morning' to someone. A moment later Alan entered the room.

'Good to see you back,' he said.

I moved papers off a chair for Alan to sit down and said, 'Thanks.'

'The room is a bit stuffy,' said Marlene. 'It's been closed for almost a year. Should I open the window to let the fresh air circulate?'

'Please do,' I said, wondering whether Amjad had brought the odour with him and Marlene was being polite.

Marlene closed the door behind her.

'I just came to say welcome back,' said Alan.

'Thanks, it's very kind of you.'

'Did you hear about Martin?'

'Yes, I did.'

'What a waste of two lives.'

'I know. How did it happen?' I asked.

'It seems they were sitting together on the sofa watching TV. First, he killed her with a single bullet through her head and then killed himself. Both were found joined together by a big clot of blood. There were no signs of an intruder, no break-in, no scuffle, no restraint. It's mind-baffling.'

'Very strange.'

'Apparently they were quite happy together,' said Alan.

'Yeah, that's what he told me. He came to my house, maybe two, three weeks ago.'

Alan thought for a moment and then said, 'I think Martin just couldn't handle lover's anxiety. He was seized by a maddening urge to stay happy. He was so happy that he became worried that his love, his felicity, might vanish. He wanted to end his life on a high and opted to become a killer rather than face the uncertainty of Connie ending the relationship.'

'Very profound!'

'The comforting thing about taking your life is that you're no longer there to feel any lasting pain. A lover hasn't got a guarantee that the end of a relationship wouldn't be the end of love.'

The conversation was veering in an uncomfortable direction for me. I fussed about with my computer mouse and Alan took the hint, leaving me pondering the question of love. It's not only the shortage, the dearth of something that kills you. Sometimes it is the abundance; an over-abundance of food, love or shelter could kill as well. I could agree with Alan: it is possible that Martin died of an excess of love, or a fear of what an excess of love would bring. Unlike Martin, my love was in short supply. Was this not a good enough reason to end my life? Or had I more resilience? Was I able to control my impulses? Or was I a coward?

An e-mail from James landed in my inbox, informing me that my complaint against Adrian Baylis for delaying the investigations was unfounded and any members present at the clinical group meeting could not substantiate a breach of confidence allegation. Therefore the complaint was closed.

I didn't feel like going through the rest of my e-mails and decided to return to my lonely home. The thought of Martin lying dead in a pool of red congealed blood along with his partner saddened me. His face must have twitched hard before he pulled the trigger, I thought. He did succeed: the end of life, the end of pain. Along with Martin, I had lost whatever he wanted to tell me further about Sandra Ashcroft.

I sat in my study and looked out at the blustery November day. Dried leaves and a brown paper bag flew about in an aimless flurry. Everything seemed to move fast except time. Guilt was brewing inside; I hadn't done anything to save Mark. Could I have done anything to prevent what happened to Martin and Connie? Was I so inadequate, so inept that I had caught no vibes and was now using this as a justification for my inability to act? I had been a perpetual failure in my life. Hyperacidity from my stomach rose to the back of my throat.

It was half-two.

Carys's card was lying on the table and had gathered a thin layer of dust. I cleared it with my finger. I had lost too many familiar faces and couldn't afford to lose any more.

I rang Carys.

'Hello, Carys,' I said. 'Hope I've not caught you at a wrong time.'

'No, no,' she said, 'I've just got home. I'm not doing anything, just peering out through the window.'

'Same here,' I said. 'How are you?'

She sighed. 'Some days I'm good and others I feel I'm back where I started. I wish some clever surgeon could dissect memories from my mind.'

I laughed. 'If you find someone, do let me know.'

'How are you?' she asked. 'You're home early, too?'

'Didn't feel like working so came home. How is Jamie?'

'I heard he got married… I didn't go.'

'Did you not want to go or were you not invited?'

There was hesitancy for a moment and then she said, 'I wasn't invited.'

'Did you sell the house?'

'I had to. Dad had re-mortgaged it. It's all done and settled.'

'Did Jamie buy it?' I asked.

'Yes, he did,' Carys said with surprise in her voice. 'I wanted a quick sale and he was the only option. How did you know?'

'My sixth sense,' I said. 'I'm sure he sold it at a hefty profit to finance his wedding.'

'Quite frankly, I don't care.'

'Carys,' I said, 'is it okay if I ring you sometimes?'

'That would be nice,' she said.

I went upstairs to Isla's office. A stack of magazines and newspapers waited for me to go through and search for any pictures taken by her. There was none in the past six months. A fear eclipsed my heart. I called her. Isla's phone rang but gave no option to leave a message.

TWENTY-FOUR

The beginnings of my medical career couldn't have been more eventful. Within a month of graduation, the medical regulator issued me with a warning. *Rohan Singh, sadly your ingenious plans backfired big time*, I said to myself.

Mr O'Reilly reported me to the regulator for improbity, citing a long list of examples. I had no doubt that O'Reilly and Demir had stuck together and cooked up such a case against me that the investigating panel reached its decision firmly. Even my appeal was rejected. The warning would be seen against my name on the regulator's website for the next five years. It was abysmal.

There was no dearth of nosy people around who had the nasty habit of browsing through the regulator's website and would learn the details of my case. As time passed, my hatred against Demir grew harder. He'd managed to wriggle out of the complaint I'd brought against him unharmed, and tangled me up in this mess. He deserved a harsh punishment, but I didn't know how it could be done.

I was able to find a foundation-year-one post. It was incredibly frustrating that because of the issues I was instructed to have a special meeting with the mug-heads of education and training on a monthly basis at each hospital placement. I didn't trust any of them or their meetings. I had no option but to endure this crap for another five years but I soon created a fake e-mail account and wrote my own references.

Ava was working in the same hospital but in a different specialty. I'd met her a couple of times on combined teaching days and I never got the impression that she was aware of my shenanigans with the regulator. I was still doting on her.

Paul said to me, 'Buddy, you can't dwell on the peck on a cheek forever. You need to make or break with Ava.'

'I know, I have to make a move.'

'Yes, you do. Take her out. Wine and dine her, and maybe try some hypnosis, which you've been practising for so long now. Stalemate is not good. If she isn't for you, move on.'

I thought that what Paul had said made perfect sense. Maybe Ava would help me to climb out of the mess I was in with the regulator. Maybe she would be able to steer the ship of my life into calm waters and settle down with my life.

I was overly excited and pleased when Ava agreed to go out with me. I booked a highest-rated Micheline-star restaurant and found the right table, not in a too discreet corner but away from crowded areas. Ava looked comfortable in my company and encouraged me to talk about my hobbies. She looked impressed with my knowledge of hypnosis and how it could help the patients with chronic pain. It was not genuinely based, all fabricated for the occasion, the seduction. As per Paul's instructions, I refilled Ava's glass with wine every time it was empty. I had lost the feeling of pre-meal anxiety, but it was succeeded by a touch of drowsiness: a head unused to alcohol, a heart unshrivelling by the warmth of her company.

As we sat in the car ready to drive home – again as Paul had told me – I leant across and gently kissed her on her lips. Ava retracted, which I put down to shyness. Her lips were soft and a little hesitant. The taste of the very first kiss; I felt vertiginous and a step closer to my conquest. Paul had advised me that if the response of the kiss was positive to take her to my room, otherwise to remain patient for a better time. He had very kindly donated me a condom. I was finding it difficult to contain myself and placed my left hand on her thigh whilst driving the car. Ava resisted and replaced my hand on the wheel, saying, 'Mind the road.'

Out of nowhere, a small dog ran out and crashed into my car. I immediately stopped and got out. The dog had a small ooze of blood from his mouth that unfurled like a red flag on the road, the tongue bitten and clamped between the teeth. The dog convulsed for a few seconds before becoming limp. There was no dog owner in the near vicinity. My mind had become a directory of all the cases, which had been referred to the medical regulator for misconduct, and the case of a doctor sprang to my mind who had been given a warning by the regulator for dangerous driving. He accidentally killed a pet deer on an A-road. I couldn't afford another warning against my name. I looked at Ava. She was peering through the windscreen. I carefully lifted the dog by its hind legs, keeping my back towards Ava, making sure his blood didn't smear me, and placed it on the grass beside the kerb.

'What happened?' Ava said, getting out of the car.

'Nothing,' I said. 'Looks like some stupid dog has committed suicide.'

'Oh my god!' said Ava, shrieking and looking frightened. 'There's blood on the number plate!' She bent down and touched it, and shouted, 'Oh my god, it's fresh blood!' She looked at me. 'What did you hit?'

'I didn't hit anyone,' I said. 'This dog came crashing into my car.'

'Did the dog die?' she asked, wiping her hand with a tissue. She was trembling with grief, as if some close relative had passed away.

'I told you,' I said. 'I didn't run over the dog. He just came running into my car, head-on. Let's go home.'

'Did the dog die?'

'Probably, yes,' I replied briefly.

She went over to the dog, trying to feel his carotids, her bag still slung over her shoulder.

She stood up silently, thinking, and said amid sobs, 'The dog's dead; you killed him.'

'I didn't run over him, he just came crashing in. Let's go.'

'We're not going anywhere. We'll wait for the owner and apologise.'

'The apology isn't going to bring the dog back,' I said, getting rattled with her insistence. Waiting for the owner would certainly raise the stakes for me.

'An apology is the least you can do,' she said, her voice sharp with bitterness.

'Let's not spoil our evening for a stupid little dog.'

'The evening's already spoilt,' said Ava with violent distaste, crying. 'I'm leaving now, you heartless crazy.' She took her mobile out and tapped on it.

'I'm sorry,' I said. 'I didn't do it purposefully. Please try to understand, it's some crazy dog. I haven't struck some innocent child.'

Ava swiped tears from her cheeks with a tissue and said in an angry voice, 'You're a disgrace to our profession. You don't seem to have any respect for life. Come on, Rohan. A life is a life, whether human or animal. You just took a life, and you're saying it's only a stupid little dog. You're unbelievable. Do you not know that hitting and killing a dog is a reportable offence? You should be reported to the police... absolutely despicable. I told you to pay attention to the road.'

'Ava, give me a chance,' I beseeched her. 'I'm sorry... You know the dog just came running from nowhere. I wasn't even speeding. Please forgive me, just for once. Please, please...'

'Why should I?'

'Because I like you... I love you. I want you...'

'You've disappointed me... I'll walk home alone. Don't you ever come near me again.'

I could see Ava slipping out of my hands, and the future of our coupledom becoming an impossibility. I had put my entire career in jeopardy just for her love. I had hoped that in some congenial season she would be mine. But she had failed to acknowledge my love and my feelings, and showed no sympathy or empathy towards me after the freak accident, and was now threatening to report me to the police. A heartless woman. My fists clenched and my jaw muscles tightened to such a degree that my teeth began to ache. She should be wounded exactly as I'd been wounded.

I took a deep breath and said, 'You must be going to see Demir.'

'What?' she said, her voice full of surprise.

I maintained calmness and said, 'How's your sex life with Demir? You like experienced guys, don't you?'

'What are you talking about?' she stammered, her eyebrows arched.

'Everybody in the medical school knows you slept with Demir to get distinctions in the exams. Didn't you?'

'You're sick,' she said, her voice trembling as she stifled tears. She waved to a passing taxi, which screeched to a stop immediately.

I took the condom out of my pocket and tossed it over to her. It fell just in front of her. 'Good luck to you, but don't forget to ask Demir to wear it. I've heard the dirty bastard is full of STIs.'

'Fuck you,' she said as she opened the taxi door.

A few weeks later, I heard that she had emigrated to Australia.

I hold that bastard Demir responsible not only for spoiling my career but also for my failing in love.

PART 2

FEBRUARY 2016–JUNE 2018

TWENTY-FIVE

I t appeared that I had no option but to have an operation. Crohn's disease had flared up with a vengeance. The link between the hyperacidity that I had suffered during and after the suspension more than seven years ago and Crohn's resurgence was a distinct possibility. The operation would involve the removal of a small part of the small bowel. My consultant surgeon colleague, Richard Smith, also promised to fix a small inguinal hernia at the same time.

Richard visited me with his medical and nursing entourage in the pre-operative ward round.

'Do you understand the operation you're going to have, along with all the risks and benefits?'

'Yes, I do.'

'Could you tell me your date of birth, confirm that this is your signature and that you've signed this consent form?' Richard showed me the form, fulfilling the rituals of the round.

I told him my date of birth, adding, 'Yes, I can confirm I've signed this consent form.'

'There are no perks in the health care service for staff,' Richard said in a cheerful humour as he squirted bacteria-zapping gel from a bottle attached to the bed end. 'But I've managed to get you this single room.'

'I'm grateful,' I said. 'The room description sounds an apt abridgement of the story of my life.'

'Sorry, I didn't mean it like that,' Richard said looking embarrassed, and there were chuckles all around.

'My regular anaesthetist has called in sick today, and the anaesthetic office has sent a replacement. I haven't worked with this chap before, but the girls tell me he's good,' he said, pointing towards two nurses accompanying him.

'Yes, he is good. He often comes to us. He also does hypnosis and maybe if you fancy, you could have your operation done without a general anaesthetic, just under hypnosis?' one of the senior nurses said, smiling.

'No, no hypnotic spell, just the good old-fashioned anaesthetic would do,' Richard replied before I could say anything. 'See you in theatre. You're first on the list.'

I waved him and his staff goodbye.

I'd operated upon thousands of patients but had never realised how unnerving it was to wait just before the operation – or was it just me? I'd known Richard for years. He had the national reputation of an excellent surgeon. *I mustn't worry*, I said to myself, *I'm in the best possible hands*. But there was an inexplicable anxiety rolling in my mind that something might go wrong. After all, complications do happen even with the most experienced surgeons. I tried to distract my mind by looking outside. It was a dismal view of the back entrance of the hospital. A truck was reversing, making a beeping noise, and a couple of porters were waiting to take the goods off. The truck stopped and the porters unloaded two big bundles of theatre scrubs wrapped in transparent plastic like kitchen cling film.

My mobile whirred and I received a message of good wishes from Olivia. She was now mainly working in Spain, having climbed several rungs in the company and become a partner. I had hardly seen her in the past few years but had remained in touch through WhatsApp. A drug rehabilitation programme had worked wonders for her, and she had had no relapses.

There was a knock at the door and a timid sort of person entered the room. He had a nicely trimmed, shiny beard; hair gelled backwards, and was wearing black-framed glasses, which were a bit large for his face.

'Mr Demir, I'm Dr Singh,' he said, extending an arm to shake hands. 'I'm consultant anaesthetist and will be putting you to sleep for today's operation.'

'Hello, Dr Singh, nice to see you,' I said, extending a hand for shaking and just managing to negotiate with his fingertips. I'm not an expert but some people claim to be able to foretell the whole personality of a person just on a mere handshake. He appeared a bit less congenial.

'I was your student some seven or eight years ago. I know you can't remember each student, but I remember you very well.'

'It's good to know that,' I said, trying to remember him, but it wasn't easy with the beard and glasses.

'I had a look at your history and blood reports and it seems you're a fit and healthy person. I'll see you in theatre,' he said, looking at me with piercing eyes. 'Do you have any questions for me?'

'No, thanks,' I said, and was trying to work out whether his unusual mannerism was the result of his cultural upbringing or something else. He had a peculiar, jack-o'-lantern kind of smile on his face.

'The nurses were telling me about your hypnosis skills, but I think I'd rather opt for the conventional anaesthetic.'

'It's okay. The research has shown that hypnosis is good for post-operative pain, should you wish to have it,' he said, still fixing his gaze on me. 'Would you like to try it?'

'No thanks, I'm not mistrusting your hypnosis skills for a moment,' I said. 'I've never thought about having hypnosis and I'm not comfortable with the idea just before the operation.'

'That's absolutely fine,' he said. 'For post-operative pain relief, I'll give you an epidural along with a general anaesthetic. Is that okay?'

'Yes,' I said. 'I suppose so. Women have epidurals all the time during labour, so it must be good for pain.'

'Yes, it's wonderful for pain, and it works for twenty-four hours. When you have an epidural, you don't need opioids with all their side effects,' said Dr Singh. 'I'll see you in theatre.'

There was something different about this anaesthetist, something unusual, but I couldn't decide what it was. I thought more than eight hours of fasting before the operation was turning my cynical button on.

The trolley was wheeled into the anaesthetic room and a young person greeted me. 'Sir,' he said, 'I'm Jason, the operating department assistant. Before we secure intravenous access and start the anaesthetic procedure, I will check your identity along with your surgeon and also any allergies you might have, and confirm your consent. It's all repetition but ensures your safety.'

'I'm aware of the WHO checklist procedure,' I said.

'That's great. In that case, I will call a member of Mr Smith's team and Dr Singh, who is our anaesthetist this morning, should be here in a minute,' said Jason.

A minute later, Richard entered the anaesthetic room and took me again through the formality of checking my identity and agreement to the operation.

'Okay, Mikel, sleep well, and I'll see you back in recovery after the op,' said Richard.

'Thanks, Rich, be good to me,' I said, joking.

'I'll try my best.' As he was about to leave the room, Dr Singh entered, and Richard said to him, 'Hi, I'm Richard Smith, we've not met before. Mikel is a good friend; please take care of him.'

'I'll take extra care of him, don't worry,' he said and lowered the protective side-grills of the trolley to start the anaesthetic procedure.

'Good to see you after such a long time, Mr Demir,' Dr Singh continued. 'You're right-handed, aren't you? I still remember you very well after all these years. Jason, maintain an intravenous access on Mr

Demir's left hand. Once you've done this, position Mr Demir for an epidural while I go and get scrubbed.' Dr Singh left the room.

Jason professionally and painlessly inserted a cannula into a vein in the back of my hand.

'Mr Demir, could you sit up and come to the edge of the bed for epidural insertion.'

'Is that far enough?'

'That's perfect,' said Jason. 'Now, if you bend your head down so that your chin touches your chest and relax your shoulders.'

'Like that?'

'Yes, that's perfect. Now Dr Singh is going to paint your back with antiseptic.'

'That's perfect.' I could hear Dr Singh in the background, unfolding some plastic sheets and making rustling noises.

'Jason, call the lab and ask them to process the coagulation screen on the blood sample sent this morning for Mr Demir. I just want to be ever so careful here. I'll start with the epidural first. Thanks for setting up the trolley.'

'Sure,' said Jason. 'Will you manage on your own for the time being?'

'Not a problem, Jason, I've been in the trade for long enough now,' said Dr Singh.

The smell of antiseptic solution reached my nostrils before I felt it rubbed over my back. After some more rustling noises, an adhesive sheet was stuck over my back.

'You'll feel a sharp scratch now,' said Dr Singh.

I said nothing and closed my eyes. It was indeed more than a sharp scratch, followed by a needle going into my spine. I immediately felt my legs getting heavy and my face flushing.

'Mr Demir, can you move your toes?'

'No.'

'Legs?'

'No, but I don't feel good. Is it normal?'

'That's exactly what I wanted. I've given you a double dose to stop your breathing,' said Dr Singh. He came and stood in front of me.

'What? Sorry?'

'Just a bit of fun. I certainly don't want you to suffer any brain damage. But if it happens, it happens.'

'What did you say?'

'I said I don't want you to suffer brain damage.'

'Sorry?'

I could feel tingling and numbness in my face.

Dr Singh helped me to lie on my back and said, 'From now on I control you. You're dependent upon me. You will do as I tell you to do.'

He held a syringe containing a white milk-like fluid and another syringe of colourless medicine attached to the intravenous access but not yet injected, and I knew that I was only seconds away from my anaesthesia. I closed my eyes.

'Open your eyes,' Dr Singh said harshly to me. 'I have waited for this moment for a very long time.'

'Who are you?' I said struggling to speak. My tongue felt heavy.

'Your worst nightmare.'

Dr Singh started injecting the fluid very slowly and I began to feel my arms, legs and then my whole body going flaccid. He'd given me a muscle relaxant. I could still hear and understand but was unable to move a muscle.

'Mr Demir, do you recall if any student has ever made a complaint about you?'

My head was spinning.

'Think again, think hard.'

I felt dizzy but could still hear.

'I'm the one who raised the complaint of sexual assault against you seven years ago… because you shagged my girlfriend, your own student.'

I wanted to shout but could not move my tongue.

Dr Singh growled. 'You used your consultant status to wriggle out of the case. Because of you, I was referred to the medical regulator and lumbered with a fucking warning. You ruined my life, my love, my career. Because of you I'm unable to find a permanent consultant post. I have endured years of mental torment just because of you and I have gone through the pain of changing my personality. Now it's time for you to feel the pain and this time I'll change your personality for good.'

He attached another syringe to my intravenous cannula. I could hear him breathing heavily. He pulled his facemask down and said, 'It's payback time, Mr Demir. You might think that I'll just paralyse you and not give you any pain relief during the anaesthetic, to make you feel the whole operation, but no, no… I'll give you an analgesic. How could I be cruel to my teacher? No, I've got something far better planned for you… I'll hypnotise you with Fentanyl to change your personality for the rest of your life… turn you into a sexual predator of a kind… well, who knows, you may like it… I know your wife abandoned you.' He laughed a loud, sarcastic laugh and said, 'I don't blame her. Who could live with a filthy asshole like you who doesn't even spare his own students? I won't do any harm to you… you yourself will self-destruct, inflict harm on yourself… you will beg, but no doctor, no psychiatrist will be able to help you… oh dear… I have waited too long for this moment.'

I tried again to speak but could not. My head was becoming muzzy and my breathing had stopped. I could see and hear Dr Singh laugh. The helplessness was debilitating. I could feel tears rolling down the side of my face.

'Oh, oh, Mr Demir is crying… I have cried too… now, it's your turn… but you're a big boy… don't cry… don't cry, my baby… I'll wipe your tears away.' He was laughing frenziedly.

I could hear the whooshing of blood in my head.

Suddenly, the door was flung open, and Jason entered the room. 'The lab has looked everywhere but the blood sample hasn't reached them yet. I'll try again later.'

A mask was firmly placed over my face. I could feel the firm grip of Dr Singh's fingers over my lower jaw, choking me.

Jason leapt towards the anaesthetic machine and said, 'Holymoly! His oxygen levels are dropping!' He opened the door and shouted at the top of his voice, 'Help needed in Theatre Seven.'

I heard the door opening and closing, people rushing in and congregating around me, faces fuzzing and intermingling, voices coming at me from a distance.

'High-spinal, intubate him,' were the last words I understood. A dense fog engulfed me.

TWENTY-SIX

I knew there would be a Serious Case Review of Demir's case. I wanted everyone to be on my side. I got on very well with everyone except Henrietta. She didn't like me. She was a senior theatre nurse, and her seniority had engendered in her an air of audacity for challenging systems and behaviours.

It was two to three weeks ago. I was adding the patient details in my database of all the patients who had undergone pregnancy terminations that morning. Looking back, it was a bit stupid of me to do this in the coffee room in the presence of all the staff. Henrietta was passing by and caught a glimpse of my open laptop.

I could see a question in her eyes. I said to her, 'I like to keep a record of all the patients I've anaesthetised. It's useful for my annual appraisal to show my workload, and also for the research project I'm doing.'

She wrinkled her nose in dissent and said, 'But you're keeping the names of the patients in your records.'

'This laptop is password-protected.'

'Still, that's loads of patient information. You may lose the laptop and someone might crack your password. All possible in this day and age. This log is only showing female patient names. Is your research only on women?'

'Yes… partly on women,' I said. My throat felt sore, as if I'd gulped a sandy drink.

Nosy bitch, I thought. *Can't she mind her own business and go away?*

But she didn't. 'I understand research and research governance. If you wish to keep a patient's record for research purposes, it has to be anonymised. I can't recall under which rules research and development allows you to collect sensitive patient details.'

'Trust me, they did allow me. I could show you an e-mail.'

'Really? Please do, and save me filling in an incident form about this.'

'Will do,' I said, and slammed shut the laptop.

That evening I spent quite a lot of time cursing Henrietta and producing a fake e-mail from research & development, and Henrietta spent a lot of time with the AA as I punctured all four of her tyres.

After the Demir incident I decided to take some time off work to show how distressing the whole incident had been for me. But I realised it was more important to go in to display my remorse to the recovery nurse, Jason, and a consultant anaesthetist, who came to help. These people would be asked to give their statements and I needed their support. I also needed to collect the earphone box, which I'd forgotten to take from the anaesthetic room.

'I just wanted to be ever so careful with him,' I said to the consultant anaesthetist, shedding genuine-looking tears. 'I feel so bad.'

'Complications do happen and will continue to happen, but it was unfortunate that it happened to Mikel. You did well in the difficult situation,' he said placing his hand on my shoulder to console me.

'I feel traumatised.'

'Do you think you need counselling?' the consultant asked, with worry for me spread over his face.

'I think so. I couldn't sleep all night.'

'Okay, I'll make arrangements for you to see someone in occupational health on an urgent basis.'

'Thanks.'

'There was a complication and you dealt with it. It would have been challenging for any one of us; thankfully, the patient is alive and well. You held your nerve, and that's the most important thing in dealing with an exceptional situation. You also called for help, which is the right thing to do in such circumstances. Don't punish yourself, you did well.'

I managed to remove the earphone box from the anaesthetics cupboard, but as I was coming out I saw Henrietta.

'Dr Singh, you're not on call by any chance?' she said. 'We're looking for an anaesthetist to do an emergency.'

'No, I'm not working today,' I said, and shrugged my shoulders. 'I shouldn't be here; just popped in to collect this box.'

'What is it?' asked Henrietta, nosy as always.

'Nothing, just my stuff,' I said, and then I accidently dropped the box, spilling earphones everywhere.

'That's a lot of earphones. What do you do with them?' Henrietta asked with surprise.

I was on all fours, frantically collecting earphones. 'It's research-related.'

'Mr Demir is transferred from ITU to ward today. He's doing okay.'

'That's fantastic, but I'm too embarrassed to face him.'

'Don't be daft. Complications do happen.'

I was pleased that everyone, including Henrietta, was talking about the incident as a complication, which should help me in the impending investigation.

I came back home feeling triumphant.

Rohan Singh, you're a lucky bastard, I thought, and laughed from deep inside my belly, like a recurrent hiccup.

The whole event filled me with a viscous pleasure. I had no regrets: he deserved it. I had never imagined even in my wildest dreams that I would be able to take revenge upon Mr Demir so easily, so unexpectedly, so surreptitiously, and with possible lifelong consequences. This qualified for a celebration until the last day of my life, I thought, as I filled the glass with vodka and lit another cigarette. I laughed in exultation but I knew I couldn't linger too long in the state of ecstasy of achievement and would soon have to enter the state of pondering, to escape unscathed. The possibility of a complaint by Demir was almost a certainty. 'Before my luck runs out,' I chuckled to myself, 'I need to move to a different hospital, far from this area, until I leave this mundane medical profession and this cold, off-putting country.'

I filled my glass again to celebrate the joyous moment when Mr Demir lay helpless, crying before me in the anaesthetic room. It was also amusing to me that Mr Demir didn't recognise me before the operation. I knew that my appearance had changed over the years. I looked too young without a beard, so had nurtured one for the last couple of years. My jet-black head and beard hair were trimmed to a size which didn't require any combing. I'd given up contact lenses for black-framed designer glasses to give myself a mature appearance and had lost lumpish student body contours to a much slimmer shape, as I'd started cycling to work. Ironically, Demir had not changed a bit, and I recognised him at the first glance. How could I forget him? Not a single day had gone past when I hadn't thought about him or hated him. The anger had coiled around me like a python, suffocating me. He charred my career and ruined my life.

I was quickly running out of enthusiasm for hospital work. The whole business of doctoring appeared incredibly repetitive and boring to me, even in the prime of my supposed honeymoon era. I was seeing my medical colleagues reduced to a pair of hands, working flat out, going home to snatch a few hours of sleep and trudging back to work again, looking sleep-deprived, burnt-out. The routines remained almost identical every day. You come to work, change into scrubs, draw the same drugs into the syringes; talk to patients in the same rehearsed tone, which you'd developed over the years. The same procedure for putting the patient to sleep, connecting to machines, keeping an eye on the monitors, and waking the patient up after the operation. You do the same to the next and the next patient until the working day is finished. How scintillating! Working every day in the hospital reinforced in me what I'd suspected earlier during my training years: to succeed as a hospital doctor or even a GP, one doesn't need a high index of intellect or inventiveness – the only attribute one needed was an ability to do the same work day in, day out, without looking weary. I felt pity for my colleagues.

I was completely disillusioned with work until I came across this business of altering personalities during anaesthetics in some wacky journal of psychiatry. The research findings energised me to come to the hospital.

From my knowledge of anaesthesiology, I knew Fentanyl was a hundred times more potent than morphine and, unsurprisingly, had been used as an elephant tranquiliser in the past. The theory behind swapping someone's personality during the Fentanyl induction of anaesthetic was that there was a phase, possibly a very tiny window, during which the whole mind was like a clean slate, and if something was introduced to the brain precisely at the right time, it would override past personality traits.

How fascinatingly plausible. I loved it.

The research could break ground and shatter skies, and would have wider implications. If the technique proved successful, there would be no need for jails in the future – instead of being locked up, all criminals with mental illnesses or compulsive behaviour could undergo a short general anaesthetic and hypnosis to rectify their behavioural issues. I thought I was getting carried away when it came to my mind that there was a potential for governments to use the technique to produce mass-scale stooges to carry out their aims, and this brought a big dollar sign into my eyes. The ornaments of democracy, freedom of people and speech are still despised in some countries. This method would sell to these countries. I wasn't prepared to sweat and toil like a doctor, to collect pennies by the end of the day and just be able to pay the bills. I wanted more out of my life, something bigger and grander. This might be my lucky breakthrough.

I needed to try out the research methods on patients. I considered doing proper research into the area but the more I read about research and development and research governance, it became clear to me that the only aim of these glorified offices was not to encourage but to deter people from doing research. The departments had created so many hoops in the name of research safety; they would put off even the most determined. The chances of getting approval from the research ethics committee for the study was non-existent, hence I was left with no option but to start the project stealthily without anyone noticing. Research has never been a clean business, after all.

The chances of success were high in middle-aged men with a history of emotional disturbances. Mr Demir was my perfect catch. Nature provided me with a platinum opportunity for taking revenge. Everything happened spontaneously, and looked natural and normal. I discarded the additional vial containing local anaesthetic into the sharps bin – a bin akin to a mind of emotional disturbances, full of needling thoughts and infected ideas, never safe for any curious brain to ferret into. I made changes to the anaesthetic clinical notes and re-wrote some with such care, as if I was reading them in front of a judge. I took my assortment of earphones home and hammered them into tiny pieces, and in the middle of the night I drove miles and deposited the shards in public waste bins.

Mr Demir wasn't my first prized prey. As my pilot study I tried hypnosis techniques with success on several celebrities or their daughters who were private patients having abortions. The research stated that the technique was more successful in men, but I guessed that no one without emotional disturbance or distress would ask for an abortion, and hoped that it would work with such a cohort as well. Some clever-arse might suggest that I was preying on vulnerable girls, but we're all vulnerable at some stage of our lives.

I chose girls with discretion; only those from the wealthy postcode areas, and preferably famous. For everything to look normal I imported skin-coloured, miniature earphones, which could be placed inside the ear canal without being noticed, and had a tampon-like thread attachment to pull it out at the end. The files playing on my mobile would be transmitted to the earphones and do the hypnotic spell. I'd pretend to read messages on the mobile, but would start and stop the hypnosis.

The combination of anaesthetics and hypnosis proved to be a triumphant success on these mademoiselles. I was becoming an accomplished hypnotist, a skill that could earn me a living in any part of the world. My prime objective was to siphon money from my subjects. It was enjoyable to see how they robbed their parents and partners to bring me cash. I was able to pay my mortgage through these girls. It was attained easily but was no more than peanuts in contrast to the money I was offered to sell the personal details I had kept on my database. An anti-abortion, pro-life group offered me a five-figure sum for patient details. Another group of punters floating around was extremely interested to get their hands on celebrity data and was prepared to pay double the amount the anti-abortion group had offered. An internet-based company offered to pay in the form of bitcoin in the stock market of my choice. It was intriguing how a few personal details could be so bountiful to these people. I had been planning to sell the same data to many interested parties or countries but before I threw the final dice, I had to have all the arrangements made and be ready to leave to the country for where even Interpol couldn't bring me back to the UK. In my calculations, the stakes were not higher than the rewards. To have sex with database girls was an additional bonus, which I admit I never enjoyed, partly as this was never my key objective, but neither they nor I minded. I think it was also in the back of my mind that if the medical regulator got a sniff of this, I could face press humiliation, an enquiry, and erasure from the medical register in no time. I had to tread extremely cautiously, and this carefulness had become a source of anxiety in my mind. I planned to voluntarily erase myself from the medical register just before leaving the country. I wasn't in any hurry to leave and wanted to take all the steps at the right time and, at the same time, make sure that no step was one too many. I wasn't convinced in my heart that hypnosis made it easy sexing up with such girls. I had achieved similar results by contacting girls through my bogus Facebook accounts and administering booze. The major difference was that hypnotised girls brought cash for me, with considerable ease.

TWENTY-SEVEN

I was discharged from hospital three days after surgery, yet I did not feel my normal self. I phoned Richard to tell him my concerns and went to see him in his office to discuss how to proceed against Dr Singh.

Richard apologised profusely, as he had to go urgently and review a patient on the ward. He asked his secretary to make a cup of tea for me.

Richard's office was the same as any other consultant's office, small like a cosy closet. On the desk was a picture of him with his wife and two children, grinning and exhibiting their teeth. Another unframed picture rested against the wall showing Richard skiing, stooping forward, ski poles under his armpits, zooming down a snow-laden slope. Scattered papers made the desktop invisible. A packed-to-capacity bookshelf stood sombrely against one wall and there was a waist-high pile of journals lying on the floor along another wall.

Suddenly, I realised that I'd brought with me two porn magazines, which I'd bought on my way to the hospital and were visible through the transparent carrier bag. It would be hugely embarrassing if someone found me with them so I placed the carrier bag under my chair, and hid it behind my feet.

Richard's secretary brought in a teacup on a tray. She was probably in her mid-twenties. She wore a knee-length green frock with black stripes. Her legs were in finely meshed black tights and black shoes with moderately high heels. She looked at the table in a contemplative mode for a moment and said, handing me the cup, 'I'd better not move any of his stuff.'

I looked away, not wanting her to notice my admiring glance, but her hand brushed my left forearm. The noise of crashing surf churned in my head. A tremor of desire rumbled up inside me, an urge I resisted strongly by placing the cup on the floor and holding my head in both hands.

'Are you okay, Mr Demir?'

'Yeah,' I said. 'I'll be fine. I sometimes get this wave of pain.'

I smiled and picked the cup up.

The smell of cigarette smoke lingered in the room after she left the room.

I was shocked by my carnality.

Richard returned and slumped heavily into his chair. 'Juniors these days don't want to take any responsibility for decision-making. I'm so looking forward to taking early retirement! How are you doing?'

'Okay,' I said briefly.

'I bumped into the histopathologist yesterday. They're still analysing the piece of the bowel I removed from you but they don't think it will be abnormal.'

'That's very reassuring,' I said. 'I think I've recovered quite well. I've begun to eat normally... no abdomen pain. It's the anaesthetic side I'm more concerned about.'

'Yes, I did discuss the case with the head of anaesthetics who spoke with Dr Singh, the ODA who was in theatre, and the nursing staff in the recovery. High-spinal is a rare but recognised complication of an epidural.'

'I know... I understand high-spinal is an anaesthetic block higher than the required area of body,' I said. 'But he deliberately caused this complication to me. He told me he'd given me double the dose. Can this not be verified by counting the number of ampoules of medicine he used during the anaesthetic?'

'First, they only keep an account of the controlled drugs, not all the medicines used. Second, there is no evidence that he used double the dose.'

'Maybe he altered the notes? Changed the prescriptions?'

'Possible, but difficult to prove. Also, Dr Singh is denying vehemently that he recognised you. It would be an open-and-shut case,' said Richard, looking firmly at me.

'Isn't he the same student who complained against me?'

'I don't know... It's your word against his. He is insistent that he didn't recognise you.'

'What about hypnosis? He has changed my personality through hypnosis,' I said, too embarrassed to tell him what happened a few minutes ago when his secretary was in the room.

'You did agree to have post-op pain relief through hypnosis, didn't you?' said Richard. 'The nurse in the recovery area thought you'd agreed to hypnosis post-operatively.'

'I didn't sign any consent for that, did I?'

'No, it was verbal consent. But Dr Singh had clearly documented in the notes that he did discuss it and you'd agreed.'

'It's a big lie.'

'Well, that's where the problem lies.'

'He made me listen to his hypnosis through an earphone for more than an hour in the recovery area, and that was not about pain relief. It was constantly hammering me with only one message...' I said, leaving my sentence unfinished.

'Well,' said Richard, 'you were in recovery for precisely three hours and twenty-three minutes. Quite a long time. Dr Singh did visit you there four times. This can only be interpreted as concern and that he was looking after you well.'

'Yes, I know,' I said. 'Just before I was about to be transferred to the ward, he came and changed the hypnosis chant to pain relief.'

'What was the other hypnosis about?' asked Richard curiously.

'It was full of erotic commands,' I said, feeling too uncomfortable to say what I wanted to say.

Richard's eyes opened wide. 'What?'

'He was implanting a message in me to seek pleasure only through sexual gratification... making it a compulsive behaviour... I don't know, but I feel that he has done something wrong with my psyche, with my thinking. I don't feel the same person as I was before. He said in the anaesthetic room that he'd changed my personality, and I think he's done it.' I looked carefully at Richard for any signs of dissent.

Richard kept his expressions neutral and appeared to be analysing the information.

I continued, 'I don't know if it's an effect of high-spinal or hypnosis.'

'I've seen quite a few cases of high-spinal but have never come across what you're describing,' said Richard.

'Nor me. I've done a thorough literature search of the complications of high-spinal and have found no evidence of what is happening to me.'

'Scary.'

'I know. He's done this so cleverly. He's vindictive and dangerous, a danger to the public. I don't think he should be allowed to practise. He's not a normal human being.'

Richard listened to me carefully and then said, 'We must have robust evidence against him that he is a danger to the public before making such a huge allegation. The medical director is aware of the high-spinal case but not of this business of hypnosis and altering your personality. I'm not too sure how to proceed against Dr Singh with this amorphous entity of changing personality. Maybe you should discuss it with your defence union and I'll speak to the medical director again. If Singh has done this the way you have described, he has done it very intelligently, without leaving any trace. We've got to tread very carefully. We don't want to do or say anything that could come back and haunt us in the future.'

'But no one is so clever to do anything wrong without leaving a trace. I've spoken with the theatre scrub nurse, Henrietta, who bumped into Rohan Singh the day after my operation. She said Singh was sneaking out of the theatre carrying a box of earphones. He wasn't in scrubs to go into the theatre and Henrietta did raise an incident form. Does it not sound fishy to you?'

'It's hardly evidence, and it could mean anything. I'm surprised Henrietta raised an incident form. You can approach the anaesthetic room through recovery without changing. We can't use this to suspend him.'

'It's so ironic! I was suspended immediately after an accusation by a medical student, and now you're searching for rock-solid evidence.' I laughed sarcastically. 'I've asked Henrietta to write down her recollections from that evening.'

'Yeah, but please try to understand…'

'Understand? I understand completely that I'm going bonkers,' I said. 'Could you please check my testosterone levels? My GP is a friend of mine, and I don't want to tell too many people what I'm suffering from.'

'Sure,' Richard said, and grabbed a biochemistry form. 'I think you need to speak to your GP. You might need a psychiatrist assessment.'

'I'll think about it,' I said.

I reached home despondent. The power of suggestion couldn't be overestimated. I remembered an interesting incident from the past. I was going to Kenya and Walter prescribed malaria prevention tablets and warned me of a rare side effect, that the tablets can give nightmares. That night I had terrible nightmares. I cursed this malaria tablet but was embarrassed to find in the morning that the box of tablets was unopened: I had not started taking the tablets.

I wanted to talk to someone who could understand my problem. Isla came to my mind and I felt aroused. I tried ringing her, but it went straight to answerphone. I shut my eyes and fantasised making love with her. It was bliss, and then the image swapped to Ava without any efforts. My hand moved hard to extract maximum gratification from my imagination. Surging endorphins were delivering a high-quality felicity and the woman now changed to Carys. I stopped abruptly, as I felt wet but hadn't reached a climax.

I was horrified to see fresh blood everywhere. I thought it was bound to happen. I had begun masturbating habitually, with a daily forensic frequency. Most likely I'd hurt myself, but there was no pain. I was bleeding from the back of my hand from where the blood sample had been taken earlier. I replaced the plaster and put a firm pressure over it to stem the bleed.

A whirlwind of sex thoughts clouded my mind again. I wanted to continue but I needed a kick to re-start. I craved porn.

'Oh fuck,' I said out loud. I had left the magazines in Richard's office. Whatever credibility I had in the hospital would now be ruined.

In frustration, I re-dialled the sex line phone number.

TWENTY-EIGHT

Physically I was getting better every day. The stitches on my skin had dissolved away, leaving a faint line-like scar that extended from the umbilicus downwards. The microscopic examination of the part of the bowel removed at surgery had confirmed Crohn's disease and no other untoward abnormality. My mental recovery, however, showed no progress. I had become very insular. I mostly stayed indoors and fought my new demons: an irresistible urge to spend time in the company of women. I was struggling to try to understand whether Dr Singh had uncovered something which had always been inside me lying dormant, or had he placed a new layer over my personality?

I tried my best: instead of six times per day, I managed to curtail calling premium-rate phone calls to three. I bought a couple of fiction novels to keep myself busy but my thoughts would always drift back to the peri-anaesthetic events. It was more than six weeks after the operation and I was legally allowed to drive, but didn't feel like it. My sick leave was extended for a further three months.

One evening, I walked into part of the city I'd never been to before. There were nightclubs inviting punters to watch peep shows and lap dancers. I gravitated towards a place called the *Fairy Heaven Club*. There was a small queue at the entrance, which was guarded by an efficient-looking woman, clad in black, who was checking some form of identity before letting people in. I took out my photo ID driving licence from my wallet and showed it to her.

'Do you have a membership card, sir?' she asked politely.

'No, I don't, but I have this ID.'

She took the card and, after carefully looking at it, said, 'The club is strictly for members only, sir. Do you wish to become a member? There are benefits of membership-subsidised drinks, complimentary evening meals. I could arrange for you to become a member immediately, if you wish, sir.'

'Okay,' I said. 'Yes, I could become a member if it's essential.'

'It is absolutely essential, sir. We have a high-security standard, which is only possible by keeping membership for select people like yourself. You'll be as safe inside the club as you are in your own home.' She spoke into the mouthpiece of her microphone. 'Please let Mr Demir in… Delta Echo Mike India Romeo.'

I was ushered through a metal detector and a blonde girl greeted me on the other side. She was skinny and scantily clad. She had an assortment of dangling earrings from each ear, which would chime if the breeze was heavy. Unsurprisingly, she also had a hanging belly-button ornament.

'Lisa will accompany you while I do the paperwork; can I have your credit card, please? It is necessary for you to inform your credit card company that you have joined the club and no one is misusing your card. I'll ring them for you to verify your presence.'

'That should be okay. I'll speak to them,' I said.

Lisa was already hovering over me, held my hand, and took me to a smaller room where all the furniture was red, including the curtains and carpet. The sound of ocean waves was slowly brewing in my head.

'We'll wait here. Can I get you a drink?' Lisa whispered, and her lips touched my ear; she intertwined her fingers with mine. The sound of ocean waves was gradually getting louder.

'I'd like to sit down,' I said, feeling uncomfortable.

'Don't look so nervous. You'll love this place so much you'll want to come every day.'

Lisa sat beside me, crossing her long legs and showing high heels.

'Let me guess. You're recently divorced?'

'No.'

'Widowed?'

'No.'

'Okay… Getting remarried after a long time?'

'No.'

'Experimenting?'

'No.'

'Seriously? Okay, now I understand, you're teasing your wife or your girlfriend?'

'Neither.'

'You don't look like a gambler to me,' she said, smiling. 'Have you received an unexpected sum of money from an inheritance or a bonus, or won the lottery?'

'No, I haven't got any unexpected sums from either of the sources you've mentioned.'

'Strange… but lovely to meet you,' she said, looking less buoyant.

The girl from the front door entered the room with a cordless phone in her hand and said, 'I'll pass you on to Mr Demir now.'

Lisa got up. 'I'll leave you to talk to the card company, then I'll be right back.'

'Okay,' I said. After going through the formality of checking my identity, the customer manager suggested increasing my credit limit from £7,500 to £15,000. I thought, *I don't need an increase*, but didn't argue, as I'd never utilised the credit limit in the past.

'Welcome aboard,' Lisa said, re-entering the room. She was holding a file containing membership paperwork, and asked me to sign on a dotted line. After I'd signed, the inviting smile on her face evaporated and she said in a business-like tone, 'You're a member now. A show is about to start in the first-floor studio. Make your way whenever you're ready. There's also a casino on the first floor if you want to try your luck at roulette.' She gave me a sticker with a handwritten membership number on it and placed it over my breast pocket.

It was a different world on the first floor. It was a large hall like a cinema with a stage on which a couple of dozen topless girls were dancing; an aerobic sort of dance to the sound of music. Their bodies changed colour under psychedelic lights. The crowd comprised men and women, who appeared very well mannered, cheering and clapping appropriately. All the waitresses were topless, scurrying around dispensing drinks. A girl ushered me to the only empty chair around a table and scanned my membership number on her mobile. Another pressed a chilled tumbler of wine into my hand.

'I hope you don't mind me sitting here,' I asked generally of the people sitting around the table, as I sat down.

'No, no,' one of the grey-headed men replied, his cheeks pink with alcohol. He continued watching the show.

The show was non-stop dancing of naked young girls. To keep it perpetually interesting, something new was happening all the time. At one stage, a small chopper descended on the set, and unsurprisingly a topless girl emerged from within. At another time, a girl was hoisted up to the ceiling. The show must have gone on for the best part of two hours. There was frantic clapping then all the girls came together on the stage, bowed, and the show finished.

I enjoyed the show without any shame or embarrassment, liking the sight of semi-naked girls. But the constant sound of sea waves was making me nauseous and spoiling the fun.

Lisa went on the stage at the end of the show and announced that the exclusive trip to Paris last week was extremely successful and another trip was arranged in a couple of weeks, for which she was taking bookings tonight. The crowd cheered and several people raised their hands to show their earnest desire to go on the trip.

I found myself compelled to join the queue that was paying. Lisa was taking the bookings; her sales-person smile re-emerged on her face. When my turn came, she asked me, 'Sir, how many places do you want?'

'Only one. How much is it?'

'It will be a chartered flight, a five-star hotel stay in the heart of Paris and a show. All-inclusive, only eighteen grand per person.'

'Quite pricey.'

'It's an exclusive trip. Food, drinks, hotel room and the cost of the show. Very good value for the money.'

The ocean sound was recurring intensely in my head again and I was finding it difficult to decide what to do. In the end I said, 'Okay, one place, please,' and gave her my credit card.

'Sir, we only take debit cards for such tours.'

Someone said in a boozy voice from behind me in the queue, 'Hurry up. Why is only one person taking bookings?'

'Sorry, sir, I'll be as quick as I can,' she said in an apologetic tone.

I handed over my debit card to Lisa, and she processed the transaction expeditiously.

'Have a good night, sir,' she said. 'I hope you enjoyed the show tonight. There's a new show every night. I'll see you tomorrow.'

'Good night,' I said and left the place.

There was another girl in place of Lisa outside. She scanned my name sticker on her mobile and said, 'There's a complimentary taxi for our new members tonight.' She hailed a taxi and swiftly opened the door for me.

The noise of crashing waves in my head was becoming unbearable. I folded my arms over my knees and put my head over them.

'Are you feeling sick, sir?' the taxi driver said in a worried voice. 'Should I open the window for some fresh air?'

'You can stop here actually,' I said, looking outside. I was barely two hundred yards from home.

'As you wish.' The taxi driver halted the taxi under a yellow streetlight. 'Goodnight, sir.'

I waved to him and slowly tramped home. The swishing noise in my head, palpitations, profuse sweats and a badly hurting big toe were making me very disinterested in this life. After reaching home, I grabbed a bottle of wine and directly decanted it inside me in a few mouthfuls. Was I becoming an alcoholic? Was there anything medically wrong with me, or was it time to extinguish this dimly lit candle of my life? I resolved to go to see Walter tomorrow. Not for a psychiatrist, but for a sick note. I didn't feel like work.

TWENTY-NINE

Lust had become the chief engine, the main driver, of my life. With child-like eagerness, I waited all day to go to the *Fairy Heaven Club*. The club visits were habit-forming. I had been going there every Friday and Saturday night for the last couple of months. Evening drinking had crept to commencing in the late mornings. I knew it wasn't the right thing to do but I couldn't care less. Despite all this, the intensity of ocean noise in my head had shown no sign of abating in loudness or frequency. In desperation, I rang Olivia to talk to her and lighten my heart but I was always greeted by an answering machine, and I left no messages. Probably she was on a yacht, gliding gently on sapphire waters with azure skies.

Thoughts of ringing Carys to ask how she was getting on with her life came to my mind. I took her card out of my wallet and noticed wrinkles on it. I placed the card on the tabletop and attempted to smooth it out. Her mobile number was handwritten carefully. I observed the way she had written the numbers with a slant angled on the top of the first word and a small line crossing the middle of sevens. Without thinking, I put her card back in my wallet and tried ringing Olivia again. No answer. As I was about to put the phone down, I noticed a different tone on my phone indicating recorded voicemails.

There were three messages from the bank. Andrew Penny, a personal banker, wished to speak to me urgently.

I returned the phone call. 'What's this about? Why is it so urgent? You could leave a message on my answering machine but not tell me what it was about… Yes, 11:30 am should be suitable for me as well.'

I deliberated over why he wanted to see me. I hoped that the aim of the meeting was not to sell me a new mortgage or some advice on an investment scheme. I would be rabidly mad if he tried to do that to me.

Andrew had said very politely that the computer automatically brought my bank account to his attention, which can happen in quite a few cases, but he would need my verbal consent to have a detailed look into my accounts, including my credit cards.

Going to the bank thwarted my plans to go through the stack of letters piling up on my desk. Maybe some other day, I thought.

Andrew Penny wore a pinstripe suit and looked quite young for his job.

He came straight to the point. 'I need to discuss some money matters with you. Should we go to this cubicle so that we could talk in private without any distractions?'

'Yes, we could,' I said. 'Just to tell you in advance, at present I won't be interested in any new products or investment schemes.'

'No, Dr Demir,' he said quite respectfully. 'I'm not here to sell you anything.' He paused. 'You hold with us a current account, a mortgage account and a credit card.' He closed the door behind him and gestured to me to take a seat.

'It seems I'm providing you with a lot of business,' I said, looking at him.

'That's absolutely fine, sir,' said Andrew hesitantly. 'We need to discuss unauthorised overdrafts, arrears and unpaid credit card bills.'

'Is this the reason you've asked me to come here?' I said with exasperation. 'You could have written me a letter or sent me my account statements.'

'I'm sorry; the bank is still sending you your monthly bank

statements. You have signed for e-mail statements. We've also written you several letters.'

'I haven't opened my e-mails for some time; that explains why.'

'I'm sorry that you couldn't check your e-mails. Your debt amounts to £36,975. I have a report about your finances from a consumer credit rating agency.'

'What? What're you saying?' I said, shocked to hear this. 'I hope this is not some kind of sick joke. Are you sure you haven't made any mistake?'

'No, sir, there aren't any mistakes. This is the most up-to-date report of your finances. Your mortgage payments are also in arrears for the last three months. You know, your house could be repossessed.'

'What? Mortgage arrears?' I said, cutting him off mid-sentence. 'Overdrawn? I didn't spend all this money, are you sure there's no identity theft here, or someone has fraudulently drawn money on my behalf? Why did you not let me know that this sum of money was going out of my accounts?' I was shocked and angry to hear the amount.

Andrew moved the knot of his slim red tie to ease it over the collar, without losing his cool, and said, 'No, sir, there does not appear to be any identity theft. All the transactions have been carried out legitimately using your debit card and PIN. We did try ringing you, but your mobile went straight to answering machine.'

I interrupted him. 'I've not been well, and don't use the mobile all the time.'

'I'm sorry to hear that, sir. Also, your landline bills each month are averaging around £4,000, which is not helping the situation as the money goes out by direct debit.'

'What? £4,000, good grief.'

'Last month it was £5,064. If you want to dispute the amount, you need to take up the issue with the phone company.'

'All these bills have been eating into my savings?'

'Precisely. We did write to inform you,' he said. 'Well, we are where we are.' He spoke with maturity beyond his age. 'As a personal banker, my advice to you would be to immediately pay off the arrears in your mortgage payments and start paying at least the minimum amount on your credit cards. Ideally, you should pay off all your credit card bills straightaway, as they come with a hefty interest rate.'

'What amount on the credit cards is outstanding?'

'£30,982, more than the credit limit of two credit cards.'

'Thirty-one grand? How and where did I spend all this money? My salary comes into the account, and I think I did have savings of more than fifty grand?'

'Yes, sir, your monthly salary is still coming into your account. The credit card statement shows all the items,' he said, showing me the current account statement. 'You paid eighteen thousand for club membership fees, and you also spent on average £2,000 each time you visited this club.'

'Have I spent all my savings?' I said, raging in anger.

'Looks like it. And your overdraft limit of two thousand,' Andrew replied quietly.

'Bloody hell,' I said. The effect of the bombshell was getting bigger. 'I've got another credit card. It's not with your bank. I've been using this lately.' I took it out of my wallet and showed him the other Mastercard.

'Sir,' said Andrew, 'this report shows both your credit cards. Let's confirm this. How do you pay for this card? By direct debit, I assume?'

'Not by direct debit,' I said, and could feel sweat flowing in my armpits. 'I write cheques, but I hadn't written one for some time.'

Andrew looked at me and said, 'I could electronically search for your recent statements if you just log in here.' There was pity for me in his eyes just before he looked away to allow me to type in my password.

'Please look for the statements, if you don't mind,' I said.

Andrew clicked a few buttons and said, 'Here are the statements for your other credit card. I'll print them off for you.'

The statements showed that I'd crossed the limit of fifteen thousand on the cards three months ago. As I had not paid even the minimum amount, there was an interest of £1,800 for each month.

Andrew clicked the calculator on his mobile and said, 'Sir, the total amount you owe for both cards, bank overdraft and mortgage payment amounts to £36,772. You need at least £6,000 to pay off your mortgage arrears and start making some payments towards your credit cards. Arrears and non-payment to the cards have negatively affected your credit ratings. Because of this we won't be able to offer you any loans. If you pay at least £26,000, then I can see whether we can consolidate the rest of your credit card bills into your mortgage. It'll inevitably increase your mortgage outgoings but perhaps that's the cheapest way to tackle these immediate issues. Failing this, I'm sorry to say you run a serious risk of losing your house.'

'So, you're saying that if I don't pay £26,000 immediately, I might be on the road?' I said.

'Without sounding too cruel,' Andrew said, 'it's a real possibility. Can someone lend you the required sum? Or can you ask your employer to pay you in advance and then deduct it monthly from the salary? However, you would have difficulty in getting a non-secured loan due to your recent credit rating. There are some lenders on the high street that may lend you that sort of money quite happily but they do charge an extortionate amount of interest rate. They're loan sharks, and I wouldn't recommend you going to them.'

'I could try to get an advance from the hospital,' I said, 'although I'm not sure they would give me the advance. I've been on sick leave for the past five months.'

'It's worth a try, sir,' said Andrew. 'Also, sir, it's none of my business, but may I take the liberty of suggesting you change your lifestyle? I can see something has happened to you recently which has caused this financial difficulty and blemished your credit rating.'

'I know,' I said. 'I've been fighting it, without much success. But as you said, I've got to do something. I don't have any other savings or assets. The only thing I can sell is my car. It's seven years old and I don't know how much it will fetch. I did spend £25,000 to purchase it.'

'Today is Friday. Could I touch base with you next Thursday so that we can pay monies into your account before the close of play next Friday. This gives you some time to speak to the finance people at your workplace. I'll leave my card with you in case you want to get in touch with me.'

'I didn't realise I was in such a big mess,' I said to Andrew, who smiled professionally in response.

I could raise twenty-six grand, which shouldn't be a big deal, I thought as I drove back. After going through a couple of drawers, I was able to find a salary slip and rang the hospital finance officer to pay £10,000 in advance. He apologised profusely and informed me that as the Trust has been going through financial difficulty for some years, the advance salary payment policy had been temporarily suspended.

I had been spending money without realising. The voyage of desire had to stop, but how? I needed to seek medical help and whilst doing that, I had no option but to sell the car. What else could I sell? I thought. The gold Rolex watch which Isla had given me as a wedding present was also lying redundant somewhere. Selling the watch should raise some funds. Isla had kept it tucked away in a wardrobe in its original packaging. I looked at the watch. I had only worn it for a couple of months before we clinicians were forced to adopt a bare-below-the-elbow policy in the health care service, and no wristwatches were allowed.

It was beginning to dawn on me that selling my car and the watch would not fetch money even close to the required sum. My head was spinning. The conversation with Alan Taylor sprang to my mind when I was effectively removed from the post of the head of workforce and my salary reduced. At that time I could never foresee that a loss in wages would make any difference to me. Now, I was thinking that if I'd continued to receive an additional seven or eight grand each year, maybe I would have had more money in my savings.

Dr Singh had successfully managed to submerge me into health and financial destruction. The prospects of raising the sum looked bleak. The house had to go. I'd be another tramp in the town. The acid was building up again in my stomach. For the first time in my life tears were rolling down my cheeks. Could my life go any lower than this? Martin had taken his life to stay at the peak of felicity. I could do the same, but finish in the depths of misery.

THIRTY

I booked a double-slot appointment with Walter. He listened to me carefully and was quite distraught to hear about the psychological and financial mess I was in. I wanted to be off work again for a long period but that would mean a reduction of my salary to half for the next six months and none after that, which I couldn't afford. The result of my blood testosterone levels was plumb normal. Walter's face was etched with concern. He raised his hands and acknowledged that he had not heard about Sudden-onset Compulsive Sexual Behaviour before and made an urgent referral to a psychiatrist.

'How long will I have to wait to be seen?' I asked.

'I don't know, I need to phone a friend,' Walter said and went out of the room to speak to someone on his mobile.

I needed urgent help. Could I afford to wait, or get it done quicker privately? But where would the finances come from to go private? The thought dismayed me.

'Not too shabby,' Walter said as he came back. 'Marcus will see you in his clinic in a week's time.'

'Not bad at all.'

'Marcus has suggested re-checking the testosterone level and to arrange an MRI of the brain, chest and abdomen. I'll request these now. The results of these investigations should be ready by the time you go to see him.'

'Walter, I'm most grateful.'

'Never mind, my friend,' Walter said. 'Marcus would also like you to go on some antidepressants.'

'What would they achieve?'

'Well, Marcus thinks antidepressants would help you.'

Reluctantly I agreed to follow the doctor's advice.

To go on the mood-flattening drugs was certainly not a step in the right direction as they made me sleep all the time. When awake I was back in the fantasy world of being with women, offering slimy, squirty libations and listening to the premium phone numbers and doing the same again.

I was really terrified of myself.

I shut myself inside the home in case I did something silly.

With a heavy, drowsy head I peered outside the window. The daily war had ensued inside me. The noise in my head got louder. The memory of Isla came from nowhere. I wished she were here, with me. I remembered the time we were together. The smiles, the fights. All the hard words she had spoken on the wretched day she left were forgotten. I regretted not keeping in touch with Isla's mum. She was certainly hard-done by, by me. Why is my learning only activated by a loss? In remorse, I rang her, and a voice message said the number was not recognised. I'd lost another contact. Life was deserting me.

The thought of taking early retirement to get the lump sum pension and settle my debts was considered and dismissed as it only meant swapping problems, not solving them.

It was heartbreaking losing the house, which Isla had decorated, but it looked like an unavoidable reality. I had to ring and tell Andrew Penny this. Perhaps I'd do that tomorrow. An appointment was made to sell the car on the coming Friday. I found the contact details of a local auctioneer to clear the furniture. I had to find some cheap bed and breakfast accommodation until I had seen Dr Marcus and completed any treatment which might be needed. I hoped I would get better, but I wasn't sure how long it would take. After the treatment, I had to decide whether to stay in the UK or go back to Turkey.

I cancelled my membership of the *Fairy Heaven Club* and broke the Internet connection. Both charged me three months' fees as a penalty for not giving notice. Every penny was precious but I had no choice.

I was still looking outside but my mind flat-lined as the sun meted out an autumn-like afternoon. Decidualised leaves cluttered the roads. The bitter reality was slowly dawning upon me that the world of the ill was different in many ways from the world of the healthy. We doctors feel battered by our daily schedules, but, in health, we still enjoy a temporal freedom that has completely disappeared for many of our patients.

I had no access to guns to follow suit with Martin Norton, or to *Propofol*, which anaesthetists steal to extinguish their lives peacefully in the comfort of their own home.

THIRTY-ONE

The phone rang and I was afraid to pick it up, dreading it might be Andrew Penny chasing me.

'Hello,' I said hesitantly, and was pleasantly surprised to find Olivia on the other end. 'Olivia, where were you? I was trying to contact you. I need to see you, I'm in trouble,' I said without any hesitation.

'Again!'

'I can't explain it over the phone,' I said. 'I need to go out and sell my car, and I'll see you afterwards.'

'Why are you selling your car? Have you ever sold anything before? Do you know how to sell a car?' She bombarded me with questions.

'I assume it should be pretty straightforward. I give them the car and they give me the cash.'

'No, you don't sell anything like that,' she said with maternal affection. 'If you sound desperate, they'll rip you off. They won't even pay you half the price your car is worth. Just give me some time to take a shower and eat something. I'll meet you at the pub in an hour for lunch. I have some news, too.'

Olivia was tired, tanned and hungry, but still in a very pleasant mood. I ordered lunch for both of us and told her about my operations, complications, hypnosis spell, and my dire financial situation.

'Unbelievable stuff. So, you're telling me that nothing could be done to prove what this bloody doctor has done to you.'

'Looks like.'

'So, he walks free and you become a hostage to your debts,' she said. 'Your plan to sell the car and the watch won't get you out of the hole you're in. There's a better solution. How much do you need straightaway?'

'Twenty-six grand.'

'I could lend you the money as long as you don't have any feeling for me,' she said, laughing. Olivia's ability to invert a situation with humour was incredible. 'I got a company dividend of fifty thousand this month. You're in luck.'

'That's very kind of you. But I won't take money from you. I'll sell my car and my watch and…' I couldn't complete my sentence.

'Okay, but for argument's sake,' said Olivia, 'say you sell the car and the watch, how much are you hoping to raise? I don't think you'll make more than five grand. You'll still be twenty grand short.'

I'd no answers but I said, 'I could do some locum work.'

'Have you gone completely bonkers?' she said. 'You can't do locums. First, you're on sick leave and if your hospital gets a sniff about your locum work, they'll sack you without any problem. Second, you're off work for almost six months, and you told me that after six months you need to work under supervision for some time. Mikel, don't make your life even more difficult. Be realistic. Take the money from me before I change my mind. You could return it with interest.'

'I think it'd be much better if I sell the house, the furniture, pay all my debts and downsize,' I said.

'Potentially,' said Olivia. 'But Mikel, your issue isn't only money but time. How can you sell your house in a week? You must cancel your membership of these strip clubs.'

'They're not strip clubs,' I said with emphasis. 'They're just clubs, and I have cancelled my membership. I know I've got to stop what I've been doing. I'm very cross with myself.'

'I could transfer the money online today, and you can sort out your finances.'

I remained pensive, and Olivia said after a pause, 'For anyone else, the best solution would be to cancel the remainder of your sick leave and rejoin the hospital. But I can't suggest this to you... You're a bloody gynaecologist, working with women all the time. The work wouldn't be a distraction for you but a minefield. I don't know what to suggest to you. It's a difficult one.'

'I need to consult the psychiatrist before I do that,' I said. 'I'll get an appointment next week. I don't want to land in any bigger problem by doing something very silly at work.'

'I agree.'

'I could kill Rohan Singh,' I said in a fury. 'Twice he has tried to ruin me.'

Olivia smirked and said, 'Well, you need to park your anger and move on, especially if he's done all this and you can't prove it.'

I said, 'I know, I feel so helpless. He's outplayed me this time.' I looked at Olivia. 'You said you had some news to tell me.'

'Yes,' Olivia said, showing a diamond ring on her left hand. 'Do you remember Albert Rossi?'

'The marine biologist? That pencil scientist?'

'Yes, be respectful towards him. I married Albert last week on the island of Capri,' said Olivia ostentatiously admiring her wedding ring.

'Congratulations,' I said, and shook hands with her. 'How wonderful! You need to tell me all the details.'

Olivia laughed out loud. 'We've been seeing each other for the last seven or eight years. He's adorable, I love listening to him.'

'You had a philosophy of fulfilling other people's dreams,' I said. 'Is this part of the same?'

'Quite the opposite,' she said. 'By marrying him, I'm fulfilling my dream of making myself happy.'

Good luck is nothing more than good people around you. Olivia was more than true to her word, and transferred the sum into my account. The mortgage arrears were paid off and all my remaining debts were consolidated and incorporated into the house mortgage.

Contrary to Olivia's advice, I sold my car and wristwatch for £5,000 and immediately transferred the whole amount into Olivia's account. She didn't like it, perhaps for not following her counsel, and sent a text back with an angry emoji.

I took Olivia and Albert out for dinner and gave them a wedding present. Albert had the curiosity and impatience of a child and unwrapped the crystal vase, inspected it from every angle, looked at the country it was manufactured in, and then thanked me profusely.

The newlywed couple appeared happy in each other's company. Olivia's magic had perked up Albert, and he'd begun to smile every now and then. With maternal affection, Olivia suggested that I should join yoga and mindfulness classes. She gave me a card for such a centre, whose annual fees were paid in advance. I was moved by her thoughtfulness. Albert straightaway seconded Olivia's idea and said how meditation had helped to transform his life. It was blatantly obvious that Albert was a very honest man; any other savvy husband would have attributed changes to his life because of his new wife and would have won several brownie points.

THIRTY-TWO

D r Marcus, the psychiatrist, appeared self-assured and experienced. He was wearing an expensive-looking dark-blue suit with a red bow tie, and neatly polished black shoes, indicating a good upbringing.

There was walnut panelling on the walls, which created a warm aura. The consultation area comprised two dark-brown leather high-back armchairs facing each other, separated by a coffee table upon which was a carved silver tray with an assortment of wrapped chocolates. Very pleasantly mannered, he showed me to one of the chairs and went to grab a file from a large desk, which was on the other side of the room.

'Okay, let's take a look at your history first,' he said, and began to take a detailed medical and family history, noting the recent history of alcoholism and occasional use of recreational drugs and was intrigued to hear about the high-spinal and the hypnosis. 'An abrupt start of such behaviour is very uncommon, and I'm considering quite a few differentials. My immediate first thought was of Kluver-Bucy Syndrome, which is brain-related. Do you know anything about it?'

'Not a clue. My area of specialisation is three to four feet lower than yours.'

Marcus smiled genially, folded his arms across his chest, and said, 'Kluver-Bucy has an association with hypersexuality and disinhibited social behaviours. I've been postulating whether your amygdala, which controls sexuality, was damaged during your profound low blood pressure during the anaesthetic complication.'

'So, you think I've got this syndrome?' I said. I didn't like Marcus calling my anaesthetic debacle a complication.

'You don't have all the features of the syndrome. I've discussed your case with a consultant neurologist colleague. Your brain MRI is normal and isn't showing a tumour. The MRI of your abdomen or pelvis is not suggestive of any testosterone-secreting tumour either. It's reassuring that no sinister pathology is detected.'

'So, where do we go from here?'

'Well… you're a bit of a diagnostic conundrum. We hold monthly multi-disciplinary meetings to discuss cases as complex as yours. I've added your case to the list for discussion.'

I came out of Marcus's clinic feeling deflated because of no diagnosis. What could I do? Had Dr Singh irreversibly damaged me? Would I have to live with this mental condition for the rest of my life?

I should explore the yoga and mindfulness centre, for which Olivia had given me a year's membership.

The centre was within walking distance from Marcus's clinic. I showed the card to the wizened old lady at the reception, who had heavily-mascaraed large eyes. A lanyard hanging around her neck gave her name as Jocelyn Warren.

'Good afternoon, you're very welcome to our centre,' she said with genuine welcoming warmth. 'You've got a premium membership card and you can use the centre at any time.'

'That's excellent.'

'Is it a birthday present?'

'No, it's not a birthday present. One of my friends gave it to me to wish me well after my operation.'

'So, you've had an operation recently?'

'Yes, a couple of months ago. Is there a problem?'

'Unfortunately, the insurance doesn't cover us for yoga if you've had an operation within the last six months. But you can join the introductory class to mindfulness if you wish. There's a class about to start in the next fifteen minutes on the first floor.'

The direction to the room was signposted. The room was like a medium-sized classroom and already there were twenty-five people there. I took the last row, closer to the door, in case it got too boring, then I could leave without being noticed. I looked around and noted that except for a couple of youths, the majority appeared to be of post-retirement age. It was still ten minutes for the class to start.

'Steve, what do you think of mindfulness?' someone asked someone.

'Not a lot. It's the latest goofy fad in a very long line of goofy fads, which Americans like. You know what Americans are like…'

There was unreserved laughter.

Surprisingly, the lady I'd met earlier at the reception came to give the talk. Jocelyn introduced herself and told us the receptionist had a hospital appointment, so she was manning the post for a little while. She allowed us to interrupt to ask any questions, which I thought was a dangerous proposition considering the comments that were made earlier. She started her talk unaided by a PowerPoint presentation or any cue cards. Her talk appeared candid and I liked the way she talked.

'On average we get about 60,000 thoughts in a day, which amount to one thought every 1.5 seconds. Our mind is all over the place. The idea of mindfulness is to cultivate attention to the present moment…'

My mind skittered away to the consultation. I hoped Marcus would be able to reach the bottom of my problem. Also, I hoped there was some easy cure to my problem, no electric shock-type treatment. That bastard Rohan Singh…

'You have to live in the present moment, the only time you have – the present. Reminiscing the past or planning for the future compresses our present. In addition to our ability to think we need to develop a capacity for awareness, cultivate attention to the present moment and to our present self. Concentrate on your breaths, each one of them.'

Someone in the front row raised his hand and said, 'This isn't a new concept. Buddha said this in 2600 BC. This is called *Vipassana* and *Anapanasati.*'

'The real true truth is eternal,' someone else replied.

'Very well said,' Jocelyn replied. 'The whole idea of mindfulness is to quieten the inner incessant chatter, to connect with life. Our educational system trains our minds to think, which is great. New ideas, new theories come through this but we shouldn't become hostage to our thoughts, we need to live in the present moment.'

Someone harrumphed and said, 'I think you're right. We're thinking, thinking and thinking, and this race of thoughts makes life miserable.'

My mobile whirred in my pocket and there was a text from Olivia asking how my consultation went. This provided me with an excellent opportunity to leave and I rang Olivia to tell her the details of my appointment.

Walking back home, I was mulling over what I'd heard in the mindfulness class. *What is so special about the present? Why have we become so fixated on it? There's no doubt that it's not a new concept.* I remembered once talking to a whirling dervish in Istanbul, twenty years ago.

'The key to the happiness in this world is to become a *sahib-e-haal.*'

'Who is this fellow?'

'A *sahib-e-haal* is a person who only dwells in today, the present moment,' the dervish said poking his lean index finger towards the ground and told a story as an example.

'A king himself went to see a prisoner who was condemned to death, and asked what his final wish was.

'The prisoner appeared totally unperturbed and said casually, "I don't have any last wish. I'm ready to die, but could you please move out of the way, you're blocking my view of the flying horse."

"Which flying horse are you talking about?" the King asked, looking around.

"The one, which is just outside. Marvellously white skin, white hair and blue eyes. It's a feast to the eyes. If you don't mind, let me enjoy this moment of my life."

"That's my horse," said the King. "He's a stunning animal but not a flying horse."

"That's what you think," replied the prisoner. "That horse is a flying horse. It just needs some training."

"Really! How long would the training last?"

"About a year."

"Are you sure?"

"Not a shred of doubt."

'Thought lines furrowed the King's forehead before he said, "Your sentence of death is reprieved for a year, but could you train my horse to fly."

'When the prisoner reached his home with the horse, his wife began to cry with tears of happiness.

'The prisoner told her that his death sentence had been postponed for a year and now his wife began to cry her eyes out with grief and said, "Time flies. This year will pass in no time."'

Whatever the convict said at that time was worth remembering, I reflected. 'Let's not spoil our today for the fear of tomorrow. Let's live and enjoy our today as this is the only asset we've got; the rest is an illusion, a mirage.'

I envied *Sahib-e-haal's* complete and profound freedom. I looked at my miserable self, like so many other clerks, my back bent with the weight of the past and the future encircling my mind, frightening me. A non-stop shuttle service flourished between the two times: the time I'd never have again and the time I might never have. A terrible headache took over my thoughts again.

THIRTY-THREE

could hardly wait for my appointment with Dr Marcus to discover the outcome of the MDT discussion.

I reached the hospital well before my appointment.

The clinic was running on time.

Marcus had a consoling smile on his face.

'So, what's the verdict?' I said.

'Not something serious. We had a detailed discussion and we all felt it is Compulsive Sexual Behaviour of nonparaphilic type, which is typical of sexual desire but excessive, out of order. The paraphilic variety is behaviour deemed socially unacceptable, with legal implications.'

'That's a relief to know. So, what could be the underlying reason for this?'

'Yes…we did consider all the possible contributing factors… well… hypnosis might have triggered it, but it's difficult to prove.'

'Can something be done to cure this?'

Marcus smiled and said, 'First, you need to draw up a sexual sobriety declaration in writing with yourself. Your dos and don'ts. Realistic and honest.'

'I think I've already done this, not in writing but in action. I've cancelled the membership of the clubs, barred all the premium-rate phone conversations. The Internet connection is gone.'

'That's good. It tells me about your motivation. Well, if you wish I could start cognitive behavioural therapy with you. I'm hopeful this will help.'

'Is there no pharmacological treatment? I'm fed up with anti-depressants and they're useless.'

'You may stop them if they're not helping you. Sometimes we do prescribe *Naltrexone*, which is an opiate antagonist and reduces the craving by blocking the euphoria receptors.'

'Is this the same medication which is given to compulsive gamblers?'

'That's right, but I'm confident we could get on top of your problem by CBT alone.'

'How long do you think it would take?'

'It depends upon you mainly, but usually requires three to six months.'

'What do you suggest? When should I resume the work?'

'Not until you're in full remission.'

'Yeah. I'm so worried that I might do something unprofessional or silly with the patients… which I've been accused of in the past.'

'Hopefully, the CBT will help you to overcome your fears,' said Marcus, rubbing his eyes without bothering to remove his glasses.

'I'm sorry, I think I'm about to sneeze and they usually come in bouts of ten to twelve.'

He did sneeze like rifle shots, twelve times.

As advised, I wrote a sexual soberness plan and started the CBT.

In the first couple of months, I didn't feel any improvement. The questions were bubbling up in my mind: had Dr Singh rendered me incurable, unsalvageable? Was life worth living?

I felt exhausted.

Marcus asked me to persevere with the treatment, but I could see that deep down he was worried about me. With no improvement in my hypersexuality symptoms and perhaps in desperation, Marcus ran another battery of blood tests and repeated the MRIs. I could now fully comprehend the frustrations of the deceased war veteran, Mark Davis, with the slow pace of treatment. But I persisted.

Marcus didn't suggest it, but I made another change to my lifestyle: I started walking everywhere. No use of Uber. I walked five or six miles each day, and some days even twelve miles. I didn't know how and why walking helped, but it did. Was it the electromagnetic waves of the field of the earth travelling from my feet to my mind and rectifying the electrical activity of my brain? Marcus laughed at my theory of walking, but it worked, so I continued.

I gave up alcohol altogether, and in addition to being teetotal, I became coffeetotal.

After a painfully slow start, the progress curve gently began to digress from the base.

THIRTY-FOUR

I t was a dim, wintry afternoon. As on most days, I maintained a blinkless vigil peering through the window of my study. The tall leafless trees stood still as if waiting, but nothing happened and spring wasn't on the horizon. A solitary raven fluttered its wings in the tree, breaking the monotony of the scene, but soon settled quietly, perhaps due to the cold weather. It was even cold inside. Without thinking, I ran my hand down my recently trimmed salt-and-pepper beard, producing a grating noise. 'I can't afford to fall into the same mess again, I've got to keep myself mentally busy,' I said to myself and tried reading a medical journal, but soon felt jaded and unable to carry on. I felt better. The noise in my head was settling. I decided to rejoin the hospital the next day after six months.

I had started drinking green tea and stashed an assortment of teas to suit any time of the day. Perhaps I needed one. On the landing I took my beanie hat off and looked in the mirror. The time had taken its toll. I looked different. My bald scalp shone with a few strands of scattered hair, which I combed with my fingers. The grey bushy eyebrows appeared as part of the frame of my glasses. I had lost some weight, and my cheeks weren't as chubby as before.

I went to the kitchen, filled the kettle and watched it come to boil as if some interesting phenomenon was happening. When the kettle had boiled, I didn't feel like having tea and went and sat in the living room. The news channel was showing film footage of a bomb blast in Syria. I muted the TV. The macabre massacre saddened but didn't shock me. Was I losing compassion? Was I becoming insensitive? I switched the TV off and stared at the blank screen.

I put my head back against the sofa and closed my eyes. The day shouldn't go to waste, I said to myself, and to keep myself mentally occupied, I became the examination committee member of the Royal College and decided to write questions for the exam for which the deadline was looming. *Okay*, I said to myself, *let me take some rest and then I'll write the questions.*

I must have dozed off for a while, as it was dark when the doorbell rang.

'Who could that be at this time?' I quietly mumbled to myself as I opened the door. The cold breeze and a familiar but strange face greeted me. Suddenly my memory recalled her. 'Is this you, Isla? Is this you? I knew you'd come back… I knew you'd come back one day.' I was shocked and overwhelmed by emotions on her unexpected, unannounced visit.

'Hope I'm not daydreaming.' I pulled and hugged her tightly.

She winced. Her eyes flooded too. She looked frail. The pallor over her face was visible through her make-up. Her shadowed eyes had a distinct tinge of sadness and seemed to drown in the eye sockets.

'Come inside, stranger,' I said.

'I was dreading you not being home,' she said. 'It's good to see you after so long.'

'Yeah,' I said. 'It's more than ten years… but forget all this now… you're here … I don't go out much these days… I'm so happy to see you.'

Isla said, looking at her wristwatch, 'I'm only here for thirty minutes. I'm on my way to the airport. My taxi is waiting outside.'

'Where're you going?'

'South Africa.'

I opened the door and looked outside. A taxi was waiting with the engine running.

'You could let the taxi go,' I said. 'I'll call another later.'

'No, don't worry,' she replied. 'That won't be possible. You don't know how we journalists travel. There's a large wooden chest, which won't fit in the boot of any normal car.'

'In that case,' I said, 'the taxi can stay and I'll come with you to the airport. Thirty minutes are too short to meet after a decade. At least we'll have a few more minutes together if I go with you to the airport.'

'Okay,' said Isla. 'That should be fine.'

Isla walked inside, turning lights on, peeking into each room.

'You've not changed any furniture,' she said, looking around. 'It seems time has frozen and I'm back where I left.'

'Well, nothing more than mere laziness,' I said facetiously.

I resisted but I wanted to tell Isla: *You were part of this furniture, trust me... you were... I couldn't change anything even if I wanted... I've walked with caution all these years in this house ... don't step over on any of your memories.*

'You know, sometimes laziness becomes our attribute.' I could hear joy oozing out of my voice. *Contain yourself, old man, hold tight,* I said to myself. She might have come to hand over the divorce papers.

Isla looked at me and said quietly, 'The beard suits you.'

'Thanks,' I said. 'Again, the laziness. I couldn't be bothered to shave every morning.'

'Did you miss me?' asked Isla.

Women like to ask questions even when they know the answer; they love an auditory confirmation.

'Yes, every now and then, but especially on Thursday evenings,' I said calmly.

'Why on Thursdays?' asked Isla, surprised.

'Well, when I was putting the rubbish bins outside for collection,' I said. 'You know how much I hated wheeling the bins outside.'

'Very funny,' she said.

'I missed you every day, every hour, you don't have to ask this,' I said quietly.

'You still love me so much?' She asked me another confirmatory question. 'I left you… for so many years. Do you?'

She took off her long coat and handed it to me. I hung the coat over my forearm and brought it close to my chest. Isla's warmth and perfume lingered inside it. A spasm of lust began to uncoil inside me. The old memories, the times of togetherness. *Contain yourself.* I was able to control myself: the CBT was working.

'I have and will always love you,' I said and held her hand to follow me upstairs. 'Come with me to your office. I'll show you something… you were always with me.' The room had pictures that I'd cut from the newspaper and stuck on all four walls. The yellowing images fluttered as I opened the door.

'These are the photographs you've taken all these years… the ones printed in the newspapers and magazines here. To read the credit of your name on those pictures gave me immense joy.'

'Wow,' she said. 'You're the biggest collector of my work.'

She went around the room, carefully looking at the pictures, and stood near one. The pallor on her face grew stronger. 'Can I take this?' she said, staring at a picture of a burning jeep.

'Of course you can.'

'This picture represents a watershed moment in my life.'

'Really?' I'd wondered about the significance of a blazing jeep. 'That wouldn't be unusual in a war zone.'

She peeled the picture off the wall and held it in her hand. 'This was the last picture I took as a war-zone photographer.'

'Tea or coffee?'

'No, nothing, just stay with me,' she said as she sat on a high-back sofa chair and I sat on a sofa, right in front of her.

There was so much silence that I could hear our heartbeats. We were immersed in our thoughts, just like two astronauts floating in space, tied with a cord, with a question, an unspoken question: Does this marriage still exist?

'Why are you going to South Africa?' I said, as I could no longer bear the silence.

'I've been offered a political editor post at the *Cape Town News*,' she replied. 'I wanted to see you before I go.'

'Not a bad idea,' I said.

'I know you've tried several times to contact me… but I didn't want to answer your calls or meet you because I wasn't sure I was ready or that it was the right thing to do.'

'Why?' I said. 'Why did you think it wasn't right? I've waited all these years just for you.' I was again finding it difficult to control my emotions.

'I know, I know. This life is very unpredictable; you plan one thing and something else happens,' she said, wiping the edges of her eyes with a folded tissue.

'You didn't give me a chance,' I said. 'We could've worked something out, together.'

'The accident, the operations, the painkiller drugs took my ability to think straight. I was off sick for six months. I couldn't decide… I wanted to come back, but I couldn't… I thought… I wasn't worthy of you… I couldn't give you the happiness you deserved. I thought I was a misfit… I wanted to tell you but I couldn't,' she said. 'Please forgive me.'

I didn't wish to interject; I wanted her to lighten her heart. She came and sat with me.

'Mikel, there isn't much time left and I need to talk to you,' she said. I noticed her index and middle finger had a lighter colour skin than the rest of her hand.

'What happened to your hand?' I asked.

'It's not only to my hand … so much has happened to me, my body, my mind,' she said with a forced smile on her face. 'This picture nearly cost me my life.' It was a picture of a flaming jeep in the middle of nowhere.

'Really… what happened?' I said, getting up to get her a drink. 'I'll get you some water.'

'Just sit down, please… I don't want anything… my flight is in three hours… I've got to go.'

'So you're going to leave me again… I won't let this happen,' I said.

'You couldn't stop me that wretched day ten years ago,' she said with a mild smile, 'and you won't succeed today either. If I stay with you, I'll be staying for all the wrong reasons.'

'Why?' I said, protesting like a child.

She ignored my question and said, 'I was telling you about this picture. This is the last picture I took… nine years ago… I was in this jeep,' she said, pointing at the picture. 'We were going to cover the footage of the war behind the enemy border… the word Press was clearly written in bold letters around and over the jeep. We were going without any problems until another fast-moving vehicle overtook us and within seconds a very low-flying jet followed us over the skies, shadowing us like a noisy, dark cloud. Our driver stopped at the roadside. The jet bombed the jeep. Shrapnel, I don't know whether it was part of the burning car or the bomb, but it was about the size of a manhole cover, came flying into our jeep and instantly tore off the roof.'

'Very frightening,' I said. 'Actually, it must be shocking and amusing at the same time… did you enjoy the fresh air?'

Her facial expression remained sombre and she looked paler and said, 'There was no time to feel the fresh air… a flaming piece of bomb… it wasn't big… just about the size of a firefly… landed in my lap,' she said, gesturing with the thumb and index finger.

'It was so hot… I instinctively picked it up to throw it away… my fingers melted away… these are prosthetics… I felt an excruciating pain in between my legs…there was a smell of burnt meat… which I can still smell… we all jumped out of the jeep and I took this picture just before I passed out… When I came round I was in hospital, I was so surprised to be alive… all the members of my team died of severe burns and shrapnel wounds… I've had several operations… I'm sorry to burden you with all this… I'm very sorry.' Tears were flooding her face.

I held both her hands, squeezing them. The prosthetic fingers were cold and lifeless like those of a doll.

'Don't be daft… I'm very sorry to hear all this,' I said. 'You don't have to worry about anything… I'll get you seen by the best surgeons here… everything will be fine… please stay with me … I'm so happy you're back.'

She laughed a hollow laugh. 'I can't stay… I must go. I've thought about you, talked to you in my imagination every day for all these years. I'm so glad to know you still love me… even though I left you… let's not throw any pebbles in the pond of our past… keep it unrippled… unperturbed… perhaps this was our destiny… one can't fight what is written up, as you used to say.'

She stopped, wiped away tears, and glanced at her wristwatch. 'We need to go now; I don't want to miss the flight.'

'Do you have to go?' I asked her again.

'Yes, I must,' she said. 'I promise I'll come back to you.'

'Okay, let's go,' I said.

'You really love me… Thank you… I'm eternally grateful… it's always nice to know,' she said. I could see a shine in her eyes, which rarely comes unless one has the reassurance of love. 'But I don't want any melodramatic scenes at the airport, promise?'

'Promise,' I said, crossing my heart.

The airport was busy as usual. Isla had already checked in online and handed over her luggage at the counter.

'Let's have coffee,' Isla said, pointing towards the Costa. It was unusual, as she never liked to have caffeine drinks before the flight and hated the onboard toilets. We sat there talking about the past. She told me she had given up fieldwork after the jeep accident. She managed the newsroom for CNN but decided to quit due to a constant difference in opinion with the head office, which in turn was under pressure from the White House.

'You like the news editor job?' I said, as photography had been her passion.

'I love it,' she said. 'Editing news is intense, thrilling but quite exhausting.' She talked to me in detail about how the news is processed before going to press or on air.

She felt comfort in talking, and I just let her talk and didn't tell her the events that had surrounded my life since she'd left. She talked and talked until we heard her name announced to go immediately to the gate.

She ignored the announcement a couple of times, saying, 'The plane can't leave without me,' and ordered another coffee.

I liked listening to her but was getting uncomfortable with the flight announcement requesting her by name to proceed for security checks.

She got up and said, 'I suppose I've to go now.' She kissed me on my lips and hugged me tightly, as she had done more than a decade ago. 'See you soon,' she said and walked away to the security gates.

'See you soon,' I said.

I noticed a change in her gait, which swayed slightly to her right. When she hugged me, I felt she had a hot-water bottle wrapped around her stomach, perhaps to soothe the pain she was experiencing. I watched her until she reached the security gate. She turned around and sent a flying kiss. I responded with a salute.

Isla had certainly had a more difficult time than I had – but I'd been the one wallowing in self-pity?

Women's habit of wittingly or unwittingly presenting men with trials and tribulations haven't ceased over the years. Isla's visit had tested me, and I had been able to curb my carnality. I was relieved to think that I could now go back to work. That was surely not a test, but a precious gift to me.

THIRTY-FIVE

This could hardly be an auspicious omen: as I left home, a seagull swooped down from nowhere and relieved himself over my shoulder, splattering onto my shoes. I had to come inside, change my shirt and clean my shoes.

I reached the hospital with a crowd of apprehensions. It wasn't already a good start to the day. I was trying my best to avoid meeting Richard Smith, in case he brought up the issue of abandoning the porn magazines in his office. The mistake still mortified me.

To do gynaecology clinic after eight months was terrifying. It was a phased return to work, doing only one clinic each week. Uninvited thoughts of examining the patients without gloves, to stroke their clitoris, to caress their labia in the name of clinical examination, jumped into my mind from some distant unknown vistas and were completely alien to me. The noise of waves crashing on the shore had returned with a painful intensity. Had Dr Singh irreparably damaged me? Had I hopped back to square one after six months of CBT? Was I even suitable to work as a gynaecologist any more?

After an unduly lengthy medical history, a patient was now getting undressed for an examination in the adjacent room, and I sat clutching my forehead, worried sick.

'Should I open the window?' said the nurse.

'No, no… could you please elbow me if you feel I'm doing something unusual or wrong to the patient?' I replied.

'Mr Demir, you've always been a very good doctor,' she said with a confident smile. 'I don't think you would ever require any nudging.'

My heart knocked hard as if I was going to perform my first-ever intimate examination. I went into the room with trembling, clammy hands hung slack at my sides. To my relief, it all went without any problems.

Patient after patient… my confidence to interact, my ability to take a succinct history and to perform a smooth internal examination had returned. I felt I was able to scrape off, slowly but surely, what Dr Singh had attempted to implant in my psyche.

Work proved a distraction but I discovered that the titanic energy, the cyclopean ambition to help patients, had withered away. The job I'd enjoyed doing had transmuted into a drag. To give up teaching medical students and trainee doctors, which had been my passion, wasn't an easy decision, but I wanted to keep my clinical and non-clinical responsibilities to an absolute minimum. I did exactly the opposite of what I had done in the past; I reduced my hours of work and began planning for early retirement.

I shouldn't let Dr Singh off the hook so easily. I began to collect evidence by speaking to other colleagues.

I met with the nurse, Henrietta. She had been my long-suffering scrub nurse and a good colleague. She concurred with me that Dr Singh was an "odd doctor" and quite possibly deliberately harmed me. She had jotted down her recollections of the events when Dr Singh came to pick up a box of earphones from the anaesthetic room. She found this out of order and was willing to act as a witness for a case against Dr Singh.

'He kept patient details on his laptop,' she said. 'He told me he was doing some sort of research and showed me an e-mail from R & D.'

I rang the R & D department to inquire about the research Dr

Singh was doing. The department had no record of his application for ethics committee approval, neither was he registered to do any research trial by himself or in collaboration with any other colleagues.

I was overjoyed with my discovery of concrete evidence.

I made an urgent appointment to meet Adrian Baylis.

Adrian was very supportive towards me for the complications I had received during the anaesthetics and the effect of hypnosis on me, but he was sceptical of the evidence against Singh.

'Henrietta, the theatre nurse, has seen him leaving with a box full of earphones.'

'That's odd but doesn't prove anything.'

'He's been hypnotising patients without informed consent.'

'How can you prove this?'

'If he's done this to me, he could have done it to anyone else.'

'That's hardly an argument. What else?'

'He's been keeping all the patient details in his laptop, including their full name.'

'Really! That's serious. Who told you that?'

'Henrietta.'

'I don't know how reliable a witness Henrietta would be in your case, as everyone in the theatre has told me you get along very well with her... and she's been your scrub nurse for years. Her witness may be regarded as loyalty towards you. What else has she told you about Dr Singh?'

'Allegedly, he was doing some research, but he hasn't registered it with R & D.'

'I'll start an investigation for breach of research governance. That's serious, and if proven, I'll come down like a ton of bricks on him. I promise he'll be referred to the regulator. But I don't know what we can do about this hypnosis business. It all appears very fluid to me.'

I waited another month.

Despite Adrian's best intentions, Dr Singh's whereabouts could not be located. He had stopped practising medicine in the UK and voluntarily erased himself from the medical register. Adrian rang the hospital Dr Singh had joined after leaving ours and was told that he'd resigned a couple of months ago and had perhaps left the country. Adrian also wrote to the medical regulator to find out whether Dr Singh had requested a Good Standing certificate, a pre-requisite for registration in another country, and was informed that no such request had been received. He had slipped away to an unknown country. It was exceedingly disappointing that no case against Dr Singh could be made.

Dr Singh did exactly what the seagull had done to me: dived down, shat on my shoulder, and flown away. I had no choice but to endure the seagull phenomenon.

THIRTY-SIX

There have been three calls from an unfamiliar phone number on my mobile. After the third call, I checked the number on Google and was alarmed that the call originated from Cape Town General Hospital. I was about to ring Isla when the same phone number rang again. The caller introduced himself as Doctor Lethabo Pillay, the medical director of Cape Town General Hospital. He said he wished to talk to me urgently but first I should check the authenticity of the call either by going on Google or by Call Trace, which I had already done. Having gone through the formalities of confirming my identity, Pillay informed me that Isla had given my name and number as next of kin.

Pillay asked me instead whether I was driving, at home or at work, and if there was someone close by.

He broke the dreaded news that Isla had passed away. She had died of post-operative sepsis. The news hit me like a dagger, straight into my heart. I sat on the floor; my legs could no longer take the weight of my body.

I had imagined so much about Isla, but never thought I'd see her lying dead. She tormented me even after death. To be her next of kin was a hammer-blow to my head... we were still married but... why not her mum?... I wished she had kept me out of this. If I had the option, I'd choose to be blissfully unaware of her death and would be happy perennially searching for news edited by her, for the rest of my life. But the door had slammed shut. No more hope. There was a surge of anger against the medical staff. How could the doctors in Cape Town not treat her infection? Died of post-operative sepsis; inexcusable. No matter how severe the infection, we have strong kill-all-infections antibiotics. The doctors who failed to treat her had failed me in my life, too.

Fifteen and a half hours of flight passed with me thinking about Isla. I had no appetite and politely refused numerous offers by the stewards of hot or cold drinks. When we landed, my eyes were burning and I had a throbbing headache. Appreciatively, the immigration formalities were painless.

The popcorn-bright day of Cape Town further compounded my grief – Isla used to love clear days with blue skies. When you're dead, it hardly matters what the weather is over your burial site. I was amazed at the speed with which it becomes totally irrelevant. I was still finding it difficult for the news of her death to sink in. I don't know how long the taxi drove. I didn't dare to look outside, and was just preparing myself to see her finally, complete the burial rituals and return to the UK, send in my resignation at work and then go somewhere very far away. I didn't know where.

The hospital was in the middle of the city and was an impressive multistorey building. I rang Dr Pillay from the hospital reception desk, and he was there in no time. Pillay had a confident face with dark, wavy hair, which was brushed backwards. He walked with a limp, perhaps due to childhood polio. He told me that he would first like me to meet the consultant urologist, Mr Brush, in his office.

It was amazing to note that the corridors were almost identical to that of UK hospitals, as if one master architect designed them. Latebo Pillay had a large office; the walls had the portraits of the past medical directors. Dr Pillay's secretary offered me tea or coffee, which I declined, and she informed Pillay that John Brush was on his way. She was absolutely right. The office door opened, and a tall person

entered, who said, 'Hello, I'm John Brush. Isla was under my care...
I'm very sorry.' He was wearing a creaseless, starched white coat. Such
coats have been long outcast from the health care service hospitals as
an infection risk.

'Isla was a very brave person,' John Brush said. 'A true fighter. She
was an amazing person. I'm so sorry we couldn't save her.'

My voice was burdened with the grief and tiredness as I said,
'I'm traumatised beyond words. It has happened so suddenly, so
unexpectedly.'

John Brush looked sympathetic and said, 'The post-mortem
report has confirmed the cause of death as sepsis.'

'Why did you have to do a PM when she died of sepsis?' I said
with a knot in my throat. The mere thought of her body cut open
and systematically chopped to pieces saddened me. I was finding it
difficult to use the word "dead" in relation to Isla.

'We had to. She died within three days of surgery, which was
very complex,' John said. 'Isla told me about you on the day of her
surgery. She had told me you weren't aware of the details of her burns:
when the piece of the bomb landed in her lap it burnt the inside
of her thighs, bladder, urethra and vagina completely. An artificial
bladder was created using her small gut in Jordan, which worked
for some time, but then she began to develop bowel problems.'
John stopped and looked at me, as if waiting for some question,
and continued. 'She had twenty-one operations performed in the
Middle East for one or another reason. Before she came to South
Africa, she had had tubes placed in each kidney to collect urine in
a bag, which was strapped to her abdomen. When I first saw her
here, she had developed an intestinal obstruction. In view of the
case complexity, we discussed her case in a joint multi-disciplinary
meeting. The consensus of opinion at the meeting was to relieve
the obstruction and close the artificially created bladder. I did the
operation along with a colo-rectal surgeon, and not surprisingly
there was intense scarring inside her tummy... the sort of scarring

I've never seen before. Absolutely rock hard. Her kidneys were not working well before the operation and stopped working altogether after the surgery… a mild chest infection just tipped her over… I'm very sorry… she was a very brave woman… she told me that she didn't want to hurt you by telling you about her burns.'

I said, 'Poor Isla. Almost two dozen surgeries; oh my god, poor Isla, why didn't she tell me all this?' I sat, thinking, why did she hide all this from me?

Pillay came to me and placed his hand on my shoulder and said, 'I'm sorry, but before we can release her body for burial, as a legal requirement, you'll have to identify her.'

'Do I have to do this?' I said.

'I'm afraid so,' said Pillay. 'It's entirely up to you whether you want to do it today or come some other time.'

'I think it's best to get all the formalities over and done with,' I said, thinking.

'It's entirely your choice,' said Pillay and dialled on his landline phone. 'Hi, Mr Demir is on his way. Could you please let him identify Isla Demir's body?'

Pillay handed me a large white envelope and said, 'This has the death certificate and the PM report. There aren't any bills to settle; the hospital and funeral expenses are all covered by her insurance. I'm afraid I've got to go to a meeting, but my secretary will take you to the morgue.'

'Thanks, Dr Pillay,' I said and shook hands with him. 'Thanks for all your help.'

I quietly walked with the secretary through the maze of corridors of the hospital.

Isla didn't put any burden on me when she was alive and now, after her death, she had paid in advance her hospital and funeral expenses. Why did she do this? Did she think I might not be able to pay for her funeral costs? Was it mistrust, or love?

The morgue was located at the back of the hospital. The secretary pressed the bell. 'Please take your time. I'll wait for you outside here,' she said, pointing towards a bench outside.

An old-looking man wearing a dirty white gown with matching hair opened the door and said, 'Mr Demir?'

'Yes, that's me.'

'Hi, I'm Bill. Come inside, please.'

The morgue was like a big hall. I didn't know whether it was the morgue or the cold that sent my body into shivers. An eye-watering smell of formaldehyde filled the room. Three-storeyed, horizontal silver fridges half-covered the walls.

Bill glanced at a large white board and said, 'Please follow me.'

I wasn't looking forward to this moment in my life, and my heart fluttered. He read the number over a fridge, opened the door and pulled the stretcher out on which Isla laid. She was wrapped in a thin, beige, coarsely woven sheet. Bill parted the sheet to expose her face. This was my Isla lying lifeless in front of me, eyes closed, lips ajar with a faint smile. I squeezed her arm; it was cold and rigid with rigor mortis. Thick streams of tears flooded my eyes. I wanted to cry, cry very loud. I had to control myself.

'Sir,' Bill said, uncovering Isla's right foot. An ID tag dangled from her big toe. 'Could you please check this?' I completed the formality of looking at Isla's identity. There was an unasked question in Bill's eyes.

'Yes, this is Isla,' I said looking at Bill.

'That's fine,' Bill said. 'Do you want some time with her alone?'

I looked at her again and said, 'No, thanks.'

Bill expeditiously covered her, and shoved the stretcher back into the fridge and closed the door. He went back to his desk and wrote something in a big blue register.

'It's all fine,' he said. 'You may inform the funeral directors to collect the body.'

'I don't know any funeral directors here.'

'No problem,' said Bill, and took out a booklet from his drawer.

'This contains a list of funeral directors and all the important information.'

I took the booklet from him and said, 'Thank you.'

I looked at the closed fridge where Isla, my Isla, lay cold, stiff with rigor mortis.

Isla was born in New York, brought up in England and laid to rest in Cape Town. After the burial, for the first time in my life, I realised how lonely and empty I was. The hopes of reuniting Isla were buried with her in Maitland Cemetery. I walked aimlessly and reached the seashore. The memories of time spent with Isla came all together in big processions. The fragrance of her skin, her smile, her laughter, the fights, the walks we had, reading books under a duvet cover, naming stars on a starry night.

'Sir, you need to move from here. The sea is getting very rough.' A rescue-team girl tapped on my shoulder and yanked me out of my thoughts. Two other guards stood beside her, arms folded on their chests, fully ready in swimsuits.

'Don't worry,' I said. 'I should, but I'm not going to jump into the water.'

The girl said, 'Could you move up the beach now? It's not safe here.'

I hadn't realised the evening dusk was engulfed in the darkness. The stone I sat on at the seafront was now half immersed in water and the incoming sea was bashing on the shore, gradually encroaching and leaving shiny shells upon receding. I looked back at the girl and wanted to tell her that the word safety had no meaning for me.

THIRTY-SEVEN

The residential home where Isla's mother was living was just outside the city. It was kept neat but, like its occupants, showed signs of old age. A young, petite girl, who must have been doing a summer job before going to university, approached me.

'How can I help you, sir?' she said and I looked at her ID badge, which read "Receptionist". Her name was Shakila. It was interesting that when you're alive an ID is hung around the neck, but it migrates to the big toes when you're dead.

'I'm Mikel Demir,' I said. 'I've come to see my mother-in-law, Josephine Bancroft.'

'Sure,' Shakila said with a professional smile. 'Could you sign the visitors' register, and I'll take you to her? She's not been well lately. Her GP visited last week. She seems okay now.'

'Thanks,' I said.

Shakila said, 'I met your wife a few months ago.'

'Did Isla come here? When?' I asked her and was surprised, as Isla didn't tell me.

'Yes, she came to sign some insurance papers for Josephine,' she said, thinking. 'I remember quite clearly. It was Saturday and I had to call our manager from home to go through all the paperwork with her.'

'Are you sure Isla was here? You might've met someone else sent in by Isla. Is that possible?'

'No,' said Shakila with conviction. 'She was here, with me, with our manager, with her mother. Why are you asking?'

I ignored her question and said, 'You said she came to sign some insurance papers?'

'You know, the insurance papers to pay for the residential home fees.'

'Yes, I know.'

Despite her illness, Isla never wanted anyone to be under financial burden, either because of her or her family.

The residential home had the peculiar smell of someone who hadn't showered for days.

A woman wearing a pink flowery gown came straight to me and said, 'I know you, you're Andy's friend. Could you please tell Andy that I'm sorry? I'm very sorry.'

Shakila said to the woman politely, 'Audrey, please go back to your room. He isn't Andy's friend.' Audrey shook her head in disbelief and very obediently walked away.

The long corridor had an old-fashioned radiator with a large silver bowl placed under its missing knob, collecting drips of dark-coloured water.

'This is Josephine's room,' said Shakila.

Her room was small. The bed was professionally made with a blanket tucked under the mattress. Josephine sat on the only available chair in the room, her elbows on the edges of the arms and her hands interlocked in front of her chest. She was bent forward and looked out through the ceiling-high window. She didn't hear me come into her room.

'Good afternoon, Josephine,' I said. 'Do you recognise me? I'm Mikel Demir, Isla's husband.' I placed a fruit basket on the table.

She looked like a screwed-up mask of Isla, the one I'd seen in the morgue. She shaded over her eyes with her left hand and said, 'I know you. You're the doctor.'

She recognised me despite her dementia. It was impressive.

I said, 'I know you like coffee; I've brought a jar for you and some fruit.'

'Yes, I do like my coffee with milk,' she said, with the happiness of a child in her voice. 'I don't like fruit. You can take it back. Fruit gives me wind.'

I said, 'I'm not going to take it back. You can give it to your friends over here.'

'Can I?' she said with excitement. 'Audrey would love it.'

I sat on her bed, closer to her. She again made a shade over her eyes and closely inspected me again and said, 'Who are you?'

The question didn't confuse me and I said, 'I'm Isla's husband. I came to tell you about Isla.' I said it loudly this time, thinking she might not have heard me before.

She began to look out again, as if ignoring me, and said with a stout curtness, 'What've you come to tell me?'

I looked around to see if there was a tissue-paper box in the room, but there wasn't any. I walked to her, held her hand, which was all bones, and said sympathetically, 'I'm very sorry to tell you... Isla has gone to a better world. She passed away last week.'

She replied quietly, without any emotion, 'I know. Isla came to tell me.'

'I think,' I said, 'Isla came to see you five, six months ago, but she passed away last week in Cape Town. I didn't think there was any point in bringing her over here to the UK for burial.'

Josephine thought for a moment and said, 'She was here last week, with me, and told me that she wasn't going to live much longer. She had suffered a lot. I think you did the right thing. I'm the last one to go... don't know when.' Her voice was devoid of any emotion or distress.

She repeated, 'I'm sorry for you. Both of you had a tough life but you've been a good husband.'

I was lost for words. She talked like a very sane person with no sign of dementia. But I wasn't sure whether she fully understood what I'd come to tell her. I said again, 'Josephine, I'm sorry to tell you the bad news; Isla is no longer alive, she died last week… Do you understand what I'm saying?'

Josephine looked at me strangely and said, 'I understood you the first time. Do *you* have difficulty understanding? I told you Isla came to tell me that she was going to die… I've cried my tears, and there's none left in my eyes.'

Her grief response was not normal, and I wasn't sure that she understood what I'd told her. I made another effort and said, 'But Isla was in South Africa and in hospital… she couldn't possibly have come to you.'

She continued to look out and said in a low voice, 'No, she did come.'

Telling her again and again about Isla seemed a futile exercise. We sat quietly in the room and then she said, 'I think you should go now; it's getting late. Thank you for coming.'

'Okay,' I said and gave her a cuddle, which she half-heartedly reciprocated, felt my face and bestowed on me a maternal kiss, which left a wet patch on my forehead.

'Could you turn the lamp on? It'll be dark soon,' she said, and closed her eyes. I turned the light on, although the sun was shining brightly outside, and sunset wasn't for another four hours.

I met Shakila at the front desk and asked her whether anyone had visited her last week. Shakila checked the register and there hadn't been any visitors for Josephine.

'She's totally blind now, and she imagines a lot of things,' said Shakila.

'Is she?' I said, and was surprised to hear this. 'She never mentioned this to me.'

Shakila said, 'Yes, she has glaucoma in both eyes and can't see. She had several consultations at the hospital but apparently, nothing could be done at this stage.'

I said that perhaps the news of her daughter's death hadn't sunk in yet and her carers needed to be aware of this, as she might show a grief reaction later on. Shakila called for the lady who had been looking after Josephine.

'Hello, I'm Josephine's son-in-law. Could you please keep an eye on her? I've just broken the bad news to her that her daughter has passed away.'

'Oh, I'm so sorry,' the lady said. 'Josephine has been crying for no reason during the past week and I thought that she might be in pain. I requested a medical review but it was normal.'

I thanked Shakila and left the home.

The metaphysical element in the mother–daughter relationship has always confused and intrigued me. When the eyes extinguish, is it possible for some other eyes to open and see what is not visible to everyone else?

I had the impression that Isla's visit six months ago was exclusive to me, but now it appeared subsidiary. The thought brought another cloud of sadness over me.

THIRTY-EIGHT

It was a fine summer's day, and complete mayhem. There were six TV broadcasting vans parked outside the hospital with reporters talking into their mics. Inquisitive patients and their relatives had gathered to see the live transmission. The presence of a TV crew outside the hospital wasn't an unusual scene. Our hospital was the major trauma and burns centre and soldiers from Afghanistan or other war zones were frequently brought here.

'What's that commotion?' I asked the nurse who helped me in the clinic.

'You don't know, Mr Demir?' she replied. 'You need to see this. Everyone is in the coffee room watching the news.'

The coffee room was crowded with nurses and auxiliary staff, watching TV on the screen. 'Our hospital is in the news again… and not for the right reasons,' a nurse said.

The new chief executive, Donald Anderson, was fielding questions from reporters. He appeared rattled and said, 'We're investigating the issue. We don't know how sensitive patient information leaked out to such groups. Our information technology team is on the case and we are fully cooperating with the police. We apologise to all the affected patients for letting them down.'

'Mr Anderson,' said a reporter, 'after this major disaster, why are you still in post?'

Donald touched the tip of his nose, squared up and stared down his interlocutor, and said, 'I'm in the job because I've got to do this job. Anyway, this all happened before I was appointed here.'

Another reporter asked, 'Mr Anderson, can you estimate how many patients might be affected?'

'No, we've no idea of the numbers at present.'

The reporter didn't want to give up and asked, again aggressively, 'We don't expect you to tell us the exact numbers, what we're asking for is an estimate. Is it dozens? Hundreds? Thousands?'

Donald took a sip of water from the bottle he was holding, licked his lips and said, 'It could be in the several hundreds.'

A reporter who had had his hand raised for some time asked, 'The amount and the details of the confidential information leaked couldn't be obtained by hacking. Is it an insider job? Only a hospital employee could have access to such sensitive information.'

'We shouldn't jump to conclusions,' said Donald. 'We need to wait for the results of the investigations.'

'Has this information leak affected both male and female patients?'

Donald replied briefly, 'It seems to be exclusively women.'

The same reporter asked, 'Are you aware that a large number of celebrities are among the patients who have had their confidential information leaked?'

'Yes, I'm aware and apologise to all of them.'

'Don't you think the head of IT, and the hospital management team, should resign as a result of this incident?' another reporter asked.

Donald looked uncomfortable with the question and said, 'We've called an emergency hospital board meeting to discuss the issue.'

A female reporter asked in a cutting, sharp tone, 'A patient of your hospital has committed suicide following this information leak. How can you give confidence to the public and patients who will be attending this hospital that this will be expeditiously investigated and nothing like this will happen again?'

Donald shifted his weight from one leg to another, looking uncomfortable, and said, 'We unreservedly apologise to the family of the deceased and send our heartfelt condolences. It's very sad and tragic. We're investigating and strengthening the IT systems so that no such events can happen in the future.' Donald clearly looked miserable with the constant onslaught of press questions, and abruptly finished the press conference.

The news showed an interview with a girl in her mid-twenties. She was holding the hand of her partner and talking amid sobs. 'This person knew all about me, my pregnancies and the two abortions I had. He was nasty and horrible. He said that he would let my husband know about the abortions unless I paid him money... I stole money from my husband's business, but it was never-ending... he demanded more and more money.' The girl looked at her husband and said, 'I did what no woman would normally do to give them money... this all happened because of the hospital... I wish I'd never come to this hospital. They've betrayed me and my trust.'

A nurse asked me, 'Mr Demir, what do you think has happened?'

I said, 'Very serious stuff. Someone has handed the confidential information of vulnerable patients to some criminal blackmail groups. It has to be for money. Very sad... it must be very serious information as someone committed suicide.'

The same nurse asked me again, 'What will happen next?'

'It's not good for the hospital's reputation and may have financial consequences,' I said. 'The clinical groups may penalise us by sending patients to the neighbouring hospital... some heads will definitely roll in management.'

'So they won't close the hospital?' the nurse asked again. 'That's okay, as long as I don't lose my job.'

After the hospital board meeting, Donald Anderson called an urgent meeting with all the consultant gynaecologists, the anaesthetist who had done the surgical abortion lists, and the senior theatre staff.

The meeting was very well attended despite the extremely short notice. Uncertainty brings all people together.

Donald began his address by highlighting the gravity of the situation. The incident had triggered an immediate visit from the National Clinical Group. To date, 364 women who were victims had contacted the hospital. The common denominator was: they all had a surgical termination of pregnancy in the operating theatre. Quite a few colleagues didn't agree to do the lists for personal or religious reasons; therefore locums mainly ran the service. There had been a good turnover of locums, which further confounded investigations. An exhaustive scrutiny would include matching the surgeon, the anaesthetist and the theatre staff with the name of the patient who had claimed their details had been leaked. It was a daunting task, and everyone in the meeting thought the culprit may not be found.

I stood up and asked, 'Has anyone checked Dr Singh... Rohan Singh?'

'Mikel, this is not the time to bring up your personal vendetta,' Adrian Baylis responded angrily.

'Who is this Dr Singh?' asked Donald. 'Is he working with us?'

'No, he isn't,' said Adrian. 'I'll explain to you later. Mikel and Dr Singh have history.'

'No, there isn't any issue of history here,' I said.

'Okay, I amend,' said Adrian. 'There isn't any history, just wrong chemistry.'

There were chuckles all around.

'The anaesthetic secretary says that Dr Singh always requested the terminations of pregnancy list,' said one of the anaesthetists. 'She was quite happy to allocate all such lists to him as no one else wanted to do them.'

'Let's not get fixated with one person,' said Donald. 'We've to investigate with an open mind.'

'When is the National Clinical Group coming?' someone asked.

'I don't know when, but they will definitely come,' said Donald.

'We'll set up a training session for all the consultants to get you ready about how to answer them.'

'I've heard,' one anaesthetist said, 'that the Government is thinking of appointing a former QC to investigate these issues.'

There was a muttering disquiet among the staff on hearing this. I overheard a consultant colleague saying, 'I need to find a job elsewhere.'

'I've not heard anything like that,' Donald said. 'Such enquiries are very protracted and could be very damning for the reputation of the Trust. Thanks for your time. Have a good evening.'

I met Adrian immediately after the meeting. He was in a foul mood.

'Mikel, it was very unprofessional of you to name a former colleague in front of everybody.'

'Adrian, he is behind this information leak. I'd told you this before.'

'The information you gained from that theatre nurse?'

'Yes. I told you that he was keeping a record of patient details. But you chose to ignore it.'

Adrian's face turned red with blistering dissent. 'Did she complete an incident form against Singh saying that he was storing patient data on his laptop?'

'I don't know.'

'No, she didn't. Listen, Mikel, I'm retiring in four weeks. Donald is a very reactive person, so please don't get me involved in any investigation at this stage. But do feel free to hurl as much shit on the fan as it pleases you, but only after four weeks, not before.'

'Oh, you only love to investigate… you're so afraid to face an investigation!'

'Don't make me say this,' Adrian said. 'I could easily send you on "gardening leave" again. The cleaners discovered porn magazines in Richard Smith's office. He says that you were the only visitor during that week. Can you deny this? If you do, then we'll suspend your pal,

Richard Smith. It's your choice – either you keep your mouth shut or I'll land one of you in deep, stinking shit.'

'That's blackmail.'

'Whatever the fuck you want to call it.' Adrian thought for a moment and said, 'I'm sorry, let's not bring other issues in... I had decided to do nothing about the magazines but, please...'

'Adrian, this guy, Dr Singh, is burning down this hospital, and you're playing games with me. It's unbelievable.'

'Listen, Mikel, you and I know that this person doesn't exist on the regulator's register any more. Six months is a long time and you know I tried to chase him, but we don't know which country he's emigrated to. Don't be neurotic about him. The reality is, we can't catch him. The other harsh reality is that we might never know who leaked the data. It's all very complex.'

'Rohan Singh is sick; he's a psychopath,' I said. 'He has every ability to do this. You need to marry up the details of patients with the days when he was anaesthetising. I can assure you all the leaked patient data would be from his lists.'

'And if he also stole patient data from some other theatre lists, how are you going to prove this? It's very complicated. We need to have solid evidence before we could point the finger of blame.'

'I suppose you don't have that evidence.'

'No, none whatsoever.'

'I still think you need to investigate Rohan Singh.'

'I think you're paranoid about this person. I'm sorry. Leave it and move on.'

I felt frustrated to hear this. 'No, he's not my paranoia. I know this person is evil, and I won't be surprised if he has exchanged the personal details of the patients for money. I think he's got enough money, and that's why he erased himself from the medical register and emigrated. You need to re-open, re-order the investigations and bring this person back to the UK through Interpol to face the charges.'

Adrian laughed and said, 'We can't send Interpol to every single country in the world. Cases are built on strong evidence, not on theories or gut feelings. I'm afraid there could be no case against him or any other anaesthetist or any ODAs. It's sad, but a fact.'

'The chief executive promised the public that the Trust would find the culprit. What're you going to tell them?'

'Nothing. We tried and tried hard,' he said calmly, 'but we didn't succeed. The public has a relatively short memory. They'll forget all about this in a couple of months. Don't worry about the public. And listen, if the press gets any sniff about your suspicions regarding Dr Singh or you bring the hospital into disrepute, this time you won't get away lightly. I promise you, Mr Demir, we'll hang you out to dry.'

Sensing hostility in his remark, I said, 'Thanks, I shall keep your threat in the forefront of my mind.'

'It's not a threat. Just friendly advice.'

THIRTY-NINE

onths passed, and a stubborn winter gave way to a timid spring. The earth became alive with a profusion of excitement; every dot of a bud sprouted and every unfurling petal was ostentatious.

It was still morning. My mobile rang, and it was a call from Carys. 'Hello, stranger, how are you? Long time, no see,' she said.

'Good to hear from you. I'm okay, as usual. You sound happy,' I said.

'Well, I'm in town, attending a conference on the life and works of Shakespeare,' she said, 'but I've no intention of going to all the talks. If you're free, we could meet.'

'Sounds quite nice. I'm free. Just tell me the address of this conference place and I'll ring you when I reach there.'

I took a taxi to the conference centre, which seemed well attended. It was a lunch break, and people were meeting and greeting old acquaintances.

It was almost eight years since we'd met. I rang her from the registration desk. People do change in their looks, and eight years was a long time. Would I be able to recognise her? After about ten minutes, my phone rang again, and it was Carys, who said, 'Where are you?'

'At the registration desk.'

'Okay, I see you… oh gosh, you've grown a beard,' said Carys and walked swiftly towards me, showing her identification badge hanging around her neck.

Carys had the stamp of her mother all over her, but I easily recognised her. 'You haven't changed a bit in all these years.'

'But you have,' she said, smiling. 'You look distinguished with that beard.'

I ran a hand over my beard, smiling.

'You're looking after yourself... you've lost weight.'

'I bike to work.'

'Bike?' Carys said with surprise. 'That's very sporty.'

We went to a restaurant for lunch. Time had moved on so much, she needed glasses to read the menu. Her glasses, perched near the tip of the nose, gave her a professorial look governed by sensibility. She had snazzy dark brown hair with golden highlights. Like before, she hardly wore any make-up. There was a hint of sorrow in her eyes, but in the background there was an electric cheerfulness in her voice, a sort of current, which I needed to kickstart my halting life.

During the conversation, it became obvious that she hadn't been in a relationship following the tragic death of her fiancé. I was struck when she said, 'I couldn't uproot his love from my heart.'

I hadn't realised there was so much in common between us.

'I know the feeling,' I said and told her, without going into the details, that Isla had passed away in Cape Town.

She shook her head in grief, stopped eating, and said, 'Oh, that's terrible. I'm so sorry.' Her eyes overflowed as she held my hand and said, 'You've been through a lot. It must be devastating for you. Are you okay?'

'Yes. As much as I could be,' I said, and tried to put a brave smile on my face. 'Just plodding on.'

'I'm so sorry.'

I smiled and remained silent.

'It's so sad... Death has been the author of our lives.'

I smiled again.

I was thinking more than talking to Carys. The tuning forks of our hearts sounded for the ones we had lost. I could feel the loneliness of her soul. Could we console each other?

Amid the conversation, I was thinking that so much time had elapsed, and we didn't have the luxury of running after each other through the labyrinth of life. We were like two electrons of the same element – the element of unfulfilled love – circling in our own orbits. Thoughts took shape in my mind.

'Carys, I've been thinking, and thinking about you…'

'Please, don't say this. I'm no longer in the habit of remaining in someone's thoughts.'

'I wanted to tell you something, which I hadn't considered before today. It may sound stupid, but please forgive me.'

Carys looked at me but didn't say anything, giving me a pure, trusting smile.

'I'm sorry if I make myself a complete fool.'

'I'll forgive you,' she said and gave me a bemused glance.

'The bright roulette of time is spinning away sharply…' I let the sentence hang, cleared my throat, and fixed my gaze on Carys.

She nodded but her tongue withheld assent.

I made up my mind and said, 'Will you… marry me?' I was impressed with my own audacity.

'Are you serious?' she said, laughing. 'Or is it some sort of trick question?'

'I'm serious, very serious,' I said. 'As someone said, *A heart to love, and in that heart, courage, to make love known.*'

'Wow, that's impressive. *Macbeth*, Act 2, Scene 3,' she said, and laughed a lengthy laugh. 'I never expected this.'

'I'm very fond of the unexpected. What do you think?'

'*Love sought is good, but given unsought is better, Twelfth Night.* Act 3, Scene 1.'

'Will you?'

'I don't know,' she said, looking pale due to some unknown

fear, which eclipsed the beauty of her face. 'I'm very afraid, and any prospect of happiness makes me frightfully sad.'

'The feeling's mutual,' I said. 'But it's equally sad when two people who are alive sit and only talk about those who are dead. We should give life another chance.'

'Perhaps,' she said quietly. 'I hope I haven't appeared too pitiful.'

'No, you haven't. Also, I hope I don't look so pathetic that you accept my proposal out of charity.'

She laughed.

'If you want to take your time to decide, you may. I won't be offended if you do decide against it. I'm not rich or famous or have any intrinsic advantages. I am what I am. What I hope is that we could care, love, provide solace to each other.'

'I'm not sure I'd be able to console anyone,' she said in a nervous voice. The pallor still dominated her face.

'I think we've caught ourselves in the horrid habit of nurturing our wounds, scratching and keeping them afresh. We could help each other to break this hurtful cycle.'

'Relations built upon needs aren't durable, are they?' she said.

'Neither is the one that is established upon false pretences,' I said. 'I hope a love – a true love – will sprout in time.'

'Your certitude frightens me. If this fails…' she said, shivering with a presentiment.

'Trust me, and trust yourself,' I said, and held her hand firmly.

'It's such a goddamned lie that time heals all things. Or perhaps I'm a slow healer!'

I laughed.

I could see on her face a heaving battle inside her mind and heart.

'You don't expect me to give you my decision right now.'

'No, I don't, but either would be acceptable to me, I promise.'

'I think I'll do what my heart is telling me to do,' she said, as her face beamed with excitement, and calmly she added, 'I do, I do.' She pulled me forward and kissed me.

I looked around and was relieved that the proposal and the acceptance had happened without any spectators.

'Life is so unpredictable,' said Carys. 'I came here to learn more about Shakespeare and I'm going back with…' She intentionally left the sentence incomplete.

'A liability,' I said, laughing.

'Maybe.'

There was another passionate cuddle, and we decided to marry the coming Saturday in the presence of our close friends.

*

I went back to work on Monday morning.

'Good morning, Mr Demir,' Marlene said. 'Good weekend?'

'Yes, an exceptionally good weekend.'

'Did you do anything interesting?'

'Yes, I did…' I said with a pause. 'I got married.'

Her eyes widened and her eyebrows arched in surprise. 'Did you plan it like that?'

'No, it just happened.'

'Congratulations,' she said, trying to overcome the shock of the news, and extended her arm to shake my hand.

'Thank you.'

EPILOGUE

FORTY

'Your tea's getting cold,' Carys said, looking at me with a smile.

'Sorry, was too engrossed reading this.'

Our life had a pattern. It was a midsummer afternoon and we sat reading together in the conservatory of our home.

'What's it about?'

'Fifty out of 120,' I read aloud, 'committed suicide in the last five years whilst facing investigations by the medical regulator. In addition, a further thirty doctors also died during the investigation, but it was difficult to ascertain whether their death was due to natural causes or suicide.'

'Investigations by a professional body could be a career-defining moment for anyone. It is the mindless no-smoke-without-a-fire culture, which can be isolating, stigmatising and worrying.'

'Truly shocking. I can relate to these statistics... I was nearly one of them.'

Carys placed her hand over mine. 'I'll make fresh tea for you.'

'No, it's okay,' I said, looking at her. 'There's no mention about the psychiatric and mental issues for which no one has bothered to keep any statistics.'

'Statisticians measure death as the ultimate end point, which is easy to measure. But I take your point, it presents an incomplete picture.'

Carys's analysis of a situation was always sympathetic, intuitive and intelligent.

A company of two makes it easier to go through the harsh realities of life.

'I've got a vague idea, but what's the usual cause that doctors are referred to the regulators for?'

'They're usually referred when there's a bad outcome or it's thought that some error is made in patient management, and the doctor's competency to practise is called into question.'

'Errors can and will happen because doctors are human, and humans are fallible.'

'The fact remains that the diseases are opaque when they develop, and aren't always clear even with a retrospective analysis. Mistakes don't happen in isolation and there is usually a mix of factors leading to a bad outcome like experience, alertness, staffing levels and skills mix, distractions… attending to nagging doubts… failure of the supporting systems. Tragedy can occur when enough small things align but, unfortunately, the last person holding the ball is held responsible.'

'From what I understand, adequate staffing is a huge problem in hospitals.'

'It is. Do you remember when we were travelling to Zurich last summer? The flight was delayed for hours at the airport because the co-pilot had called in sick.'

'You were totally cool about it but there were incredulous gasps and arms thrown in the air from the other passengers.'

'I wasn't annoyed at it, as this is almost an everyday scenario in hospital practice. I was struck by the airline for two reasons: the airline contacted off-duty pilots to substitute, but only if they were well rested and willing to take an additional flight. The airline didn't cut safety corners by saying it's only a short flight and almost all modern planes fly on an autopilot and this flight could fly without a co-pilot. We medics are obsessed with comparing safety standards with the airline industry. In fact, a flight will not take off until all the crew, including the cabin crew, are present. In hospital practice, corners are cut regularly. Doctors, rested or unrested, just plough on with the work if a colleague is off sick.'

'Doctors by their very nature are highly sensitive individuals,' Carys said, intertwining her fingers with mine. 'The suicide statistics show that investigation into their practice signals a harsh criticism of their work. But to take their own lives during an investigation seems an extreme step when quite possibly they may be exonerated.'

'Or rehabilitated,' I said. 'Another contributing factor to death is the press. It's the defamation that kills you. I remember the time and the emotions when I was the subject of inquiry and can easily recall a couple of occasions when I could have killed myself.'

'Is there no help available in such circumstances?'

'There's a telephone helpline arrangement with an industrial organisation. I don't know how effective it is.'

The suicide statistics were loudly shouting that something more than a telephone helpline was needed.

I made an appointment to meet with the president of the Royal College of Women's Health in London.

The president was a gaunt person with a lifetime of patience inscribed on his face. He sat with his fingers knotted in his lap, wearing half-moon glasses behind which were intelligent piercing eyes.

I wanted to set up a college committee to provide support to the doctors facing the regulator. The president was thrilled to hear about my idea and said, 'If we could save a doctor's life, perhaps we could save the lives of thousands of patients.' His book-trawled eyes were sharp and unsentimental. There was no element of indecision. He agreed to set up a support committee for doctors on an urgent basis under the supervision of the vice-president.

Unsurprisingly, the work of the committee expanded exponentially, and was soon dealing with more than 300 cases. The committee's role was to provide information, support and guidance for doctors and a three-pronged approach was adopted. I would meet them face to face, go through a case and answer any queries. After seeing me, the doctor was assessed by a clinical psychologist who would screen for signs of depression and suicidal tendencies. The third step was to provide the medical director of the relevant hospital with a confidential report on the case and if depression or suicidal tendencies were noted, a recommendation was made for an urgent referral to occupational health and a psychiatrist. Strategies to cope with the adverse media publicity were made a part of committee work. The statistics of doctors undergoing investigations confessing to the use of illicit drugs and alcoholism was a *déjà vu* moment. The pressure of stress was so enormous that "gin twice a week" became "gin every night", and if this didn't relieve stress, they resorted to drugs.

The reputation of our support committee grew and I was invited by royal colleges in other disciplines to provide guidance to set up similar committees. This activity further increased my workload. At the age of fifty-nine, I took retirement from the hospital to do committee work on a full-time basis. Carys moved to London with me and got a senior lecturer job at the Royal University. We were happily living together but, in my heart, I knew that this might not last forever.

The committee work was interesting, frustrating and rewarding at the same time. Last week a doctor insisted on seeing me without making an appointment. I rarely turned anyone away. His unshaven face was the colour of cold ashes, and his eyes were red as if he had severe conjunctivitis.

'I'm struck off,' he said, with tears at the back of his voice.

'I'm very sorry to hear that.'

'What do I do now?' He was irate and agitated. 'Fill shelves in a supermarket? Drive a taxi? How do I earn my living? I've got a family… two children.'

'Yes, it's a huge issue, but currently the regulator…'

He interrupted me mid-sentence and said, 'Don't tell me about the regulator! They know only one thing. Take fees from us and in return fuck us hard. They don't give a shit whether we live or die.'

'I understand,' I said. 'If you'll let me finish. The regulator at present accepts no responsibility for the financial consequences of erasure. I've written to the business school to see if they can provide a fast-track degree for such doctors, but haven't heard back from them yet. Perhaps I need to chase them again. I'll keep you posted.'

The doctor calmed down a bit and said, 'All those years of studying and training to become a doctor puts an inerasable seal on the mind and heart. The medical profession binds us with unbreakable shackles. We become programmed to do only one job... to work as a doctor. But if I can't work as a doctor, I still need to earn money.'

I wish I had the answer to all the questions.

Alan Taylor never lost contact and rang to congratulate me when he heard the news of my OBE award. 'How do you feel, embiggened by Her Majesty?' I could imagine a spacious smile on his face.

'The same,' I replied.

A letter from a doctor-in-investigation who had thanked me for saving his life when he was on the verge of taking it mattered more to me than the OBE.

It was a sunny late afternoon. I went out to sit on a bench beside the well-manicured college lawn. The buds on the trees had unfolded into shiny, flapping leaves. Time flies, whether you realise or not.

A white cat lurked about inquisitively.

From nowhere, reminiscences of the past welled up like spring water, faster than I could handle them.

Memories of Isla resided permanently in my heart along with three newly implanted coronary stents. Thoughts about Isla still saddened me. Sometimes we are just too harsh on ourselves, pointlessly fighting with "the shadows". Early in life, we learn that some behaviours are rewarded and make us successful, whilst others are punished or provide no benefit. We develop behaviours that are related to success and suppress those that aren't. These suppressed feelings become hidden in the unconscious and become our demons – the shadows. We fight a perpetual fight with our beasts and like to presume things with conviction. I wished Isla had opened her heart to me about the accident when it happened.

The cat munched on a few grass blades, clearly not enjoying it, and made faces as if tasting a bitter medicine.

I wished I'd been a bit more proactive in my life and gone to see Amjad Chaudry before he passed away last year. Some neurological condition had rendered him faecally incontinent and he had to go back into nappies. Every possible available treatment was attempted, but nothing worked for him. He stopped eating and became cachectic. A common friend told me that he had regarded his illness as some sort of comeuppance for not helping me. I felt bad when I heard this and wanted to go and console him but somehow things got delayed, and then it was too late.

I felt overwhelmed to think about the fantastic speciality that has enabled me to help mothers during childbirth and to bring thousands of children into this world. Thankfully, the extraordinary circumstances in which Solomon's son was born never happened again. I really hope all the children did well and will play a role in keeping the embers of hope and optimism glowing in this world.

Memories of Martin have remained seared on my mind. Despite his profligate enthusiasm to decode the enigma of love and life – the marvellous puzzle has remained unanswered as before. The strange ways of love make you find souls, but sometimes it makes you lose. An ailing cat has an instinct to switch its carnivorous nature to help it get better, but we humans have lost such a switch somewhere along the evolutionary course.

The day was coming to a close. The last glimmers of the sun searched through the layers of haze hovering over the tall trees. The committee work was never-ending, but I knew I'd better do whatever I had to do today and go home. It was Carys's fiftieth birthday.

ABOUT THE AUTHOR

Najum is a full-time consultant gynaecologist and an educator. He lives in Birmingham with his family.

ALSO BY THE AUTHOR

A PHENOMENAL STORY

'An engaging and compelling book; was an utter page turner, with an unusually unique story line and realistic characters.'

Birmingham Mail

MYSTICISM AT ITS BEST

'Clever, engaging and refreshing. A life-like experience of three asian generations living in the UK, so close to heart that you can feel a heartbeat.'

Sunday Mercury

ACKNOWLEDGEMENTS

I am grateful to a lot of people: David Wake (New Street Authors), Chris Morgan (Cannon Hill writing group), Dr Khalid Hassan (consultant anaesthetist, University Hospital Birmingham).

My special thanks to Jenny Warren (Betterwrite), who was wonderful to work with for editorial assistance despite her health issues and bereavement.

**Matador**